The
PROPOSAL

A Novel

Martha Silver

Yankee Clipper Press

Published by Yankee Clipper Press
www.yankeeclipperpress.com
Edition ISBNs
Trade Paperback: 978-0-9881980-2-9
e-book: 978-0-9881980-3-6

Cover design by Derek Murphy
Book design by Christopher Fisher

Printed in the United States of America

The
PROPOSAL

Prologue

The call came at 11:54 p.m. Tully Gordon had watched the 11 o'clock news and drifted off to sleep. The sharp chime of the telephone penetrated her dream and she awoke, startled by the sound. Shaking off the remnants of slumber, she reached for the phone. At first, she heard only sobs amid garbled words, and then, slowly, she recognized the voice of her fiancé's mother.

"It's Scott ... It's Scott ... He's gone."

Tully didn't understand. Was Scott missing? Had he gone away?

"Margaret, what do you mean? Where's Scott?"

Tully heard only sobs, and then nothing. Moments later, the silence was replaced with the choked voice of Scott's father.

"Tully ... I'm sorry ... Scott was in an accident tonight ... on his motorcycle. He didn't make it."

Chapter 1

The early-morning sun streamed through the kitchen window, radiating its light over Tully Gordon as she cleared away the breakfast dishes. For just a moment, everything seemed normal again.

"I'm glad you insisted I come down here," Tully told her sister, Lauren.

"I'm glad you finally relented. We've been so worried about you. Christmas wasn't the same last year without you here."

"I wasn't ready then to be around family. I would have put a damper on everyone's fun."

"Is it getting any easier for you? You know—about Scott."

Tully sighed. She wanted to say yes, but it would be a lie. Instead, she mumbled, "A little." Yet it felt good to be back in her childhood hometown for the Christmas holidays, away from the raw New York City weather. The warm Florida air, mixed with the warmth of her sister's family, made her feel almost happy. No, not happy. Content. Helping her niece and nephew unwrap their Christmas presents stacked high under the plastic fir tree. Listening to their chatter about friends and school. Lying on the couch as Lauren's fingers kneaded her neck and back, loosening the muscles that seemed to be in a perpetual state of contraction. Laughing during the Christmas meal as Lauren's husband, Ted, a pediatrician, related the lame jokes he'd tell his young patients to cheer them up. At those times, she felt like she had before—before that devastating phone call fifteen months earlier.

Lauren rinsed each dish Tully retrieved from the table and then placed it in the dishwasher. "Do you think you'll be ready to start dating again soon?"

Startled by Lauren's question, Tully's body stiffened and she glanced downward. "Oh, no. I couldn't, I just couldn't."

Lauren turned the faucet off and stared at her sister. Gently she said, "You need to move on. It's not healthy, you know it's not. Scott wouldn't have wanted this for you."

Tully felt the quickening of her heart, then the skipped beats that sometimes followed thoughts of Scott. It had frightened her at first. Fears of her own death flooded through her when she first experienced the acrobatic dance within her chest. Now she understood it would pass. Her heart, if not her life, would settle into a normal rhythm once she pushed thoughts of Scott away. Never gone but residing silently in the darkest corner of her mind.

"We could have been twins, we were so much alike," she said quietly. "Everything I wanted, he wanted. Everything I liked, he liked. I never thought it was possible to be so happy. I was lucky to have found him. And unlucky that he was taken away. I have to accept that. You don't find your perfect match a second time."

Lauren reached out for Tully's hand and led her back to the kitchen table. "Sit," she said as she pointed to the antique Shaker ladder-back chair before sitting down herself. "I know how much you loved Scott, but there are other men who could make you happy. You need to be open to that possibility."

"I'm sure there are men I'd be comfortable with. But happy? I don't think so." Tully pushed her long wavy hair back from her face, a nervous gesture she'd been prone to since childhood. "Besides, it's not easy to meet men in Manhattan. I hate going to bars, I hate making small talk. I always feel awkward with people I don't know. You're the social butterfly, not me."

"What about at work? Aren't there single men there?"

Tully snickered. "Are you kidding? There are no single men in publishing."

"Well, then, you could—"

"Lauren, enough already," Tully said, the volume of her voice rising. "I don't want to meet anyone else. Not now. Maybe not ever."

The silence lasted for only seconds, although it seemed like minutes, until Lauren asked softly, "And children? You don't want children either? You're so good with Bonnie and Max, and they're crazy about you."

Tully sighed. She did yearn for children. Scott had felt the same way. They both wanted to try for a family soon after their marriage. But Scott was dead. Tully could still hear the words of Scott's father, the sound of his voice burned into her memory. "A stupid accident," he'd said. "It wasn't Scott's fault. He was always careful on his motorcycle."

"Yes, I want children." *That's all I want now. A child to love. A child to protect.*

The weather in central Florida varied in December, cloudy days with temperatures in the fifties alternating with bright, clear skies and temperatures high enough for swimming. Two days after Christmas, with the sun high overhead and the temperature at a perfect seventy-five degrees, Tully and Lauren sat on a bench in Minnewaska Park, where they had taken Max and Bonnie to romp in the playground. Completed only the previous year, it consisted of the usual swings and seesaws as well as an elaborate wooden maze of climbing steps, slides, ropes and bar swings, round holes, square holes, and turrets, all built on top of sand. Peals of laughter mingled with the cries of toddlers who fought for dominion over their desired space.

Tully followed the children in their play while Lauren engaged in conversation with her friend and neighbor Molly Sanders. Molly's two daughters were on the jungle gym with Bonnie, each seeing who could go the farthest. Max, performing acrobatics on the wooden maze, ignored Molly's three-year-old nephew, visiting with his father for the holidays.

Life seemed so simple in childhood, Tully thought. But it doesn't stay that way. She knew Lauren wanted her to move back to Middleton, start over again. At times she wondered if doing so would help lift the melancholy that had settled over her after Scott's accident and, like an unwelcome guest, refused to leave. At night, though, in the quiet of her bedroom, she knew it didn't matter whether she was in Middleton or her closet-size Manhattan apartment. Wherever she was, she'd still be alone.

Tully watched Max in his gymnastics and the three girls, who'd moved on to follow the leader, but lost sight of Molly's nephew. Scanning the playground, she noticed him playing silently with his pail in the sand. A slight child, with sandy brown hair that drooped over his forehead and sad eyes, he had the look of an abandoned puppy. Tully remembered Molly saying his mother had died. She felt drawn to him and let her gaze linger as he gathered up buckets of sand and dumped them into a large pile. As she watched, she saw an older child march over to him and grab the shovel and pail forcibly from his hands. At first startled, he quietly began crying without moving from his spot. Realizing Molly was deep in an animated conversation with Lauren and unaware of the boy's distress, Tully ran over to comfort the child.

"He was a mean boy," she said. "Do you want me to get your pail back?" He nodded, and after Tully returned with his pail, he smiled tentatively at her while wiping away his tears.

"What's your name?"

"Cody."

"Are you visiting your Aunt Molly?"

Again, he nodded.

"Would you like me to help you build a house in the sand?" she asked and received another nod in response.

Tully sat down in the sand and played with him as she had so often with her niece and nephew. "The best way to build a sand house is to add water." Tully pulled a water bottle out of her pocket and poured a little onto the sand. "What kind of house should we build?"

"Can we build a castle?" Cody whispered.

"That's my specialty." As they worked together shaping mounds of wet sand into a turreted castle, Tully sang to Cody, songs she remembered from her own childhood.

When she began singing "Old MacDonald's Farm," Cody smiled. "I know that song," he said and hesitantly joined in with the animal sounds, mooing like a cow, baaing like a sheep. "Woof, woof," Cody sang out loudly as he jumped up and stomped around their castle. "Quack, quack," he shouted with glee as they sang the last verse.

Tully told him stories she'd made up and Cody responded with stories of his own until they were both laughing at the silliness of their tales. When Molly called over to Cody that it was time to leave, he threw his arms around Tully and said, "I wish you were my mommy."

Tully hugged him hard as her eyes misted.

Chapter 2

As she dressed for a dinner party at Molly Sanders' home, Tully once again pleaded with her sister to leave her behind. "They're your friends and it's very gracious of them to include me, but really, it's not necessary. I'm perfectly happy staying home with a good book. And then you won't need a baby-sitter for the kids."

"Don't be silly. You met Molly at the park yesterday and she really liked you. In fact, she made a point of telling me she wanted you to come."

Tully didn't understand why her sister had always pushed so hard to include her. Growing up, Lauren had played to perfection the role of the protective older sister. Others complained about their siblings, but never Lauren. Despite their difference in age, they had always been close.

Quickly, Tully finished dressing, kissed Bonnie and Max good night, and got into the backseat of Lauren's car. The Sanders' house was only a few blocks away, yet they drove nevertheless. It was so different in Manhattan, where cars were a luxury and city dwellers walked everywhere rather than contend with the constant traffic jams. Ted was on call, though, and had to have his car nearby in case he was needed at the hospital.

"You know, Tully, you're welcome to stay here as long as you'd like," Ted said on the way over. "Maybe you can take another week's vacation."

Tully had always gotten along well with Ted. He had dated Lauren since they were undergraduates together. With his easygoing personality and corny sense of humor he had quickly endeared himself to Lauren's family. "I appreciate that, Ted, but I have to get back to work."

As they pulled up to the Sanders' house, Tully took in the large and meticulously landscaped lawn. Molly greeted them warmly at the door and took Tully's arm in hers. "I'm so glad you came. Cody hasn't stopped talking about you to my brother, and he's looking forward to meeting you," she said as she waltzed Tully into the living room and led her to a group of men gathered by the marble fireplace.

The room was furnished with functional pieces that were both comfortable for adults and sturdy enough to withstand the rough treatment of young children. But every piece fit together, creating a feeling of warmth. The walls were painted a honey beige that made the room feel alive without being overpowering, and the wide-plank wood floor was covered with two Oriental rugs in deep, rich hues. Tully couldn't help but envy the lavish homes of her sister and Molly. The disparity between their dwellings and her cramped apartment was just too great.

"Mack, this is Tully Gordon, Cody's friend from the park."

Mack Bryson had a smile that immediately drew Tully to him. Instantly recognizable as the father of the little boy she'd befriended at the park, he had the same sandy brown hair drooping over his forehead. His piercing green eyes, the color of a mountain lake, also had a touch of sadness, not as pronounced as his son's but there nevertheless. With a nose that turned slightly downward and lips a little too thin, he wasn't classically handsome, but he was undeniably attractive. At just over six feet tall, he had the taut, trim body of an athlete, although the creases framing his eyes and the flecks of gray in his hair said youth had departed years ago.

Mack held out his hand and locked his gaze on Tully. "So

you're the angel Cody hasn't stopped talking about. You made quite an impression on him. Now I can see why."

Tully smiled as she remembered the little boy and the fun she'd had with him.

"Thank you for paying so much attention to him yesterday," Mack said. "His cousins haven't been too interested in him, and I think he's been feeling a bit lonely."

"It was easy spending time with Cody. He's a lovely child."

"You're very kind. Tell me, is 'Tully' short for something?"

"Natalie. When I was a baby, Lauren couldn't say the whole name. It came out as 'Tully' and the name just stuck."

"I like that."

Mack introduced Tully to the two men standing next to him and rejoined their conversation about the upcoming college bowl games. As he chatted with the men, it seemed clear he was both comfortable with himself and at ease with others.

I wish I could be like that. I wish I didn't always feel like an outsider whenever I'm with a group of people. Knowing nothing about college sports and feeling uncomfortable standing among a group of men who were oblivious to her presence, Tully wandered off to seek Lauren. She found her with a group of women discussing their children. Tully didn't need to be a mother to listen appreciatively to the stories of their little ones' exploits. As she stood there quietly, she looked around at the circle of women, their hair perfectly styled, their makeup expertly applied. Tully glanced back across the room at Mack. She wished she had taken more care with her unruly curls, their ends frizzed by the Florida humidity, and regretted her lack of sophistication with cosmetics. A dab of blush on her cheeks and a touch of Maybelline strawberry cream on her lips were all she'd been able to muster.

When everyone was called to the large dining room, she was pleased to discover herself seated next to Mack.

"I hope you don't mind," Mack said, "but I asked Molly to seat me next to you. I wanted to get to know you better."

As dinner was served, the room filled with conversations, some engaging the entire group and others between individuals seated near each other. But for Tully, it was all background blur, indistinct and unintelligible. She saw and heard only Mack. For the first time in fifteen months, she stopped thinking about Scott.

"I married my high-school sweetheart right after I graduated from college," Tully answered when Mack asked if she were married. "We both realized it was a mistake from the outset. We were divorced before the year was out."

"What went wrong?" Mack asked.

"Oh, I suppose we were too young. After we married, Bobby became more and more jealous of any time I spent with others. If I didn't come straight home from work, he'd be furious. He never wanted me to spend time with girlfriends, even with Lauren. And if I even glanced at another man, it would send him into a rage."

"And since then?"

"Well, he's remarried, even has a child, I understand. I've heard through the grapevine that he's less controlling now, more like the Bobby I knew in high school. He still lives here, in Middleton."

"And you? Are you seeing anyone?"

Tully hesitated. She never talked about Scott anymore. His death was her own private pain. "This week should have been my one-year anniversary. My fiancé was killed in a motorcycle accident three months before our wedding. They say there's one perfect mate for everyone, and I'd found mine. I just didn't get to keep him for very long."

Mack reached over and took Tully's hand in his. "I'm sorry. I know how it feels to lose someone you love. Cody's mother died a year after he was born."

"How terrible, for both of you."

They ate in silence for a while, and then Mack asked about her work.

"I'm an assistant editor at Mangrove Publishing, in New York."

"Sounds impressive."

"No, really, it's just a step above secretary, but I enjoy it. I started out as an editorial assistant, so I'm slowly making progress. My dream has been to write fiction, and reading manuscripts, both good and bad, has helped my own writing. Not that I've written much."

"It must have been difficult for you to leave your home, though, and your sister and friends."

Tully nodded. "It was hard leaving Lauren and her kids. I'm crazy about Bonnie and Max."

"I hear you're a natural with children. I bet you'll make a wonderful mother someday."

"I want children, but I don't know if I'll ever have any. I think some people are meant to be lucky and others unlucky and I fit into the latter category." Tully caught herself, suddenly aware of how negative she sounded—and with a relative stranger. "Here I've just met you and I sound like I'm auditioning for a soap opera. I'm sorry. It's just been a difficult year for me. I can't believe you've gotten me to talk so much about myself."

The rattling of the dishes being removed from the table to make room for the next course cut off their private conversation. Tully was flooded with relief. She knew she'd been rambling and welcomed the interruption. After a heated discussion around the table about the upcoming presidential election, Tully turned back to Mack and asked him about his work.

"I own and run a media company. It's called Big Sky Communications. We create programming services that are exhibited on cable and satellite."

"Do I know any of the programs?"

"Sportsman's World was our first. It's a twenty-four-hour video channel devoted to fishing and hunting throughout the world."

Tully's face lighted up. "Sportsman's World is yours? That was Scott's favorite channel. He would watch it obsessively. He'd gone fly-fishing with his father as a child and he said that watching those shows always brought back memories of how close he felt to him on those trips."

"I had the same experience with my father. Those memories were my motivation for creating the channel."

They continued talking, and at the end of the evening

Mack asked if she was going to the New Year's Eve party at the Middleton Country Club.

Tully groaned. "Yes, I have to. Lauren and Ted insisted I join them even though I'd prefer staying home and baby-sitting the children."

"I'm glad you'll be there. Now I have something to look forward to."

Tully felt her pulse quicken. Suddenly, Middleton seemed the perfect place to be.

Back at Lauren's house, Tully waited until her sister had checked each of the children's bedrooms to ensure they were sleeping, straightened the covers they'd kicked off and kissed their foreheads before asking, "What do you know about Molly's brother?"

"Aha—so there *is* a spark in you. I told you there are other men out there you could like," Lauren said with a laugh. Her smile dimmed quickly, though. "But not Mack—he's not someone to get your hopes up over."

"Believe me, I'm not. Besides, you know I'm not ready to get involved with someone, and even if I were, I'm not in Mack's league."

Tully believed she was pretty, but in an ordinary sort of way. Her brown eyes were neither large nor small, her nose neither aquiline nor pug, her lips neither thin nor full. Rather, all her features were nicely proportioned and fit together well. Her best feature was her hair, long, thick dark brown waves, mostly uncontrollable unless tamed by her hairdresser but nevertheless luxuriant. Yes, she recognized she was pretty—after all, Bobby had wanted to marry her and he'd been the star quarterback and voted most popular at their high school. Yet she also knew she wasn't beautiful and certainly not sophisticated.

"You're being silly again," Lauren said. "Of course you're good enough for him. You're always selling yourself short. I meant because he's a notorious womanizer. And, according to Molly, he's vowed to never marry again. His wife, Joanna, was drop-dead gorgeous, although I guess I shouldn't use that expression. She was one of those women who look perfect without a stitch of makeup, even dressed in the grungiest clothes. She died in a car accident when Cody was a year old, and Mack was devastated."

"Did you ever meet her?"

"Once, when they visited Molly shortly after Cody was born. I can understand why Mack would be reluctant to marry again. No woman could measure up to Joanna. Beautiful, smart, everyone loved her—she had the whole package."

"Well, I'm not looking to get involved, really I'm not. But I enjoyed talking to him tonight and came away realizing I don't know very much about him. That's all."

In fact, that wasn't all. He was charming and interesting. He adored his son. He was a successful businessman. But Tully wondered about the tinge of melancholy she'd seen in his eyes, the faintest hint of something hidden beneath his veneer of self-assurance. Perhaps it was the death of his wife. She could certainly understand that. But she couldn't shake the feeling that it was something more than that.

Tully firmly believed she had no chance with a man like Mack—he was older, wealthy, used to women far more sophisticated than she. It didn't matter. She wanted to learn everything she could about him, even if there weren't the remotest possibility she'd ever see him after her week in Middleton. Speaking to him this evening made her feel more alive than she'd thought possible just a few short days ago.

"Well then," Lauren said, "he owns a programming company in Denver and has a large ranch in Montana, mostly for fishing, but I think he has horses there, too. He's older than Molly, so I'd guess he's in his early forties."

"How do you know this?"

"Molly idolizes her brother. She talks about him a lot. Raves about him, to be more precise. Apparently he's a whiz in business. What else do you want to know?"

"I don't know. Nothing, I guess. There was just something about him I was drawn to."

Lauren smirked. "Yeah, you and every other woman alive. He's easy to look at, sexy, and rich. What's not to love?"

"It was more than that. He seemed unaffected, and very secure with himself. I liked him. That's all."

Tully fell asleep that night thinking about Mack Bryson, confused by the tumult of emotions she felt, both excitement and guilt, for someone she'd just met.

Mack sat in the darkened bedroom and stared at the limp body of his son, asleep on one side of the king-size bed. Even in sleep, with his raggedy teddy bear clutched tightly in his arm and his eyes squeezed closed, an aura of sadness hung over Cody. They were sharing the guest bedroom in Molly's house despite Molly's offer to double up her daughters and give Cody his own bedroom. Mack knew that even if Cody started out there, he'd end up in Mack's bed anyway, awakened by a nightmare that could be erased only by his father's closeness. No point in disrupting his niece when her bed would end up empty.

Mack often watched Cody asleep in his bedroom at home, watched his soft body rise and fall with his gentle breathing. *How can I make him happy? Childhood is the time for joy, not sadness.* He would do anything for Cody. The intense love he felt for his little boy often left him breathless. He thought back to the moment of Cody's birth. In the delivery room with his wife, Mack had watched the crown of his son's head make its appearance, followed swiftly by his squirming body covered with a slippery mucus, and then the bawl of his first cries. Within moments of his birth, Cody seemed alert and intensely aware of his new environment. After the nurse cleaned him off and put him in Mack's arms, Cody's eyes widened and locked onto his father's face, and Mack felt a tidal wave of affection course through his body.

Mack reached out and stroked Cody's hair, brushing aside the strands fallen over his eyes. His skin was still buttery soft, yet to be hardened by life's journey. *I know what you want. I know what you need to be happy. What every little boy wants. A mother.*

Mack had seen many women since Joanna's death. They flocked to him, some because of his wealth, others drawn to his good looks. Although he had no qualms about sleeping with them, he avoided emotional entanglements. He would do anything for Cody, anything but fall in love again.

Mack quietly slipped out of his clothes and crawled into the other side of the bed. As he lay in the dark, he thought about the woman he'd met that evening. Cody had come home from the playground the day before bursting with more enthusiasm than Mack had seen in months. He'd chattered nonstop about "the nice lady" and then asked the question that froze Mack in his tracks: "Was my mommy like that lady?"

Tully seemed to be nothing like Joanna. Joanna had been strikingly beautiful, with a magnetic personality that mesmerized everyone she met. Tully was quietly pretty but seemed tentative, almost withdrawn when the whole group engaged in conversation. Yet he could understand why Cody was drawn to her. When just the two of them spoke, she emitted genuine warmth that shone in her eyes and a sweetness that radiated in her face. Talking to her during dinner, he'd felt more at ease than he'd been with any of the women he dated after Joanna's death. Perhaps it was because he wasn't attracted to her. Without the overlay of flirtation, he could relax. *Not that she isn't pretty. Just not my type. Too wholesome. Still, she's the kind who'd make a great mother if I were willing to marry again. But I'm not. I can't.*

Chapter 3

Downtown Middleton consisted of four blocks, with family-owned stores and restaurants side by side with the town hall, the public library, and the post office. Considering that most towns in Florida were composed of sterile strip malls scattered along roads and highways, four blocks was enough to create a sense of community. It was the kind of town where it was more surprising to not see someone familiar than to run into a friendly face. Shopping with Lauren at Middletown Merchandise for a dress to wear New Year's Eve, Tully heard a shrill voice behind her.

"Tully Gordon, is that you?"

Tully looked around and saw her mother's friend Sally Winston. "Hi, Mrs. Winston."

"I haven't seen you since your mother's funeral, may she rest in peace. Why, you seem so gaunt now," she clucked as she looked Tully over. "Is everything all right, dear?"

Tully cringed. She never understood how her mother had remained friends with Sally Winston for so many years. Although the two women had vastly different personalities, they had been friends since the fourth grade. Perhaps the familiarity that comes with longevity had kept them together. Mrs. Winston was a spindly woman, with thinning hair pulled back in a knot, who gabbed incessantly about the minutiae of daily life. It was always hard to get a word in edgewise once she began her chatter and nearly impossible to get away from her.

"Of course, everything's fine. Lauren and I are just doing some shopping."

"Lauren is here, too?" She peered over the garment rack at the opposite end of the store and spotted Lauren in the children's section. "Yoo-hoo, Lauren, we're over here. Come say hello," she called out over the din of shoppers.

Lauren remained planted in the same spot, her back to Mrs. Winston, and Tully was certain she'd deliberately ignored the loud call.

The elder woman turned back to Tully. "My, my, the older you get, the more you look like your mother. But everyone must tell you that, I suppose. God bless her, she was a saint. Janie was always willing to do for others. Such a hard worker. It's a shame she didn't have more joy in her life."

"I wouldn't—"

"Well, of course, you and Lauren brought her immense pleasure, especially Lauren's children. She couldn't get enough of them. But I saw how hard it was for her, raising you both by herself after your father died. Of course, she never complained. I'm sure she would have liked to have someone take care of her, though, not always be the person everyone relied upon. She often told me how relieved she was that Lauren married a doctor. She knew she wouldn't have to worry about her." Mrs. Winston paused to take a breath and then continued quickly before Tully could speak. "I heard about the terrible tragedy you suffered. So sad. But you must go on, right? Are you seeing someone new? I know it would have been a great comfort to your mother to see you married well. And she did so want to see you have children."

"Someday," Tully muttered. She looked down at her hands, her fingers locked so tightly together that pain radiated down to her wrists.

"Well, you can't wait too long. I've read about these young women who get caught up in their careers and when they're ready to settle down and have babies, suddenly find they're too old to get pregnant. It'd be a shame if that happened to you. It's too bad your first marriage didn't work out. We were all surprised it ended so quickly. I know it troubled your mother deeply, not that she would let on. No, she always put a happy spin on everything."

"Well, we both knew it was a mistake. No need to compound it further by staying together."

"Yes, that's what your mother said. Still, I know it would have been a comfort to your mother if you were married. She didn't enjoy seeing you struggle so hard. It probably reminded her too much of her own life. Now, my Nancy married very well, very well indeed. Did you know she's expecting her third child? She's building a new ..."

Tully caught Lauren's eye across the room and silently pleaded for help. When Lauren waved her arm for Tully to join her, Tully broke into the ongoing monologue. "Excuse me. I think Lauren needs me over there. It was wonderful seeing you again, Mrs. Winston. Please give my best to Nancy." Tully quickly turned away and walked toward her sister before Mrs. Winston could object. She felt like she couldn't breathe in the store's stale air, and beads of perspiration broke out on her forehead. Listening to Mrs. Winston had brought back thoughts of Scott and a stark reminder of all she had lost with his death.

Readying herself for the New Year's Eve party, Tully fidgeted with the straps of her dress. She had picked out a simple but elegant sleeveless black satin sheath on her shopping trip but couldn't get the straps to lie flat.

"Hold still," Lauren said as she straightened them. "What are you so nervous about?"

"Nothing. I'm not nervous."

"Something's up. You look like you swallowed Mexican jumping beans."

"Don't be silly. I'm just looking forward to the party."

"Well, that's a first for you. Is this about Mack? Is it because you'll see him again tonight?"

"No." *Yes, I do want to see Mack. Just as a friend, that's all.*

Tully slipped her feet into the shoes Lauren had lent her— black satin sandals with skinny three-inch heels, higher than any shoes Tully had ever worn before but undeniably sexy. A single strand of pearls, also borrowed from Lauren, hung around her neck.

Tully knew Lauren and Ted would be at the same table as Molly and her husband, Phil. That meant she'd be at the same table as Mack. As they entered the ornate ballroom of the country club, with its crystal chandeliers, stained-glass windows, and gilded trim, she heard first the blaring of horns. Looking around the room, she spotted the twelve-piece orchestra playing at one end and an ice sculpture of a champagne bottle, encircled by sculptured ice champagne glasses, at the other. Surrounding the dance floor were tables for ten or twelve, each covered with black linen tablecloths gracefully draped down to the floor. Place settings of bone white china and sterling silver utensils were laid on the tables, along with centerpieces of two dozen blood-red long-stem roses. As Ted waited to get their table assignment from one of the two women dressed in black tuxedos and top hats, Tully scanned the room to see if she could spot Mack. Instead, she saw Bobby Highland, her ex-husband, with his obviously pregnant wife and his parents.

Surprised at feeling pleased to see him, she walked over to his group to say hello. "I see congratulations are in order," she said as she came up behind Bobby.

Bobby spun around and grinned widely on seeing Tully. "Oh my God, Tully. I can't believe you're here. How have you been? Oh, sorry, this is my wife, Janice, and, of course, you know my parents." Tully saw that Janice, despite being pregnant, was very pretty, with alabaster skin and shiny, almost black straight hair hanging below her shoulders. The type, thought Tully, that had no doubt been at the center of the popular group in high school. The type the high-school football hero was supposed to be with.

Tully turned to shake Janice's hand. "It's nice to meet you, Janice. I'm OK," she said as she turned back to Bobby. "I've been visiting Lauren and her family for the holidays. I heard how well you're doing, but I didn't know you were expecting a second child. That's wonderful. I'm really happy for you."

"Thank you. We're very excited. Our son is almost four and he's becoming Mr. Independent. We've both missed having a baby to hold. This one's a girl."

Bobby looked Tully over. "You look great. What have you been doing? Have you bowled over the publishing world? I'm sure you have, you're so talented. New York has probably laid out the red carpet for you."

"No, hardly that," Tully said. "It's such an intense city. Not at all like Middleton. I've been promoted to assistant editor, and that's good, but sometimes I wonder if it's the right place for me. I mean, whether New York is right for me." She wondered why she was telling this to Bobby and then realized that despite the problems they'd had during their marriage, Bobby had been the one person besides her sister to whom she'd confided her hopes and worries.

"How about your writing? How's that coming along? Still working on your novel?"

"I've been working so hard at my job I don't have time to write." As soon as she'd answered, Tully realized that wasn't true. Before Scott's death, she'd written in the evenings and after work when she wasn't seeing Scott. Small pieces: essays, short stories. Ideas for a novel always swirled through her head but hadn't taken sufficient form to put them down on paper. Since the accident, though, she hadn't written a word.

Tully smiled ruefully, finished with some small talk and wished Bobby and Janice well before winding her way through the crowded room back to Lauren and Ted. The exuberance she'd felt on entering the room had dissipated. She could feel the beginnings of the melancholy, which had started to lift when she got to Middleton, roll in like the gentle ripples of Lake Jefferson. Although she recognized she couldn't have remained married to Bobby, if she had, she'd be a mother by now, not just a favorite aunt.

"C'mon, we're this way," Ted said as he led the women into the ballroom. The music grew louder and the voices blended into a cacophonous hum as they entered the large room. As they approached their table, Tully saw Mack, striking in his black tuxedo, already seated between two women. Disappointed that she would not be sitting next to him, she smiled and said hello as she sat down.

"You look lovely tonight," Mack said before turning his attention back to the women on either side of him. As the table filled in with Lauren's friends, Tully attempted to join in their conversation, all the while wishing she could crawl under the blankets of her bed in New York instead. Mack, seemingly oblivious to Tully, engaged in conversation with the two women and took turns dancing with each while their husbands talked about investment strategies. Occasionally, Tully heard snippets of the women's conversation, patches of laughter, Mack being as charming with them as he'd been with her a few days ago. *Why am I so upset that Mack's ignoring me? After all, we just met, and anyway, I don't want to get involved with anyone. Dammit, though, he shouldn't have made me feel he liked me.*

When the two women moved onto the dance floor with their husbands, Mack asked Tully to dance. She nodded without enthusiasm and followed him to the center of the ballroom.

"You seem a bit blue tonight," Mack said.

"Oh. I ran into my ex-husband here, with his new wife. They're having their second child soon and I guess it brought up a lot of feelings about what I'm missing."

"You'll have that someday."

Tully shook her head. "No. I don't think it's going to happen for me."

Tully's run-in with Bobby, which had started so pleasantly, reminded her of what she had waiting in New York: an empty apartment with little reminders of Scott scattered throughout—his spare set of toiletries in the bathroom, his favorite CDs, his Flintstones coffee mug. She'd been unable to discard them after his death.

"You don't mean that. You've suffered a terrible loss, and this time of year it's especially difficult to be alone."

"Is it for you?"

Mack smiled. "I'm not alone. I have Cody." When the dance ended, he took Tully's hand. "Let's go outside for a walk."

The grounds of the country club were as grand as the ballroom, with exotic flowers and plants amid the lush green lawn and curving walkways lined with palm trees, their leafy fronds providing a canopy. The evening air was still balmy, and a gentle breeze pushed the wispy clouds away from the full moon. As they walked along a lighted path, Mack took Tully's arm in his. Their words flowed easily, this time Tully taking the lead.

"It has to be difficult for you raising Cody by yourself. Especially with the pressure you must have as the head of a company."

"Well, I'm not really doing it alone. He has a nanny at home. Actually, the third nanny since he was born. It's not easy finding the right person."

"Cody must miss his mother."

"He doesn't even remember his mother."

The light from the full moon shone on Mack's face, and Tully could see the furrow in his brow deepen. "He's lucky to have you, though. Not all fathers are as devoted to their children."

"Sometimes I wonder if I'm enough. He's become more reserved with other children, and lately he's been waking up at night crying, and I can't seem to console him unless I take him into my bed."

Remembering the sadness she'd seen in Cody's eyes, she wanted to comfort Mack. "I'm sure that's just a stage all children go through."

Suddenly, Mack stopped and turned to Tully. "You're so easy to talk to." He paused, then took a deep breath. "I've been toying with a thought since I met you that seemed preposterous at first, but now, well, I guess it's still preposterous but ..." He put his hands on Tully's shoulders and turned her toward him. "I need to say this carefully. I don't want you to be insulted, but it's important you don't misconstrue what I'm saying. You know Cody means the world to me and I would do anything to ensure his happiness. I think I can raise him well by myself, but he's obviously missing something by not having a mother. I don't want to remarry, not now, not ever—I'm not prepared to make the emotional commitment needed to make a marriage work, and frankly, although I never cheated on Joanna while we were married, I'm no longer willing to be faithful to one woman."

Mack took Tully's hand in his. "You're a warm, nurturing woman who'll make a wonderful mother, but right now you've given up on the hope of meeting and marrying the right man. You're wrong, of course, but I'm selfish enough to take advantage of your vulnerability and suggest this: Let's enter into, for lack of better words, a 'contract marriage.' We'll be legally married, with a prenuptial agreement, and we'll live together, but without sex, kind of a platonic marriage. Sex with someone I'm living with would only create emotional entanglements I don't want. To the outside world, we'll be a normal married couple. We'll raise Cody together. You'll have time to write. If you're any good, I certainly have contacts that can help you. You'll have all the financial benefits and social status that come with being Mrs. Mackenzie Bryson, plus I'll give you an annual 'allowance' that equals your salary at your current job. And, of course, you'll have no expenses. If you stay in the marriage until Cody enters college, then I'll pay you a bonus of two million dollars."

Mack paused to take a breath. "Please understand, I'm not making this crazy proposal because I think you're not worthy of a real marriage. You are, and I'd be taking you away from some unknown someone who'd probably make you very happy. But you'll be free to have affairs with anyone you want as long as you're discreet about them, just as I would. Besides, if I'm already married, then my sexual partners may stop harboring illusions that our affair can lead to something different."

"But—" Tully felt as if the ground had tilted under her feet and her equilibrium had disappeared.

"Let me get this all out before you say anything. After Cody is in college, you'll be financially secure and still young enough to marry someone truly worthy of you if you want. There are even women having children at that age if you want your own at that point. But you'll be giving up the hope of your own children while you're still young."

Tully didn't know whether to laugh or cry and so just stood there shaking her head.

"Don't make any decisions now. Just think about it," Mack said.

"You don't want a wife. You want a nanny."

"No, Cody has a nanny, and she'll stay on if you agree to marry me. But a nanny doesn't love a child the way a mother does. A nanny doesn't feel the commitment to stay the way a mother does. A nanny doesn't ache when her child is unhappy. And the child knows the difference between a mother and a nanny. I want a mother for Cody. He's already fond of you and I think you're fond of him. In the little time we've spent together, it's clear we'd be comfortable with each other. Please—think it over."

"I need to sit down." Tully could feel her hands tremble. She laced her fingers together to stop the shaking, but nothing could halt the racing of her heart.

"There's a bench by the lake. Let's walk over there."

"No, I need to be by myself now. This is overwhelming, as I'm sure you can imagine."

"Of course. Should I go back inside?"

Tully nodded.

"Are you sure you're all right? I can wait out here for you."

"No, really, I'm fine. I'd just like to spend a few moments by myself." She smiled cautiously. "You've certainly given me a lot to think about."

"I don't expect an answer tonight. I know this is sudden."

Tully squeezed his hand and then gently pushed him back toward the clubhouse. "Go. I'll be fine."

As she walked down the cobblestone path to the lake, her head spun. Mack's proposal was startling. Not only unexpected but surely preposterous. She sat on the bench and tried to imagine what her life would be if she accepted his offer. Could she live with a man and share his life but not his bed? Was it possible to share a love for his son but not each other? She hadn't wanted to think of marrying again, not ever, but what else did she have? All that was left was a one-bedroom apartment in a fifth-floor walk-up she'd return to alone each night.

Conflicting thoughts tumbled through her mind as she considered Mack's proposal. *This is crazy. He must be crazy. How could I go off with a stranger? Shouldn't I say no to Mack? But I can't deny it—I wanted to see him again tonight. I like him. We share a bond, a common tragedy. He understands me. No, I should go back to New York, maybe look for a new job, maybe something where I can write. But maybe this is my chance to avoid a life alone, to have companionship.*

Underpinning everything was the recognition that she yearned for a child. Yes, she could adopt a child, perhaps even conceive a child through artificial insemination, but she'd be a single parent earning a low salary, struggling to spend time with her son or daughter. Mrs. Winston was right: Her mother's life had been difficult. If she married Mack, it's true she would give up some things, but her life wouldn't be difficult, not financially, at least. She'd have the time to write, maybe even start on that novel she knew was in her. And more than anything else, she would become a mother, in an instant able to pour her love into Mack's beautiful son.

Tully made her way back to the clubhouse. The music still blared, the dance floor crowded with gyrating bodies. Their table was empty and she scanned the room looking for Mack. He stood at the bar alone, surrounded by men and women jostling for the bartender's attention. She walked over and tapped Mack's arm. When he turned and saw her, Tully could see the hope in his eyes. She locked her gaze on his. "I don't need to think it over any longer. The answer is yes."

Chapter 4

Mack took Tully in his arms, hugged her close and whispered, "Thank you."

Tully lingered in his arms a moment and then pulled away. "Everyone's going to think we're crazy, you know. Maybe we are crazy."

Mack shrugged. "Maybe. But I think we can make this work for both of us, and most importantly for Cody. How can that be crazy?"

Tully knew it wasn't as simple as that. She could just imagine her sister's reaction. A rush of relief flooded through her when Mack seemed to understand her thoughts.

"We won't tell anyone about this now. There's plenty of time to tell our families tomorrow. And you can sleep on your decision."

"I won't change my mind," Tully said, "but I'll understand if you change yours."

Mack smiled at her. "No. My gut says this is right, and I've gotten where I am by trusting my instincts."

Tully took Mack's hand in hers and pulled him toward the front door of the clubhouse. "I can't go back to the table yet. I'm too excited—or nervous. Or both. Let's go walk outside again."

It seemed like eons ago that they had walked off the dance floor and strolled along the pristine shoreline of the man-made lake. She had left the clubhouse then confused about her feelings for Mack. Now, she felt no confusion as she held the hand of the man she'd agreed to marry.

Tully lay on the cushioned chaise lounge in Lauren's backyard, waiting for her sister to join her after checking on the children. The sky was ablaze with pinpoint-clear stars, like daggers in a celestial sphere, and the full moon bore a resemblance to a kindly old man looking down on her and nodding his approval. The light from the moon was bright enough to illuminate the hibiscus lining the pathway to the pool and the roses, lilies, and birds of paradise planted in the garden. The profusion of colors muted by the evening sky mingled with the perfume of the blossoms and made Tully feel as if she had stepped into Alice's wonderland, only it wasn't a fairy tale and it wasn't a nightmare. It was real and she was scared, but she was content, too.

Mack wanted Tully to sleep on her decision before sharing the news with her family, but Tully knew she couldn't go to bed without confiding in her sister. She hoped Lauren would understand.

"Tully, Tully, what have you done?" Lauren said on hearing the news. "This is nuts."

"I don't think it's crazy. Look, I know what it's like to have a bad marriage. I've lived through one. And I know what it feels like to find the right person. Scott wasn't perfect, but he was perfect for me, and I won't find that again. Any man I married I'd measure against Scott. That wouldn't be fair to my husband. He'd end up resenting me and I wouldn't blame him. With Mack, there are no expectations and no disappointment."

"There's more than one man who's perfect for you."

"No, there's not."

"At some point, maybe you're not ready yet, but down the road, you're going to open your eyes and realize you're wrong. And if you're married to Mack, it'll be too late for you. Can't you just wait and see what happens?"

"I don't want to go back to New York and be alone again."

"Stay here, stay with us."

"No. I've made up my mind. Besides, maybe it's better this way."

"Better? How could it be better?"

"Sis, I know you and Ted are happy, but really, look at the divorce rate. On their wedding day, couples always believe they'll be married forever, so something must happen to poison that feeling for an awful lot of them. It happened with Bobby and me. And it happens over and over. I bet a lot of your married friends look at their spouses and wonder how they could have chosen them but feel stuck because of the kids. Maybe it's because they started out expecting the world and instead got dirty diapers. Maybe having no expectations is the way to be happy."

"You're wrong, you're so wrong. Sure, some marriages don't work out, for lots of different reasons. Maybe they mistook passion for love, maybe they were too young, and yes, maybe their expectations were unrealistic. But—"

"I'd hoped you'd be happy for me."

"I want you to be happy. This isn't the way. There must be something wrong with a man who would even ask this of you."

"Why? Because he loves his son? It's just unusual, that's all."

"That's all? No one would agree to this. No sane man would want this."

"That's not true. In fact, I just read in a magazine—*Time*, I think—about a growing number of single men who invite a woman to live in their home rent-free. In exchange, the woman keeps the house tidy and takes care of personal chores for them. They don't want to pay a housekeeper or have the emotional commitment of a lover. Mack can afford a housekeeper but he wants a mother for his son. Why is that so different?"

"Well, for one thing, in those other situations, the woman can just leave if it's not working out."

"So can I. I'm not an indentured servant."

"But there's a little boy involved here, with little-boy emotions."

Tully sighed. "I know that. I wouldn't be cavalier about leaving him. But I think it can work out. I think it will work out."

Lauren shook her head. "I know you. I watched you these past few days. You're attracted to Mack. You don't want to admit it, but I can see. You think he'll change after you're married, that he'll love you, but he won't. I know about men like him. You deserve a real marriage, a real husband."

"You're wrong. I don't want a real husband any longer. I wanted Scott, but he's gone."

"You've been depressed for so long now, you think running away will make everything better, but it won't. You can handle this. You can be happy on your own until you meet someone else. Even if you don't meet someone else, although you will, I know you will. It won't always hurt this much. Please reconsider. You're so pretty and so smart. You'll find another Scott, you'll have your own children. Don't give up the hope of that. You're only twenty-nine. That's still so young."

It was strange. Tully knew that everything her sister had said made sense. Yet as she looked around Lauren's spacious lawn, the inviting pool and the beautiful house and thought about her niece and nephew, how much she loved them, how much she missed having her own child to love, she felt completely at ease with her decision.

True, Cody would not be her flesh and blood, but that was the case with all adopted children, and their parents felt a deep and enduring love for them nevertheless. True, she would be deprived of intimacy with her husband, but all the magazines told her that after several years, the burning passion of newlyweds fades and, in successful marriages, a different kind of intimacy is left in its place: trust, companionship, devotion. That's what she would have with Mack. Of course, she understood sex was part of a normal marriage, but at the moment, sex was the last thing on her mind. If, later, she met someone she was attracted to, well, she'd deal with it then.

She felt comfortable with Mack. She already felt fond of Cody. She would be moving into a leisurely life with a wealthy husband and a child who needed her. She would leave behind her life in a city where she was a stranger and where the thought of entering the dating game again caused her stomach to churn. And, too, in a quiet corner of her heart, she recognized that by marrying Mack, by removing the possibility of falling in love again, she would never risk betraying the memory of Scott. Yes, despite Lauren's objections, she was untroubled by her decision and, dare she think it, even happy with it.

Tully would tell others they had both been taken by surprise at the swiftness and intensity of their feelings for each other, but she couldn't have lied to Lauren. Lauren had been her rock and her shield throughout childhood, the person who provided succor when she felt despondent and who shared her happiness when she felt jubilant. She extracted Lauren's promise that her secret would be kept, particularly from Molly.

A good night's sleep was the last thing Tully expected after the startling events of the evening, but she awoke the next morning feeling more refreshed than she'd felt in a long time. After downing breakfast with Lauren and her family, Tully met Mack at a nearby Starbucks for a second cup of coffee.

"So, have you changed your mind since last night?" he asked after they sat down.

"Not about the concept of getting married, but I've thought some more about the particulars."

Mack look puzzled. "What do you mean?"

"Well, if you just pay me my current salary for fifteen years, it won't take into account my earnings potential, not to mention inflation."

"You'll have no expenses as my wife. Your salary may be the same, but you'll be provided food and shelter. That has a tremendous value."

"Yes, but as you've pointed out, I'm giving up a great deal as well. That should be compensated more than a mere job."

Mack leaned back in his chair. "What do you propose?"

"My current salary is forty-five thousand a year. I think I should receive fifty-five thousand a year and that amount should be adjusted for inflation annually. And the two million-dollar bonus should be adjusted for inflation as well. Also, you said I'd get the bonus if I stay in the marriage until Cody starts college. What if Cody decides not to go to college? What if he decides to travel or go into your business or climb Mount Everest or do anything before deciding to go to college?"

"You're right. You should get the bonus if we're still married when Cody finishes high school or turns eighteen."

"And what happens if, despite what you say, you *do* find someone you truly want to marry and divorce me before that time? What if you died before then? Shouldn't I still get a bonus?"

Mack smiled. "I guess I shouldn't have underestimated you. I took you for a timid southern girl and instead you're a crack negotiator."

"Well, I guess after living in New York City for three years I've learned a few things. Does that bother you?"

"On the contrary," Mack said. "I'm happy the woman I've offered to share my home and child with has a sharp mind. And I'm relieved you're treating this as a business proposition. How about this: I'll give you fifty-thousand dollars each year for your personal spending money and increase it annually for inflation. The bonus will be indexed for inflation as well, and you'll be paid it on our fifteenth wedding anniversary."

"And if you die before then?"

"Well, presuming you haven't knocked me off, I'll include in my will a provision giving you the full bonus."

"You still haven't answered what would happen if you want to end our marriage, for whatever reason, earlier than fifteen years."

"The whole point of this arrangement is because I don't want a real marriage. I just want Cody to have a mother."

Tully knew how easy it was for circumstances to change. A week earlier, she couldn't imagine even considering such an outlandish proposal. "You say that now, but fifteen years is a long time."

Mack picked up his cup of coffee and took a long sip, then leaned back in his seat. "I'll tell you what. If a meteor hits me in the head, causing a complete rewiring of my brain, and I suddenly want to marry someone else, you'll get a pro-rata portion of the bonus based on the number of years we've been married. How's that?"

"Well, I guess that makes sense. But I have to warn you, I want the full bonus. I'm going to do my best to sabotage any woman who tries to entice you away."

Mack laughed. "I'm counting on that."

As they finished their coffee, they worked out the logistics of the wedding. It would take place in Middleton in six weeks. This would give Tully time to wrap up her life in New York City and find a sublet for her apartment. It would also give them time to work out the details of a prenuptial agreement. The wedding would be a small family gathering. Her co-worker and best friend, Haley Edmonds, would be the only friend invited by Tully. Nick Hanover, Mack's closest friend and Big Sky's executive vice president and general counsel, along with his wife, Lizzie, would be the only friends invited by Mack.

It seems so real now, not like last night, when it felt like a dream. But I've just planned my wedding, and I know I should feel nervous. Instead, I feel relieved, like my life is now settled. I don't have to wonder what's going to happen anymore.

When Mack arrived back at Molly's home, he shared with her the news of his impending nuptials.

"Mack, I'm happy for you, and Tully certainly seems sweet, but isn't this a little fast? Oh, I should shut up. Before she even knew you she certainly took a shine to Cody. This is wonderful, really. I'm thrilled. Surprised, but thrilled."

Cody's reaction was unequivocal when Mack told him he and Tully would be married and Tully would become his mother. "Will she always stay with us?" he asked. When Mack answered "yes," Cody threw his arms around his father's neck and said, "I love you, Daddy."

◆　◆　◆

The next day, Mack and Tully took Cody to Sea World in Orlando. Cody was overwhelmed by the seemingly endless attractions at the marine park, running off first in one direction and then another until Tully took his hand and suggested they start with the dolphin nursery, where they were able to watch new dolphin mothers and their calves swim around in an underwater tank.

"See the small dolphin there?" Tully said to Cody, after reading the description on the wall. "That's a baby dolphin. He's only six months old."

"He doesn't look like a baby."

"Well, there are all kinds of babies. People babies and dog babies and horse babies and dolphin babies."

"And do they all have mothers?"

"Yes, they all have mothers."

"I have a mother, too, now."

They went to see the sea lions and harbor seals and watched as some playfully dived and swam and a large fat sea lion stretched out on a rock, sleeping under the warm sun. They saw a pirate show with Clyde the sea lion and an adventure show with Shamu the killer whale. They took the moving walkway through the penguin colony, watched the penguins jump, slide and dive into and out of the water, and traveled through the underwater tunnel to see sharks, eels, and barracudas. Cody's favorite show was "Pets Ahoy!" with dogs, cats, birds, rats, pigs and various other animals engaged in comic performances. They ate cotton candy and cherry snow cones and rode the roller coaster, with Mack and Tully holding Cody tight between them.

At dusk, they left the park and found a small Italian restaurant, where Cody attacked his plate of spaghetti and meatballs and Mack and Tully sipped Chianti over their shared antipasto plate and lobster ravioli.

"Can I go back with you to Molly's house?" Tully said when they'd finished. "I'd like to tuck Cody into bed. It's the last time I'll see him before the wedding."

"Of course. He'll like that."

Back in Cody's bedroom, she read him the books he'd chosen:

Goodnight Moon and *Jamberry*, his eyes becoming increasingly droopy with each story.

"I love you, Cody," she said after the last and kissed him good night.

"I wished you were my mommy," he said as he closed his eyes, "and now you will be."

Chapter 5

Back in Denver, Mack asked Nick Hanover to draft the prenuptial agreement. As his best friend since their college days at Stanford, Mack was prepared for Nick's reaction. "Are you out of your fucking mind?" Nick shouted. "You've been impulsive before, but this is nuts! You don't know anything about her. She could be an ax murderer for all you know."

Mack chuckled. He frankly wondered himself whether he was crazy. He recognized he'd been incautious in asking Tully to marry him. He knew little about her—but did it matter? He knew enough to be convinced she would be a loving mother to Cody. And he felt certain that Cody did need a mother. He wouldn't let himself fall in love again, though, so how else could Cody get what he needed? The more time he spent with Tully, the more certain he became that his seemingly imprudent proposal was actually sensible.

Nick reluctantly agreed to Mack's request and then closed the office door behind them. "We've got a problem. Internal audit flagged some inconsistencies in accounting last month that needed investigation. I didn't want to involve you until we had more information, but it seems Agnes has embezzled almost one million dollars from the company."

Mack was shaken. "I don't believe it. There must be a mistake."

"I know how you feel, but we've checked and double-checked. It's not a mistake. She did it through a series of fraudulent contracts and invoices."

"Either the invoices are legitimate or someone is making it look like they came from Agnes. She just wouldn't do it." Agnes Woodman had been Mack's assistant from the beginning of Big Sky Communications and, with an annual salary of a hundred thousand dollars, was paid as well as his middle managers. Not only was she indispensable to him, but he also considered her a friend.

"Your signature is on the contracts, but they're for services we've never used with companies that don't exist. It started about a year ago. A handwriting expert checked a letter Agnes signed with your signature against those on the contracts. There's no doubt the same person signed both."

"How would Agnes get money from that?"

"Agnes sent accounting the phony contracts and then signed off on the requisition form authorizing payment of the invoices. Accounting cut the checks, sent them out to the phony company, and, so far, that's where the money trail ends. No bank accounts or records identifying the owners of the phony businesses, but it seems clear she's somehow connected with them. With the SEC and the IRS scrutinizing us on our prospectus filings, we can't hide this under the rug. We've got to call in the police."

Mack couldn't believe what he heard. There had to be an explanation for the missing money. Agnes, a plain big-boned woman, had married for the first time just after her fiftieth birthday, almost five years ago. From the outset, Mack thought Henry Woodman wasn't deserving of her. A brutish-looking man with greasy hair turning gray at the edges, he seemed to overwhelm the normally outspoken and clear-eyed woman. However, at work Agnes remained the queen bee of the office, taking command of the administrative tasks and efficiently reining in the behavior of the younger secretaries when they slacked off.

"If this is true, wouldn't it be sufficient to fire her?" he asked.

"Not in today's corporate environment. We're taking the

company public. If you merely fire her, you bring your own conduct under question, with potential allegations that you find it acceptable to waste the corporation's assets. Executives of public companies are going to jail for that conduct. You can't risk being softhearted."

The prenuptial agreement had arrived at her New York apartment earlier in the week, and over her protests, Mack insisted Tully have her own attorney review it on her behalf. He wouldn't even recommend one, to ensure that no loyalty would be displayed toward him. Sam Horowitz, her boss at Mangrove Publishing, had called around and given her the number for Dean Goodman, a matrimonial attorney in the midsize Manhattan law firm Goodman, Latham and Jackson. Tully had met him when she dropped the original off at his midtown office. His shiny bald head and swath of frizzy carrot-red hair along the back seemed mismatched with his impeccable custom-tailored suit and erect bearing. His studious expression gave him an air of confidence that made Tully feel comfortable that he would protect her interests.

Now, waiting for her lawyer in his small conference room, Tully glanced over the formal document once again. The contract had a lot of legal mumbo jumbo, but the paragraphs she reread seemed, to her untrained eye, to contain the heart of what they'd agreed on.

Tully had quickly found a tenant for her apartment, her listing on Craigslist bringing a dozen responses the next day. She agreed to sublet the apartment, furnished, to a young couple moving in together for the first time, he a teacher at a New York City public high school and she an emergency-room nurse. They seemed responsible. They had excellent references from their current landlords and were clearly in love. Tully hoped they had better luck in the apartment than she'd had and appreciated that she felt no wistfulness leaving behind the promise—of love, of career advancement—that New York had held out for her when she arrived three years earlier. The only task remaining was to finalize the prenuptial agreement.

Mr. Goodman's assistant interrupted Tully's reading. "Mr. Goodman is ready for you now," she said, motioning Tully to follow her down the hallway.

"I have to say, this is a most unusual arrangement," Dean Goodman said as Tully entered his office. Tully sat in front of his large mahogany desk, papers meticulously stacked in color-coded piles on the right side. A framed photograph of him, with his wife and two young children, was on a credenza behind the desk. On the walls were his diploma from New York University Law School, his certificates of admission to practice in the federal and state courts of New York, and several lithographs of southwestern art. The corner office on the sixty-eighth floor of the seventy-story office building at Forty-Ninth Street and Park Avenue had floor-to-ceiling windows looking south toward the empty space that once housed the twin towers of the World Trade Center and east toward the East River and the Queensboro Bridge. "Why would you be paid an allowance each year? Is your fiancé so tight-fisted he needs to contractually control your spending? And why in the world would you agree adultery is OK?"

Tully explained to Dean the circumstances of her marriage.

"I see," he said, his brow furrowed in consternation. "Yes, it is most unusual indeed. Well, if this is what you want and you're sure about it, there seem to be some holes in the agreement that haven't been addressed. For instance, will you adopt Cody?"

"I don't know. We haven't discussed that. Does it make a difference?"

"It certainly does. If you don't adopt him and the agreement is silent, you'll have no rights with respect to him. Your fiancé is quite a bit older than you, you've said. What if he should die? If you've raised Cody for ten years, let's say, and he's always thought of you as his mother, are you comfortable turning his care over to someone else, such as Mr. Bryson's sister? Are you willing to become entangled in a custody fight after you've lost the man you've lived with for ten years?"

The attorney paused to adjust his rimless glasses. "And if Mr. Bryson predeceases you while Cody is still a minor, his estate will no doubt be placed in a trust for Cody. Who will be the trustee of that trust, making financial decisions for Cody? If you retain custody, you might find it awkward to have to go to someone else to finance his needs. On the other hand, Mr. Bryson might not be comfortable giving you control over his substantial assets on behalf of his son. It's an important issue you need to address with him.

"And in this paragraph 6(b), *egregious conduct* is too vague. It would be easy for him to claim any conduct on your part was 'egregious' to avoid paying you the bonus money. At the least, we should require that a court determine the conduct is egregious, based on a 'reasonable person' standard."

"What does that mean—a 'reasonable person' standard?"

"It means a judge or a jury would have to agree your conduct exceeds behavior considered acceptable by a reasonable person. Also, the money you're paid annually—you need to consider what expenses you'll be responsible for with that money. This arrangement is so extraordinary I wouldn't presume your living expenses will be covered."

"Well, of course my living expenses are covered. I'll be living in his house."

"Living expenses are more than food and shelter. Who'll pay for medical expenses? Who'll pay for your beauty-parlor visits and tennis lessons and even your gowns for the various charity events he no doubt attends. These are all activities you'll be expected to engage in as Mr. Bryson's wife, and they're costly. Fifty thousand dollars may seem like a lot of money to you when you're not responsible for rent and food, but it won't make a dent in the type of lavish lifestyle you'll be enjoying. I'll notify your fiancé's attorney of my comments, but you really need to talk directly to Mr. Bryson to address these issues."

♦ ♦ ♦

"I think the most important thing for us to discuss is Cody," Tully said on the telephone with Mack that night.

"It is, but I haven't thought about that 'what if' before, and I need time to think it over." Mack had done a lot of thinking since he'd returned to Colorado. Encapsulated in the closeness of his sister's family, intoxicated by the fragrant summery air, his proposal seemed a splendid solution to his dilemma. Now back at work, with daily bombardments from Nick about the irrationality of his judgment, away from Tully's gentle sweetness, he'd begun to question the soundness of his proposition.

And yet, at home, watching Cody play with his toys, gazing at his sweet face as he slept through the night undisturbed by the nightmares that had so recently sent him into Mack's bed each evening, Mack's instincts told him his decision would work out.

Allowing Tully to adopt Cody was a whole other ballgame, though. Perhaps in the future, if she and Cody truly did grow to love each other. But it was too uncertain now to risk committing the care of his son to someone on a "hunch." Tully would just have to trust him that at the right time, if it made sense, he would name her as Cody's guardian in his will.

The other changes her lawyer requested were easy, including specifying that he would pay for all reasonable living expenses. It had always been his intention that the monthly stipend he paid Tully would be her savings, preferably invested wisely so that when their marriage was dissolved, she would be financially secure. Tully told Mack she understood his protectiveness of Cody, and they both signed the agreement, contractually committing to their future together.

Chapter 6

Tully arrived at her sister's home two weeks before her wedding date. Her apartment was turned over to the sub-tenants and her clothes and belongings were packed away, ready to be shipped to Colorado. Accepting the inevitable, Lauren ceased her attempts to persuade Tully to call off the nuptials and instead devoted the two weeks to simply having fun with her sister. They watched old movies together, listened and danced to seventies rock music, even went to Disney World with Max and Bonnie, where Tully enjoyed the rides at least as much as her niece and nephew did. At night, after the children were asleep and Ted had retired to the master bedroom, the women reminisced about their childhood, laughing at the things they'd done to aggravate their mother.

It had been a good two weeks, and Tully almost felt ready to face Mack's friends. She would meet them for the first time that night at the wedding party's rehearsal dinner.

"Why are you so jittery?" Lauren asked as she sat on Tully's bed and watched her fumble with her earrings. "You're not marrying his friends, you're marrying Mack."

"Nick and Lizzie are Mack's closest friends. He's known Nick since college. It's important that they like me."

"Let's face it, yours is not exactly a conventional marriage. If his friends don't like you, then too bad. As long as Cody likes you, Mack will be happy."

Tully wasn't so sure. She knew that Nick was familiar with their arrangement, having drafted the prenuptial agreement. She didn't need to be told he opposed the marriage. As Mack's best friend, he had to be suspicious of her. "Dammit, I knew I should never have pierced my ears. This is impossible."

Lauren watched her sister continue to poke her earlobe with the gold post of an earring. "Here, let me help you with that." Lauren easily slid the post through Tully's ear and then, with the second earring, did it again on the other side. "Relax. You'll be fine."

"Did you know that Nick and Lizzie live only a few blocks away from Mack?"

"Yes," Lauren sighed. "You've mentioned that once or twice."

"What if Lizzie's told all her neighbors that our marriage is a sham? I'll feel humiliated just walking outside."

"Nick's a lawyer. It's doubtful he told Lizzie anything, and even if he did, she wouldn't pass it on. She'd be violating Nick's trust and he'd be in deep trouble for letting a client's secret get out."

Lauren got off the bed, took Tully's hand, and led her out of the room. "You look great. If we don't leave now, we'll be late."

Thank goodness Haley will be there. She's so easy to be with—she's bound to charm the Hanovers.

At the restaurant, with everyone settled into their seats around the table, Tully realized her fears had been unwarranted. She and Lizzie hit it off instantly. They chatted comfortably throughout the meal as if they were old friends.

"I can tell already you're just what Mack needs," Lizzie said as they finished their desserts.

Nick nodded. "Amen to that. Mack will tell you I was a bit skeptical. Well, that's probably an understatement, but it's easy to see why Mack proposed, and Cody absolutely glows in your presence."

Mack and Tully smiled at each other. Relieved that she had

passed muster with his friends, she looked forward to starting their life together.

Now, dressing for her wedding in a knee-length spaghetti-strap dress of off-white silk twill, Tully felt the jitters of a bride. A single white orchid was pinned to her hair, which hung loosely down her neck.

"I'm still amazed you fell in love so quickly," Haley said as she put on Tully's makeup. "Aside from the obvious—his yummy looks—Mack seems like a great guy. You've really hit the jackpot. I'm *so* jealous of you."

Tully expected that her friend would not be jealous if she knew the truth. It would have been easier for Tully to live their lie if Mack were less attractive, less charming, less considerate. Then she wouldn't be faced with the knowledge that she almost had so much when she really had so little.

Tully shoved those thoughts aside when Lauren opened the door of the dressing room and announced it was time to go. Together, the three women walked outside into the bright sunshine. Tully and Mack had chosen to be married at the country club where Mack had proposed, before a local judge, with the reception in a private room at the club. Chairs were set up outside near one of the lakes, with a red carpet leading down the path to the altar, a profusion of orchids, gardenias, and lilies of the valley lining each side.

Haley made her way over to the chairs while Lauren waited by Tully's side. Tully saw Cody waiting with Mack across the lawn. Looking very serious, Cody held the small pillow on which the wedding bands rested.

"It's not too late to change your mind, you know," Lauren said as she waited by Tully's side.

"I wish you'd said that before I married Bobby."

"Then I was just your maid of honor. Now I'm your matron of honor, and that means I'm supposed to be imbued with a fount of wisdom."

"Well, Ms. Fount of Wisdom, I'm going ahead with this. And I'm happy, really I am."

As she said those words, Tully wondered if they were true. She should be walking down the aisle toward Scott. She should be marrying the man who was her perfect mate. Her father should be by her side, holding her arm as he walked her down the aisle. Instead, she'd walk alone. Her mother should be sitting in the front row, surrounded by friends and family. Suddenly, Tully felt as if she were in another universe. Nothing seemed real—not the idyllic setting or the bouquet of flowers in her hands or the strands of music that lingered in the air.

"It's almost time," Lauren said.

"What?"

"I said it's almost time. Are you OK? You look lost."

Tully straightened up, smoothed her dress, and smiled. "I'm fine. I'm ready."

A single violinist played an adagio by Albinoni while Tully walked down the aisle toward Mack, Cody standing by his side with the wedding rings. As she took the slow deliberate steps toward the altar, she saw her sister sitting with her husband, flanked by their children. They were a family. A unit. She reached the altar and stood next to Mack. He stood erect in his dark navy suit, a bead of sweat on his forehead. Tully smiled at Cody. He looked like a little man in his toddler's suit and bright red bow tie. She slipped her hand into Mack's and felt her heart flutter.

Tully's mind seemed numb as the judge somberly intoned words she heard only as a blur, until those final words, which she heard with ringing clarity: "Do you, Natalie Gordon, take Mackenzie Bryson to be your lawfully wedded husband?" Tully peered into Mack's eyes, saw him look at her kindly but without love, and then glanced at Cody, steadfastly holding the ring pillow, and said, "I do."

Chapter 7

Mack had pronounced the necessity of a honeymoon to maintain the pretense of normalcy for their marriage, and he chose the destination—Chamonix—and made the necessary arrangements.

Living in Colorado, Mack had long been an expert skier and in fact had already introduced Cody to the sport. "I'm not a beach person," he had told her. "I can last about fifteen minutes lying in the sun and then I go nuts." Tully had never skied; it was a sport for rich people, not a struggling family in Florida. But Mack had assured her that Chamonix had slopes for beginners and that he would hire a private ski instructor for her. "If you don't care for skiing, there are plenty of other things to do to keep you entertained," he'd said. Tully hadn't expected a honeymoon, and so anyplace Mack wanted to go would be an adventure for her.

Cody had returned to Denver with Nick and Lizzie, who would take him back to his nanny, while Tully and Mack flew to New York. Mack had scheduled a business meeting before their overnight flight to Geneva, and so when they arrived at John F. Kennedy airport, they took a taxi into Manhattan. The taxi driver dropped Tully off first, at Paragon Sports. "Take my credit card and go shopping for ski clothes while I'm busy," Mack told her. "Here's a list of items you'll need. Let's meet up at the

Four Seasons at five for a quick bite before we head back to the airport."

Tully completed her shopping and then wandered over to Rockefeller Center to watch the ice skaters before meeting Mack. When she got to the restaurant, he was waiting at the bar.

"Hi," she said as she came up behind him.

Mack spun his stool around and smiled at her. "I see you've managed to find some things," he said as he pointed to the shopping bags in her hands. "Good. Let's go get our table now."

The maître d' quickly seated them and handed them menus. "May I get madam a drink?" he asked. Tully nodded and asked for a glass of pinot grigio.

After ordering, Mack spoke about Chamonix. "I first fell in love with the area when I climbed the Mont Blanc massif one summer during college. I know there are ritzier ski resorts in Europe, but this one has my heart."

"I know I'll love it."

"Chamonix is a great town. Instead of the glitz of St. Moritz or Davos, it's held on to its alpine traditions. It looks like it's right out of a picture book from a hundred years ago."

With traffic always a question mark on New York City highways, they skipped dessert and hailed a taxi back to the airport, where they arrived with an hour to spare before their scheduled departure. To pass the time, Mack took her to the first-class lounge of Swiss Air. The quiet rooms were filled with plush leather couches and chairs. Platters of cheeses, nuts and pretzels were set out, and a bar provided complimentary drinks. Television monitors were placed in certain rooms, while other areas were designated as "quiet rooms." Mack settled into a chair and perused documents from his meeting while Tully wandered about the lounge, impressed by the opulence.

On boarding the airplane, Tully was struck by the disparity between coach and first class, which she'd never flown before. The indulgence of the flight attendants and the luxuriousness of the seats in first class astonished her. Settling into her spacious window seat, she was immediately offered warm nuts and a

Champagne cocktail. Gushing at the sumptuousness, she played with the seat, putting the back down and the footrest up. "A footrest, Mack!" she squealed as she made a perfectly flat bed for herself. She lifted her personal DVD player from inside the armrest and read through the list of more than a hundred choices of movies to watch at her command.

Mack laughed at her innocence. "You know," he said, "once you get used to flying first class, you'll never want to return to coach."

"I guess that'll give you insurance I won't leave Cody early."

Later, after the plane took flight, the attendant brought her a menu. When the meal she'd chosen was ready to be served, he placed a white linen tablecloth on her tray, set with a linen napkin and silver utensils. Unlike the single tray of food provided to the coach passengers, dinner was a five-course meal, accompanied by wine and finished with a platter of cheeses and fruit. When Tully felt drowsy, she placed her seat in the bed position, put on the warm socks and eye mask provided by the attendants, and drifted off to sleep. When she awakened, it was to the aroma of warm croissants, hot coffee, and Belgian waffles covered with strawberries. Yes, she certainly could get used to first class.

A limousine driver awaited them at the Geneva airport to take them to Chamonix, across the border in France. Tully slept during the ride and so arrived at Le Chateau Philippe, the hotel where they would spend the week, refreshed and ready to experience her first foray in Europe. The traditionally styled wood-and-granite alpine chalet had the appearance of an elegant country manor set in expansive park-like grounds. Although still early in the morning, they were shown to their two-bedroom chalet without delay. The large bedrooms, one with a king-size bed and the other with two double beds, were made up with Frette linens and heavy down comforters, and each had its own marble bathroom and balcony with a view of Mount Blanc. The comfortably furnished living room had a large stone fireplace on one wall and a fifty-inch plasma television screen on another.

"Which bedroom would you like?" Mack asked after the bell-hop had deposited their bags.

"I'll take the double beds. I'm smaller than you." She didn't tell Mack a king-size bed reminded her of Scott, reminded her that a year ago she had expected to be honeymooning with him.

After unpacking, Mack suggested they head to the slopes and meet the private instructor he had hired for her. If the first revelation of this trip had been that first-class living is seductive, revelation number two was that living as a married couple and leading separate lives was going to be different from what Tully had expected. Although Jean-Luc had ostensibly been hired as a ski instructor for Tully, it quickly became apparent that he was to be her companion for the week while Mack pursued his own interests. Those interests included Lily, his skiing guide in Chamonix.

"The glory of Chamonix is the off-trail skiing or, as they say here, *off piste,* and Lily has been my guide each time I've skied here. She highly recommended Jean-Luc. He's excellent at teaching beginners and speaks English flawlessly. The women all love him, I'm told. He'll take you to the different slopes, and if you want to take a break from skiing, then he can be your tour guide as well."

"Will I see you at dinnertime?"

"We'll have dinner together tonight, but I can't promise for the rest of the week. Lily and I are old friends and don't see each other very often. But Jean-Luc will keep you company for dinner when I'm not here. I may be back very late some nights, and Jean-Luc will entertain you for as long as you like."

Tully understood Mack's unspoken words: Honeymoon or no, this was to be the pattern of their relationship—this was what she'd agreed to. With a sinking feeling, she nevertheless smiled at Mack. "I've never been to Europe before, and I can't wait to start exploring Chamonix," she said. "You go and enjoy yourself and don't worry about me. I'll be fine."

Jean-Luc was everything Mack had promised: mid-thirties, wavy blond hair and pale blue eyes, with the slim, toned body of some-one who'd skied for his entire life. He was both easy to look at and easy to be with. "Let's get you skis and boots, and then we'll go over to La Tour for some basic instruction. You'll be surprised. I'll have you skiing down a beginner's slope by this afternoon. When you get comfortable on skis, we can try snowboarding as well."

Once on the slopes, Jean-Luc was exceedingly patient with Tully, and patience was what she needed. "My sister is such a great athlete, but I'm so uncoordinated. You'd hardly know we were related." She watched the other beginners with their in-structors and thought they were all catching on more quickly than she. "There are children here who look no more than three or four, and they're skiing so effortlessly—they're not even using poles. How do they do it?"

"It's easier when you learn as a child. Your center of gravity is different; your body is more limber and you're less afraid."

Tully knew it was time to call it a day when she barreled down the bunny slope, unable to stop, and crashed into a young child. But the real humiliation came when another child, no more than five, skied over to her and asked, "Can I help you up?"

"You're doing fine," Jean-Luc said. "Don't be so hard on yourself. Skiing is not intuitive, and attempting it for the first time as an adult is challenging. You think you're—what do you Americans call it?—a klutz. But really, you've made a lot of prog-ress. With skiing, you have to keep doing it over and over and suddenly it clicks and you realize you've gotten the movement down pat. Let's try another run."

Jean-Luc smiled so kindly that it was impossible to refuse him. And he was right—by the afternoon, she had mastered the snow-plow and was taking hesitant but upright runs down the novice slope. Afterward, they celebrated her achievement over drinks at the base lodge. As she sat in front of the large stone hearth in a deep-cushioned club chair and sipped a hot toddy, she thought about her first day of skiing. Schussing down a mountain, breathing in the crisp air, her long hair flying behind her, had given her a feeling of exhilaration, even on the easy, short beginner's run. And the mountains! Peak after jagged peak surrounded the Mont Blanc massif, the highest in western Europe, all covered with snow and dusty glaciers reaching toward the tops. The rugged majesty both diminished her and filled her with a sense of grandeur. She could scarcely comprehend how such beauty existed in the world, a world she'd seen so little of.

Sitting in the lodge, Tully watched the skiers come in at the end of the day, laughing with their friends, their faces ruddy from exposure to the wind and sun. All of them were in groups or couples. Many waved to Jean-Luc as they passed by, some stopping to chat briefly with him.

"My, you're popular," Tully said.

Jean-Luc shrugged. "I live on the slopes. Regulars get to know me."

"More than just know you. It's clear you're well-liked."

"When I have clients, it's my job to have them like me. Otherwise they won't come back, and then where would I be? Just a ski bum, and that's no good. Beautiful women don't want a bum, right?"

"Oh, I don't know. It depends on the bum."

After a while, Jean-Luc drove Tully back to her hotel and arranged to pick her up early the next morning for their continued lessons. Exhausted from the day, overcome by jet lag, Tully took a hot bath in the whirlpool tub and then promptly fell into a deep sleep. Two hours later, Mack awakened her in time for dinner at the Michelin-rated restaurant in their hotel.

"So, how did your first day go?" he asked after ordering for them both from the French menu.

Sitting across the small table from Mack in a dim room lighted with candlelight and with faint violin music in the background,

Tully silently marveled that she was here with a man so accomplished, so self-assured. Not only sitting at the same table with him but as his wife.

"It was great. I can't believe how beautiful it is here. And I thought I'd be cold outdoors all day. I'm so used to Florida weather, and even though New York is cold in the winter, I was always indoors there. But today I even felt warm at times. And Jean-Luc couldn't be nicer. He was so patient with me, and I actually skied! I couldn't believe it. He says in a few days I should be on the intermediate slopes."

"I'm glad you're enjoying yourself. Today was a warm-up day for me, but tomorrow Lily and I are going over to Le Grands Montets for *off piste* skiing. We'll be pretty late, so I've asked Jean-Luc to accompany you to dinner tomorrow night. I hope you don't mind."

"Yes, of course. If he doesn't mind, that is."

"Jean-Luc often has dinner with his clients and shows them the nightlife in Chamonix as well. In fact, I spoke to him while you were sleeping and he found you to be very charming and pretty. He's delighted to keep you company. You should stay out as long as you like, and don't wait up for me. I probably won't be back until quite late."

Tully was under no illusion as to what Mack meant: He would be spending the evening, and perhaps the night, with Lily. Given their arrangement, Tully knew she shouldn't be surprised, yet she had thought, naively, that his liaisons wouldn't be so evident, at least not on their honeymoon. Of course, he was being discreet in a fashion—he wasn't announcing his intentions explicitly, and he was being considerate of Tully, ensuring that she wouldn't be left alone. *He's doing exactly what he said he would. Why then do I feel so wretched?*

Stifling her feelings, she asked Mack about his day. They chatted comfortably throughout the exquisite meal of artichoke-truffle soup and roast squab with turnips, topped off with crispy lemon-lime crepes and, for Mack, double espresso. "I still can't believe you've never had coffee," Mack said.

"It's true. Probably the only thing about me that's unique."

They lingered in the dining room, content to sit back and let the wine from dinner, the fire from the hearth, and the music from the violinist relax their bodies. When they returned to their chalet, Mack kissed Tully gently on her cheek.

"Good night, Mrs. Bryson," he said before walking into his own bedroom and closing the door behind him.

Still on eastern standard time, Tully struggled to awaken at nine the next morning for her ten o'clock meeting with Jean-Luc. It was at times like this that she wished she'd developed a taste for coffee. A jolt of caffeine was what she needed to get her going. After brushing her teeth, she lingered in the shower, letting the hot water soothe her muscles. Reluctantly, she left the steamy enclosure and got dressed for another day of skiing.

When she opened her bedroom door, Tully saw that Mack's door was open as well. A quick glance around the living room told her she was alone in the chalet. On the table was a platter of fruit and croissants. As she strolled closer, she saw a note leaning against a pitcher of orange juice.

"I'm off to an early start. Didn't want to wake you. Enjoy your day of skiing. Mack."

That was it. No "Love, Mack." No "Yours, Mack." Just "Mack." Another reminder of the deal she'd made. She poured a glass of orange juice and stared at the note.

"Well, so be it," she said aloud to the empty room. "I'm here to have fun and that's just what I'm going to do. With or without Mack." She finished breakfast and left to meet Jean-Luc at the ski lodge.

"I'm so sore," she groaned upon seeing her instructor.

Jean-Luc smiled. "That's DOMS."

"DOMS? What's that?"

"Delayed-onset muscle soreness. You'll feel worse over the next thirty-six hours, and then you'll gradually recover."

"Can I still ski today?"

"*Mais oui.* We'll pick up some ibuprofen for you and we'll take it easy today. You learned a lot yesterday, so you won't be straining your muscles as much now."

It was easier on the slopes the second day. Jean-Luc introduced her to some longer yet still gentle trails and taught her the stem christie turn. By early afternoon, she became sufficiently confident in her turns and her balance to allow herself the glorious feeling of speed as she descended the deep-powder slopes. And she never lost the sense of awe she had felt since arriving in Chamonix. In every direction she looked, she was surrounded by jagged peaks, their tips disappearing into the cottony puffs of clouds in the cobalt sky. It was another exhilarating day, and she felt a sense of accomplishment and deep satisfaction.

Jean-Luc brought Tully back to her hotel early enough for her to soak in the hot whirlpool bathtub and take a nap before he picked her up for dinner. He took her to a local café, bursting with noise and energy, and told her she couldn't leave Chamonix without trying raclette.

"Melted cheese?" she said.

"*Oui.* But a tradition in Switzerland and this part of France. It's from the French word meaning 'to scrape off.' The cheese is melted and then scraped onto a hot plate. It's brought to our table still hot, and there'll be boiled potatoes and gherkins already at the table to add to the plate. Trust me—if you like French cheese, you'll love raclette."

They both ordered the dish and started with a selection of assorted cured meats as an appetizer. Jean-Luc ordered a chardonnay, and after the second bottle had been finished, Tully realized she hadn't thought about Mack all evening.

After dinner, Jean-Luc took Tully to the Bar du Monde, crammed with beautiful people energized after a day on the slopes, regaling each other with their day's adventures, laughter everywhere, throbbing music coming from a corner of the smoke-filled room, a multitude of languages mixing together into an indistinguishable melange of sound.

As Jean-Luc headed off to the bar for drinks, Tully surveyed the large space in wonderment that she—Natalie Gordon, from a small town in Florida—was in a *happening* bar in Europe with a handsome guy everyone seemed to know and like. Jean-Luc returned with apple martinis and two other couples in tow.

"I've found some friends of mine. Tully, this is Thibaud and Marie, Georges and Bettine. Let's find a table together."

Their English was as flawless as Jean-Luc's. All four were ski instructors and guides at Chamonix as well, and they regaled Tully with their experiences coaching and guiding rich Americans and especially their teenage offspring. Each story was more amusing than the last, and Tully laughed along with the group. The wine from dinner and the drinks from the bar had infused her with a warm tingling feeling. She knew she had drunk too much but felt only mellow and lightheaded. She looked at Jean-Luc, animatedly telling one of his guiding tales, and wondered if one day she would be one of his stories but didn't care. She was enjoying herself, enjoying the company, enjoying life.

Later, as the others said their au-revoirs, Jean-Luc took Tully's arm in his and, instead of heading back to her hotel, said, "My apartment is close by. Let's stop in for one last nightcap. I can show you how a ski bum lives."

Tully wanted the pleasure of the evening to continue, the feeling of camaraderie, of belonging, and so nodded her head and accompanied Jean-Luc down the quiet cobblestone street, past the four- and five-story buildings with their red-tiled roofs. When they arrived at his apartment two blocks later, she followed him up the dark stairs to the third-floor landing. Jean-Luc unlocked the door and turned to Tully.

"You are so pretty, *tres jolie*. Your skin is so soft. All evening I've wanted to touch you, to make love to you," he whispered into her ear.

Still intoxicated from the evening, she put her fingertips on Jean-Luc's lips and then brought her mouth to his. She kissed him gently at first and then harder, responding to his tongue inside her mouth, his hands on her breasts.

"Come, let's go inside," Jean-Luc said as he held out his hand.

Suddenly, Tully no longer felt woozy. Her head had cleared like a cloud passing over the sun. She had missed being kissed, passionately kissed, and hadn't realized it until now. She knew that Mack wouldn't care if she walked inside the door, but sex and love had always been intertwined for her. The thought of separating them now felt like a betrayal of her love for Scott.

"No. This is wrong. I'm sorry, I can't. I just can't," Tully said as she stepped back from Jean-Luc.

Jean-Luc shrugged and smiled. "You cannot blame a man for trying, *c'est vrai?*" Some women I teach want more than an instructor. We're still friends, *oui?*"

"Yes," Tully answered. "Can you take me back to my hotel now?"

Jean-Luc walked her back to her chalet and saw her safely inside. She got into bed, exhausted from the skiing and sleepy from the alcohol but alert enough to register Mack's open bedroom door, signaling that he had not yet returned from his evening. Before falling asleep, she was struck with realization number three: She missed physical intimacy. For the first time since Scott's death, she could imagine making love to another man.

Mack still hadn't returned by the time Tully left to meet Jean-Luc the next morning. "I cannot move without extreme pain," she said when she saw her ski instructor.

Jean-Luc laughed. "I told you it would be worse today. I have a suggestion. Let's take the day off from skiing and I'll show you the sights. Grab your passport."

They began their day with a ride up the cable car to the Aiguille du Midi, at a height of over eleven thousand feet—the highest Tully had ever been. They stayed at the top for a while, looking down at the picture-postcard town of Chamonix and across at the ring of mountains surrounding the valley.

After taking the cable car back down, Jean-Luc took her to a group of dogsleds, each hitched to six beautiful huskies. "Let's get in," he said after arranging with the operator to guide them. Tully cuddled up next to Jean-Luc, warm woolen blankets covering their bodies, while the musher led the team of dogs.

During the thrilling ride over snow, around glaciers, up and down the mountainside, their driver talked about the history of dogsledding and the training of sled dogs. "At one time, hundreds of years ago, dogsleds were the primary means of transportation in arctic regions, carrying supplies as well as people. In fact, researchers believe that without sled dogs, people in those regions wouldn't have survived. It was only later they began to be used recreationally. In fact, the first dogsled race wasn't until the middle of the nineteenth century."

Next, they went to Argentiere and browsed in the quaint shops, and then Jean-Luc said he had a special restaurant to take her to for lunch. "I hope you like Italian food."

"We're in France—shouldn't we be eating French food?"

"Ah, but that's my surprise for you." Driving off, they headed into a long tunnel and emerged on the other side in Courmayeur. "We're in Italy now. It's just a tunnel away from Chamonix. In fact, the cable car we rode up to Aiguille du Midi connects at the top with other cable cars that continue over the mountains to Courmayeur."

Tully was amazed. She could drive for two days straight from Florida to New York and still be in the United States. In ten minutes, she had passed from one country to another, with a different language, a different government and, not long ago, a different currency. Jean-Luc took her to a tiny restaurant, tucked away on a side street, with only five tables inside, each covered with a red-checkered tablecloth. The garlic aroma from the kitchen permeated the small room. "*Bongiorno, bongiorno,*" the rotund proprietor said with a beaming smile as he gave Jean-Luc a bear hug. The food was delicious and they lingered over their lunch and Chianti for hours. The proprietor joined them at times, with Jean-Luc translating for Tully. By the time they returned to Chamonix, Tully felt exhausted despite the sedentary day.

"I know just what you need," said Jean-Luc. "A soak in the hot tub."

"But there's only an outdoor hot tub. It's too cold, isn't it?"

"*Mais non*. It's perfect when it's cold outside. The hot water relaxes the muscles and raises the body's temperature. When you get out of the tub, you'll still feel warm despite the cold air."

Tully was learning something new every day. Soaking in the hotel's hot tub with Jean-Luc, sipping Champagne, she felt the aches in her legs and arms and neck dissipate. They stayed until their skin began to wrinkle, luxuriating in the hot steamy swirls of foam.

Later, after Jean-Luc had gone, Mack returned and took Tully out for dinner. "Lily recommended this place," he said.

While sipping their wine and awaiting their first course, Mack asked, "How's it going with Jean-Luc?"

"It's going great. Yesterday I learned to do stem turns and I can pretty much make it down a beginner's slope without falling … well, not falling too often. I still get rattled when I go over a mogul. But I've gotten down pat how to get up after I fall."

"That's very good for just three days of skiing."

"Oh, we didn't go skiing today. I was so sore from the first two days that with every step some part of my body screamed at me to stop, so Jean-Luc showed me some of the sights. We even had lunch in Italy."

"I'm glad it's working out well. You're sore because you're not used to exercising. You should start a regular program when we get home. I've got a gym in our house. If you'd like, I'll arrange for you to have sessions with a personal trainer."

"Maybe. I'm not sure how I feel about working out. The people I saw going into gyms in Manhattan seemed like jocks—you know, really muscled."

"Fitness is healthy for everyone. But you can decide for yourself when we're home. And how was dinner with Jean-Luc last night?"

Tully remembered Jean-Luc's kiss and she felt her face redden. Thankfully, the lights in the restaurant were dim. *Why should I feel so guilty? I didn't do anything wrong.* Tully steadied her voice. "Terrific. He's easy to be around. After dinner last night, we went

to a local bar and I met some of his friends. It was a lot of fun."
The conversation made Tully uncomfortable, and she decided to
change its direction. "Tell me what you've been doing."

"We went over to the Grands Montets today. The conditions
couldn't have been more perfect. Lily and I skied La Pendant, and
Point de Vue—it must have had a foot of fresh powder. I keep
forgetting how much I enjoy this mountain."

Tully sat back in her seat and studied Mack's face, ruddy from
skiing the sun-drenched slopes. The sadness she'd noticed in his
eyes when they'd first met was almost gone, but not quite. Traces
of something—she didn't know what—lingered.

"By the afternoon, we tried some off-trail skiing. Lily took
me to some new places, areas I've never skied before. Lots of
moguls and cliffs." Mack leaned back in his seat and sipped his
pinot noir. "Nothing beats a day of skiing in perfect weather
with perfect snow. Capped off by a delicious meal with a perfect
companion." He smiled at Tully.

Jean-Luc wasn't mentioned again, to Tully's relief. The rest of
the evening was comfortable, as it might be with a brother and
sister who didn't have a need to impress each other.

The remainder of the honeymoon continued in the same vein.
Tully spent her days skiing with Jean-Luc, progressing to the
intermediate level by week's end, and evenings were spent with
Mack when he was around or Jean-Luc when Mack was not. By
the end of the week, Tully was ready to return to Denver, see
Cody again, and begin her life as his mother and Mack's wife.

On the flight home, after they'd been served their five-course
lunch—now expected by Tully, who quickly adapted to the as-
sumptions of the rich—Mack turned to Tully. "I have something
to confess. You're going to be upset and I realize now it was a mistake, but I hope you'll understand my motivation." He reached
into his jacket pocket and handed Tully some photographs.

She took them hesitantly, unsure of what she would see. The
first photographs were of her and Jean-Luc at Bar du Monde,

her head thrown back in laughter, followed by photographs of them walking down the street. The last pictures were of Tully and Jean-Luc, on the landing of Jean-Luc's apartment, next to his front door. One showed Tully leaning in to kiss Jean-Luc; another showed them locked in a passionate embrace.

Her body froze, numb from the shock of what she saw. Surely she had done nothing wrong. Who could have taken these pictures? "How did you get these? Why?" she asked, her voice barely a whisper.

"I had you followed."

"What! Why would you do that?"

"I shouldn't have. I realized that after your first night with Jean-Luc."

With barely controlled fury, Tully asked again. "I still don't understand. Why would you do this to me? You encouraged me to go out with Jean-Luc. I have no delusions about where you were the nights you didn't come home."

"Because of Cody."

Tully was still confused. "Cody?"

Mack took a deep breath. "I know you've signed a prenuptial agreement, but if you decided to end our arrangement, the agreement won't stop you from bringing a lawsuit to try to undo it. I didn't want to put Cody through that and I thought, foolishly, if you knew I had pictures suggestive of adultery, it would prevent you from trying that."

Tully couldn't believe what she was hearing. "Did you ask Jean-Luc to seduce me?"

"No, not that. But I knew his reputation. I expected he would try something."

Tully turned away from Mack, too angry to speak to him and appalled that he would do something so horrid.

Mack reached over for her hand and she pulled it away. "Tully, I'm sorry. I shouldn't have treated you that way. I'm only showing these to you now because—well, because I don't want you to somehow find out about them later. If we came back to Chamonix, I mean."

Tully remained silent. As she pushed her seat back into a reclining position, she was hit with revelation number four: She knew nothing about the man she'd married.

Chapter 8

The gray, intermittently rainy sky matched Tully's mood as the limousine drove her and Mack from Denver International Airport to his home—their home—in suburban Stonington Village. They had barely spoken on the flight home. Tully still seethed over Mack's incomprehensible behavior. Two hours before landing, he tried to placate her, but she wasn't ready to forgive him.

"I've told you I'm sorry," he said. "What more can I do?"

"I know we have an unusual marriage. I know we won't share the intimacy enjoyed by most married couples. But if this arrangement is going to work, we have to be able to trust each other. And I don't trust you right now."

"Tully, you must admit we barely know each other. Entering into this agreement was a leap of faith—for both of us. But where Cody is concerned, I won't leave anything to chance. I'm sorry I had you followed, but it was only because I didn't want Cody to get hurt. Please try to understand."

Tully didn't want to understand. She thought she had understood the life she'd agreed to for the next fifteen years, but she felt both furious and confused by his stunt. *How can I live like this, never knowing if my every move is being watched? But ... could I be overreacting? He knows now it was wrong. And it's true—he* doesn't *really know me, and how could he know I wouldn't go back on our agreement? Damn it, he should have given himself time to get to know me. He always could have done something later if I gave him any indication I couldn't be trusted. Now how can I trust him?*

As these thoughts swirled through her head, underlying her questioning was the recognition that she found it easy to adapt to the lifestyle of the wealthy. And this awareness about herself infuriated her further, reigniting her anger at Mack. Now that they were close to arriving home, she knew she had to change her mood for Cody's sake.

Soon after going through the gated entrance of Belle Vista Estates, the limousine pulled into the long driveway to his house—her house, she had to keep reminding herself—and she gasped. Although she had expected it to be grand, its sheer size made her sister's home look like a bungalow.

With views of the Rocky Mountains, the two-story home, set on almost three acres, was nestled among tall evergreen trees, stately maples and oaks. A large portico extended from the house over the driveway in front, so despite the rain, they remained dry while walking into the house. The front door burst open and out ran Cody.

"Daddy, Daddy, I missed you so much," he shouted as he ran up to his father, holding up his arms to be lifted into Mack's.

"I missed you too, buddy. Give me a big kiss."

Looking at Cody, Tully reminded herself why she had entered into this strange arrangement. It was for Cody, to become his mother and love him as her own. She felt her anger recede as she bent down and wrapped her arms around his small body. "I missed you, too, sweetie. I'm so happy to be home with you."

As she stood up, she noticed a dark-haired, middle-aged woman standing behind Cody.

"Tully, this is Rosetta, Cody's nanny," Mack said.

Tully held out her hand to Rosetta. "Oh, I'm so happy to meet you. I'm looking forward to getting to know you."

Inside, she was immediately taken by the warmth and charm of the home. Despite having over eight thousand square feet of space, it had a feeling of comfortable intimacy. The two-story foyer opened into a grand family room, with a stone fireplace and a wall of glass offering a view of the mountains.

Rosetta took their coats and then, with Cody in hand, disappeared into the kitchen.

"Mmm," Tully said. "What's that delicious smell?"

"One of Rosetta's creations. She's a great cook. Would you like a tour of the house, or do you want to get settled in first?"

Despite her fatigue from the flight, Tully was curious to learn about her new home. "The tour, if you don't mind."

She followed Mack as he showed her first the formal living and dining rooms. The first floor also had a separate media room, a paneled study, and a library filled with built-in floor-to-ceiling bookshelves.

"This is my favorite room. I spend a lot of time here by myself."

Tully glanced at some of the volumes stacked on the shelves—Will and Ariel Durant's *The History of Civilization*, a six-volume history of World War II by Winston Churchill, Carl Sandburg's series on Abraham Lincoln. The books had the patina of age but were in pristine condition.

"Are you a history buff?" Tully asked.

"My father was. I inherited those books from him."

Before heading upstairs, Mack pointed toward a room, its door closed, behind the eat-in kitchen. "That's Rosetta's room. In addition to taking care of Cody, she cooks our meals and does some light cleaning. I have a service twice a week for the heavy cleaning."

Tully leaned close to Mack. "Does she know about our arrangement?"

Mack nodded. "Not everything, of course. Not the financial arrangement. But she knows we have an 'unusual relationship' and that we'll be using separate bedrooms. It would have been impossible to hide it from her. She's completely trustworthy, though. The other nannies may sit around and gossip, but Rosetta is older and understands the value of discretion. And the value of the higher salary I pay her for that discretion."

They walked up the curved staircase in the foyer to the second floor, where Mack pointed out five additional bedrooms and Cody's playroom. The master bedroom suite had a marble bathroom, two walk-in closets, and a separate office outfitted with all the electronics needed for Mack to keep on top of his business even when at home: computer, fax, copier, and a bank of phones.

Mack showed Tully her bedroom, next door to his. "Feel free to decorate it as you'd like. In fact, if there's anything in the house you'd like to change, other than the library and my bedroom, just let me know first, but I'm not wedded to anything here. I want you to make this your home."

"Oh, but your home is so beautiful. I can't imagine that I could improve on it."

Mack shrugged. "Whatever. It's up to you."

After Mack disappeared into his office, Tully spent the remainder of the afternoon getting to know Rosetta.

"You tell me what you like and I can do it, Mrs. Bryson," Rosetta said when Tully found her still in the kitchen. Cody was perched on a stool at the counter, crayon in hand, scribbling into a coloring book filled with dinosaur pictures.

"Tully. Please call me Tully."

"No, that would be disrespectful, senora."

"It's fine. Really, I'd prefer you call me Tully."

Rosetta hesitated. "Well, maybe I call you Tully when no one else is around, no one but Cody, I mean. But I call you Mrs. Bryson the other times. OK?"

"OK. I'm really counting on your help with Cody. Motherhood is new for me."

As Rosetta finished preparing dinner for the family, she told Tully about Cody's routine.

"Do you have family of your own?" Tully asked.

"*Si,* senora. My daughters are all grown up now and married. I keep waiting for a grandchild, but they are stubborn, my daughters. They say they are not ready to be changing diapers."

Tully felt a tug at her skirt. "Would you like to see my toys?" Cody asked.

Tully smiled and held out her hand to Cody. He led her upstairs to his playroom and introduced Tully to his favorite playthings. Later, a bell rang out signifying that the meal was ready and Mack joined the family in the formal dining room. Rosetta prepared a plate for herself in the kitchen. As she struggled to stay awake over dinner, Tully realized how tired she was. After Cody fell asleep, so did she, both physically and emotionally exhausted.

She tossed and turned throughout the night, perhaps from the jet lag combined with the wine at dinner, or perhaps from the realization that her life had changed forever. During her periods of wakefulness, she ruminated over how little she knew her husband. She knew he was a successful businessman, was devoted to his son, and loved the outdoors. She knew his first wife had died and he wanted to avoid emotional entanglements. That was it—the sum total of her knowledge about the man she had promised to live with for the next fifteen years. What were his other interests? Did he enjoy reading, theater, movies, music? What kind? She knew he enjoyed skiing, fishing and riding, but did he also like tennis, golf, bowling, swimming? Was he interested in politics? She didn't even know if he was Democrat or Republican, liberal or conservative. She'd met his closest friends, but did he have many friends or just a few? What were his values?

As she drifted off to sleep, Tully vowed she would try to penetrate Mack's veneer and learn what kind of person she'd married. And she vowed he would get to know her and never again have doubts about his decision.

Chapter 9

"She's been offered a plea bargain but won't take it," Nick said. Mack sat hunched over the massive dark cherry desk in his corner office at Big Sky Communications, his hands pressed against his temples, his mouth tightened in a grimace. Nick, seated in one of the two leather-and-chrome sling chairs in front of Mack's desk, had just updated Mack on the status of the criminal charges against Agnes Woodman. Seated on the brown leather couch along one wall was Vince Magee, the company's head of security.

Agnes had been stoic when Mack confronted her. She never acknowledged or denied her culpability, merely looked Mack in the eye and said, "I had hoped for more from you." Vince walked her out of the office. Mack had not spoken to her since.

Now, three months later, charged with felony theft, Agnes faced ten to fifteen years in prison, perhaps more. "The district attorney's office believes Agnes was acting in concert with her husband," said Vince. A heavyset man of fifty, still with a thick mop of dark brown hair, a handlebar mustache, and deep-set brown eyes, Vince had retired after twenty years with the Denver police force, having reached the rank of lieutenant. Like many of his colleagues, he was happy to collect his pension and work at a cushier job in the corporate world.

"In fact, they believe Henry Woodman was behind the

scheme, that he planned it, created the false contracts, and instructed Agnes to sign the payment authorizations. It doesn't appear to be either his or Agnes's signature endorsing the checks, though. Henry's known to be a big gambler, and they think he dug himself a hole, his money lenders put the squeeze on him, and he convinced Agnes to go along to save his life. The checks were probably turned over to some thug he owed money to, who endorsed them with a phony name, and that's why they can't identify the signature. They've offered Agnes a reduced plea, with max one to three in jail, and restitution, provided she gives evidence against her husband. She's stonewalling them, though. Won't say diddly about him."

"This is unbelievable," Mack said. "She's been my right hand for so long she's part of my family." He shook his head. "I had a bad feeling about her husband since I first met him. Maybe if I spoke to Agnes I could convince her Henry isn't worth saving."

"You can't do that," Nick said. "You have to divorce yourself from any involvement with Agnes at this time. I know it troubles you, but I really have to insist. You don't want anyone to misconstrue your involvement as interference with their case."

"But I'm trying to help resolve their case."

"It doesn't matter. You have to stay out of it."

Distraught over the matter, Mack wished he had not succumbed to Nick's plea to press criminal charges, but it seemed too late to turn back. He knew he should be angry at Agnes's betrayal of his trust, but he understood now the pressure she must have felt. Alone for so much of her life, Henry must have seemed her last chance at personal happiness, blinding her to any acknowledgment of his limitations. Thrust involuntarily into the underground world of gambling and loan sharks, she had to have been terrified by the threat of violence to her husband. Henry had rescued her from living the rest of her life alone, from dying alone. Mack shuddered at the thought of Agnes spending even one year in jail, much less fifteen, because of a choice made out of desperation.

Had Agnes's plight not weighed so heavily on him, Mack

would have readily admitted to being the happiest he'd been in years. The plans for taking Big Sky public were proceeding smoothly, internal discussions had begun on launching a new channel—always the time when his creative juices were in full gear and his enjoyment at work was at its peak—and his arrangement with Tully exceeded his expectations. Once they'd settled in at home, he worked hard to reassure her that his stunt in Chamonix had been a temporary lapse in judgment. Gradually, her fury had dissipated and together they had burned the pictures. Since then, she had been the perfect companion. Cody adored her, and the nights Mack spent at home, when he was in the mood to talk, she was a willing listener. She'd even been a helpful sounding board for his frustration over the Agnes mess, calming him down when he got too worked up over her predicament.

Of course, many nights he was out, lately with Janine, a freelance producer who'd pitched a program to him. Although he didn't buy the program idea, he did buy her dinner, followed by many dinners and late night tête-à-têtes. She was young, savvy, sexy, and undemanding, fully aware and accepting of his marital status. And it was true that on those nights he was home, he was often too tired to converse and so just had a late dinner by himself and retired to his room for the few quiet moments of solitude he allowed himself. But when he was home and did want conversation, Tully was engaging. She filled him in on Cody's activities, what he was learning, and the friends he was making. She kept up on what was going on outside their privileged environment, too; he could always count on a thoughtful discussion with her about national and worldwide issues, controversial or otherwise. Yes, things couldn't be going better, he thought, pleased at how well his calculated risk had turned out.

Tully couldn't decide if she was ecstatic or miserable and reluctantly had to admit it was both. They had been living together now for almost two months. She and Cody bonded with each other like steel to a magnet. Although Tully adored her niece and nephew, the instantaneous love she felt for Cody astonished her, so intense and all-consuming. Perhaps it resulted from Cody's immediate acceptance of her as his mother and the purity of his love for her. In her short time with him, she had been pleased—no, thrilled—watching Cody begin to blossom, tentatively reaching out to join other children in their play and becoming comfortable wandering away from Tully's side. He was regularly sleeping through the night, without the nightmares that had been sending him into Mack's bedroom for soothing. Cody had even begun exhibiting the demanding temper tantrums more typical of younger children but which, until recently, he'd been too timid to express.

Tully was also pleased Lizzie Hanover had taken her under her wing. Not only did Lizzie live in Belle Vista Estates, but Mack and Nick had adjoining ranches just south of Livingston, Montana, in Paradise Valley, where they often spent weekends fishing and riding. Lizzie had introduced Tully to her friends and included her in their bridge games and shopping trips. Tully had felt awkward with them at first. Encouraged by the zeitgeist applicable to their socio-economic class, they were by and large woman who had attended Ivy League universities, worked at prestigious jobs until they had their first children, and then readily chose to stay home, with the knowledge that their successful husbands could keep the family financially secure. They all had nannies and housekeepers, personal trainers and personal shoppers, tennis instructors and ski instructors. Their nails were impeccably manicured, their hair perfectly colored and coiffed, their skin luminescent and their bodies tanned.

Tully had initially felt inadequate in their presence, but as she became more familiar with them, she realized that the difference between her and them was the length of time they'd spent with wealthy husbands and often wealthy fathers as well. As Mack's wife, she could never be an object of their scorn, at least not in her presence, and so Tully found, for the first time in her life, that she was actually part of a social group.

Each of the women lived in Belle Vista Estates, each was

married to a successful businessman, physician, lawyer, or architect, each had at least two children, some with the requisite dog to complete the ideal family, and each belonged to the Stonington Country Club, where their husbands played golf together. They had dubbed themselves the "Lenape Lane Ladies," named for the long meandering street in their development along which most of their homes were set. The Lenape Lane Ladies got together regularly. They were always accompanied by their children's nannies, who watched over their charges as they played in another room. During their occasional games of bridge and shopping forays as well as their weekly luncheons, their primary entertainment was gossiping about those not part of their group. When there was nothing malicious they could find to say about a neighbor, they'd say it about their neighbors' children, at the same time extolling the virtues of their own. Silent at first, Tully began questioning them about Joanna Bryson.

Susie Howard, a slightly plump woman with a sweet nature who was married to an even more plump dentist with an equally sweet nature, smiled as she thought of her late friend. "Joanna? Why, she was just perfect, you know, a perfect friend, a perfect wife, a perfect mother. She was incredibly beautiful, like a model or an actress, and had impeccable taste in clothes, with the figure to wear just about anything, whether it was cutoff jeans or an evening gown. Mack adored her. All the husbands adored her. If she wasn't such a great girl and so much fun to be around, we'd all have been jealous of her."

"Mack was devastated when she died, wouldn't go to the club or join the men in golf for six months," Karen Harding added. "Barely spoke to anyone, except Nick, I guess, since he works with him. None of us thought he'd ever marry again, he was so devoted to Joanna."

The color drained from Tully's face as she listened to her new friends' description. She had known Joanna was special, but since their first dinner at his sister's home, Mack never spoke of her, not even to Cody. His silence spoke volumes, though, and Tully sensed her presence in every room. Hearing Susie speak so glowingly of her late friend made her spectral presence in Tully's life all the more real.

Tully understood from her own experience how Mack's memory of Joanna could shut out the possibility of all other emotional entanglements. Yet in the few months she'd lived with him and Cody, she had become like the fiddler crab, shedding its hard shell in order to grow. As she did so, she found herself becoming more and more drawn to her husband. Perhaps loving Cody had opened her to the possibility of love again. Although she had tried to deny her initial attraction to Mack, living with him had intensified that attraction.

Seeing Tully's reaction, Angie Johansen, thin, pretty, with steely blue eyes laser-like in their intensity, and always quick with a sharp note, chimed in, with just an undertone of cattiness, "But we're so glad he did. You're very different from Joanna, but Mack must have known he'd never find anyone like her again, and I'm sure you make him happy."

Tully glanced at Lizzie, who sat silently in the group, contributing nothing to their discussion of Joanna. Tully felt both admiration and gratitude for Lizzie—admiration because she never spoke ill of anyone and gratitude because, from the outset, she had treated Tully with warmth and kindness. Lizzie provided a buffer of sanity, enabling her to laugh inwardly at the stereotypical behavior of these leisure-class women and still take satisfaction in their acceptance of her as a wife and mother. Tully realized she needed that recognition, that reinforcement, to keep her from feeling as if her life were freakish.

Freakish is what Tully felt when she wasn't caring for Cody or socializing with her new friends. Freakish and lonely. Her relationship with Mack was much different from what she'd expected, more isolated, more distant. Although she was more than a nanny to Cody, she wondered if Mack made that distinction. He was often not home for dinner, and when he did arrive in time to join her and Cody, he was frequently distracted, his conversation perfunctory.

Those evenings when Mack didn't disappear into his office

after dinner, though, but instead engaged her in conversation, he was so charming, so clever, so sincere, his eyes twinkling over a joke he'd heard or shrouded when describing his concerns at work. When they attended parties at the homes of his friends or at the country club, Mack, ever the focus of everyone's interest, was attentive and considerate toward Tully, always making sure she was enjoying herself.

Weekends were family time, with Cody the center of their attention, and the time when Tully was happiest. They'd all gone skiing in Aspen and Telluride, Tully pleased with how adept she'd become in such a short time and amazed at Cody's proficiency, and taken Cody to the movies (and marveled at how much of children's animated films were geared toward their parents) and to children's concerts by the *Sesame Street* cast and *Barney and Friends*. They'd gone to the Children's Museum, the zoo, and, on the first unnaturally warm spring day, the botanical gardens, and they'd cheered on Nick and Lizzie's sons at their soccer matches.

Weekends were the rudder that propelled her feelings for Mack. As her affection for Mack grew, his disinterest in a real relationship became increasingly more painful. Tully almost preferred when Mack ignored her; it was easier to accept than the fact that she was a mere appendage in his life. But when they were together, dancing at the club, joking with friends, Mack casually holding her hand or rubbing her shoulder, she understood with stark clarity what she was missing and that she wanted it from Mack. That was not what she'd agreed to, though. Mack did not want emotional entanglements, not with her, not with anyone. She felt obligated by her agreement to hide her growing affection from him, to suppress it in herself, and doing so made her miserable.

Yet there were undeniable benefits to being Mrs. Mackenzie Bryson. Tully had grown up in a household where there was never enough money and assisting in everyday chores was a requirement, not an option. She and her sister shared the cooking and cleaning with their mother and contributed to the family income when they were old enough to work after school. Working to support herself was something she took for granted, and the concept of "marrying rich" was as foreign to her as it was to have not only a nanny but a housekeeper, too. Yet she *had* married rich, and Mack was generous with his wealth.

"Come shopping with us," Lizzie said one afternoon.

Tully always hated shopping—the crowds, the noise, the expense. "I don't know."

"It'll be fun. You can get a dress for the Children's Hospital fund-raiser."

As Mack's wife, she had already attended a few fund-raisers. It was clear her existing wardrobe was inadequate.

"What about Cody?"

"That's what Rosetta is for. Really, it's OK for you to leave him with her once in a while."

Tully had to admit that her first experience shopping with "the ladies" was a hoot. Lizzie and her friends took her to Saks Fifth Avenue. Tully, of course, had walked by the original Saks in New York City many times, gazing at the expensive clothes in the window but never daring to step inside, knowing the prices were well out of her reach. Now, walking in as if she owned the place, Angie, an anorexic size two with perfectly applied makeup and straight bleached platinum-blond hair falling just below her chin, led Tully and the other women to the designer dress section on the second floor. Angie grabbed the first saleswoman she saw. "We've got Cinderella here, and we're going to turn her into a princess," she said. "Show us your very best."

It took Tully only twenty minutes to find a simple gown for charity functions. She was ready to leave, but her new friends wouldn't hear of it and dragged her throughout the store, drowning her in clothes—slacks, skirts, blouses, dresses.

"You've got an adorable figure, Tully. Don't be afraid to show it off," Susie said when Tully demurred over a slinky form-fitting black jersey-knit dress with a plunging-V neckline.

They hit the shoe department, and she loaded up on stylish footwear. "You can never have too many boots and shoes," Karen said.

Tully tried to resist the lingerie department. After all, who would see her in sheer negligees? "You must *always* keep buying new lingerie," Angie said. "Our husbands live for that."

They finished up with costume jewelry, the one department where Tully felt at ease.

"Never buy the good stuff yourself," Lizzie said. "That's the only thing husbands feel comfortable picking out for us. If you buy it yourself, they feel they don't need to."

When they left the store, Tully had charged over six thousand dollars to Mack's credit card. With enormous guilt, she told Mack about the purchases when he arrived home that night, promising she'd reimburse him from her "allowance."

Mack shrugged. "Don't worry about it. I want you to be well-dressed."

Yes, of course, thought Tully, the perfect ornamental wife must look the part to maintain the façade. The problem was, for Tully it was no longer a façade.

Chapter 10

The dim lights of the seedy bar in Chaffee Park muted the unattractiveness of its few occupants. Mostly men down on their luck inhabited the premises during this happy hour, when drinks were half-price and conversations could be had undisturbed. Henry Woodman sat in a booth at the back corner, across from Julio Martinez, his bookie. Each man had a cold bottle of beer before him, with six empty bottles pushed to the side.

"Put a thousand down on Lucky Lucy to win in the eighth," Henry said.

"Sorry, man, I can't front you no more. You're in too deep, and your money bag is locked away."

Henry glared at Julio. "You little shit," he hissed. "I'm trying to get her out, and I can't do that without cash. She's been sitting in jail almost four months because I couldn't come up with the bail bond. Her attorney is no help—she's stuck with a kid from the Public Defender's office. He looks like he's just out of diapers, still has pimples on his face. She doesn't have a chance unless I get her a real lawyer. This race is a sure thing. I got a tip on it."

"You get lots of tips, and they're all for shit."

Henry lunged across the table and grabbed Julio by his shirt. "I'm not a fuckin' loser."

Julio pushed Henry's hands off him. "I didn't say you were. Just a run of bad luck. Don't get so hot under the collar."

Henry slumped in his seat, his head bent over. "Shit. I am a loser, through and through. The only woman who ever thought I was worth anything is sitting in a goddamn prison cell because of me."

He picked up his beer and took a chug. "I wasn't always a loser. I did well enough in school—decent grades, everybody liked me. I was always good for a party on a Friday night that'd last till Sunday, but then I'd be back to the grind Monday morning, ready to roll. If it hadn't been for the accident, I'd be something today. I would've been on top, a hero probably."

He had wanted to be a policeman, and he could have been, too. He was smart enough, brawny enough. It was a tough break getting into that car accident driving home after the graduation celebration. Sure, he'd had a little too much to drink, but who hadn't? At least no one was killed. He'd already dropped off his passengers when he hit the telephone pole at sixty miles per hour. But he was left with a slight limp, and though it didn't affect him much, the police department was such a bureaucracy. No exceptions—100 percent fit or goodbye, Charlie.

Henry held his Budweiser in his hands as he thought about how his life had turned out so wrong. It was the sports betting that started him on this downward spiral to worthlessness, calculating the assets and liabilities of each team to make an "educated" pick and the sweet feeling of success that came with collecting the rewards of his astute choices. He was good at it, and it was an easy way to finance his partying, his wheels, his snazzy clothes. Instead of taking the policeman's exam, he took a job after high school in the stock room of Wal-Mart. It was lousy pay and lousy work, but it gave him enough time to study the teams and know the players, and his bets became bigger and more lucrative. He had plenty of money to impress the ladies, and hadn't yet added those extra pounds around his belt.

Twenty years later, Henry was no longer the good-looking kid with money to burn. He'd had a series of dead-end jobs, always managing to earn a living without really having enough to enjoy life. The adrenaline rush from sports betting brought him to the racetrack and then to the poker tables. Although he'd held his own for many years, the compulsive betting finally caught up to him. After his losses had started to regularly exceed his wins, he began burglarizing houses to pay off his bookie. Married at the time to a frizzy-haired manicurist he'd known since high school, she dumped him after he was caught the third time, and even the bleeding-heart-liberal judge had to throw him in jail.

Some men can do time easily; for others every day is torture, emotional if not physical. Henry was in the latter group, and when he was released five years later, at the age of forty-five, he was determined to turn his life around and never again see the inside of a prison.

When he met Agnes four years later, he'd been clear of gambling since his release from prison. He'd been with a lot of women during that time, most of them younger and prettier than Agnes, but he knew right away there was something special about her. She wasn't just some bimbo out for a good time. She had a head on her shoulders and a solid job and—this is what really got to him—knew about his past and admired his ability to pick himself up and start over again.

Agnes, a big-boned woman, was a year older than Henry and certainly not a looker, with her receding chin and her thin brown hair tinged with gray and pulled back in a knot. But she wasn't ugly either—Henry wouldn't be seen with someone ugly, even though he certainly no longer had the casual good looks of his youth. Her eyes were special, a luminescent sea-green framed by still-thick black lashes. When she wore her hair down, freshly washed, the sun shining on it, she was almost attractive. Henry knew, though, that inside, in her heart, Agnes was the most beautiful woman he'd known.

When he'd asked Agnes to marry him, he didn't know how much she earned. He knew only that she owned her own home, small but well kept, in a good neighborhood. He was astounded when he discovered she made over a hundred grand a year. With his average earnings of fifty grand a year from construction work, they together would have more income than he'd ever dreamed possible. Henry initially wondered what he could give this woman who already had a good income, good friends, and a comfortable life, but soon knew he was giving her something she'd never had: someone who loved her.

Henry did love her, more than he'd ever loved another woman, but the thought of returning to prison made him catatonic. Agnes didn't deserve to be sitting in jail now, and Henry would do anything to get her out, but he just couldn't return to jail himself. Even if it *should* be him sitting there, he simply couldn't. Agnes, bless her heart, understood him.

They'd been married a few years when a construction buddy invited him to a friendly poker game. What the hell, he thought. Something happened to him when he played that night, just a friendly group of guys sitting around a table with plenty of beer and nuts and poker chips, just a game to everyone else, but more than that to Henry. It was serious business to him, and he was good at it, leaving with everyone else's money.

He began seeking out the serious players again, joining higher- and higher-stakes games, sometimes winning, sometimes losing, but mostly coming out ahead. Before he knew it, he was back at the track, booking bets with Julio on horse races, then pro ballgames, college ballgames, almost anything a bookie would take a bet on. Each time he lost, he wagered a larger amount to cover the loss and try to come out ahead. Each time he dug a deeper hole for himself.

"Your markers are no good to me," Julio had said. "Don't matter how high the interest is, nothing on nothing is nothing. I don't operate alone, you know. I got people I answer to and they need to see something from you. A big something."

Henry knew Agnes had savings of her own, a separate account that was fairly substantial. He also knew she never touched that money, never looked at her bank statements, just filed them away when they came. He hated himself for needing her money; he felt degraded and dirty. Agnes had such faith in him. There was no way he could ask her for the money. It was better to just take it, forge her signature, and he'd make it back, plus more. When he didn't make it back but instead accumulated such a big nut he knew he'd *never* be able to make it back, he broke down and confessed to Agnes, sobbing like a baby.

"They're going to kill me if I don't pay them back," he said. "I don't know what to do. Even if we take out a second mortgage on our house, it won't come close to raising the amount I owe."

Agnes sat stiffly for minutes, her hands unmoving in her lap, before she answered. "Don't worry," she said. "We'll figure this out. You're sick, no different than an alcoholic. If you agree to get counseling for your addiction, I'll help you. I'll find a way."

"Anything, anything you say. I know I need help, and I'll go every day if that's what it takes, I promise. You're the best thing that ever happened to me and I'll do anything to keep you. I love you, you know that, right?"

Now Agnes was paying the price for his sickness. He took another chug of beer. "I swear, Julio, I'm gonna get Agnes out of jail or someone will be sorry."

Tony Capriccio sat across from Agnes in the jail's interview room, a small airless box with a plain wooden table and two metal chairs, one of many in a row of rooms. A metal door, its lock remotely controlled from a distance, provided the only access to the rooms, and a uniformed guard was seated outside, readily available if an inmate erupted in a burst of anger.

"I gotta tell you, Agnes, I don't get nervous much. My friends got nervous before their exams in law school. Not me. Some of the other public defenders, especially the new ones, feel nervous going to trial. Not me. What makes me nervous are clients who ignore a favorable plea deal when the evidence is stacked against them. Right now, Agnes, you're making me very nervous."

Agnes sat silently and stared at her young attorney, with his pockmarked face and eager expression. He'd told Agnes he was twenty-eight but looked years younger to her.

"I don't think you realize what you're facing here, Agnes. They've charged you with a separate count of felony theft for each time you forged an invoice and obtained an improper check. That's twelve counts, and each one has a potential sentence of fifteen years. The judge can sentence you consecutively, not concurrently, which means you'd serve one fifteen-year sentence and then start the next, twelve times. You'll never see the outside again.

"Now we can go to trial, but you haven't given me much to work on. They have the burden of proving it's your signature on the contracts and the payment authorization forms, but they have an expert who can tie you to it, you had the means and opportunity, and Mack will testify it's not his signature. We'll show that none of the proceeds ever appeared in any of your bank accounts, that your lifestyle and purchases didn't change, but frankly, you could have hidden the money anywhere, or, more likely, they'll bring in a witness who'll testify that your husband was a notorious gambler who had rung up big debts."

Agnes sat erect in her seat, her face composed. Although dressed in prison garb, she looked out of place in the barren room. "I've worked hard my whole life. I've never been in trouble before. Won't that count for anything?"

"Your lack of a criminal record and good service to the company may help mitigate the sentencing, hopefully convince the judge to impose concurrent terms rather than consecutive, but you'll still be looking at ten to fifteen years. If you give up your husband, you can get out in a year, and you'll get credit for the time already served. If you don't, they're only offering fifteen years on one count and the others go away. If your husband loves you, then I don't understand why he would let you protect him like this. Life in state prison is not like it is here in the county jail. It's hard time, and fifteen years is very long, especially at your age."

Agnes shook her head. "We've already gone over this. I won't accept any plea that involves Henry. I'm prepared to go to trial and take my chances. Aren't I presumed innocent? Doesn't the state have the burden of proof?"

"Only on paper, Agnes, only on paper. The truth is, a jury looks at you in the defendant's seat and they start out thinking, 'Why would the police have arrested her if she were innocent?' Unless you can bring me evidence that someone else signed those contracts and authorized the payments, then the jury will have to work hard to brush away their ingrained assumption that the police know what they're doing."

"Can you get me a plea bargain that doesn't involve Henry? I can do more than one year, maybe a few years, but I won't testify against Henry."

"I'll try, but they seem pretty intent on getting Henry."

Agnes knew that most people would think her foolish. After all, she'd been married to Henry for only five years. Those five years had been her happiest, though. Of course, the house would have to be sold as part of the restitution she'd be required to make. The thought of returning home to a small apartment—alone, without the job she'd had for fifteen years—while Henry languished in prison, confirmed her resolve to take the full punishment herself. Although Henry had created the need for money, it was she alone who had made the excruciating decision to steal from her boss and friend.

Agnes had come up with the scheme to embezzle money from Big Sky. Although she idolized Mack, her husband came first. She knew the money would be insignificant to Mack. Now she sat in prison, facing the prospect of ending her life there, and the district attorney had offered her a way out: exchange her freedom for her husband's. He obviously didn't know the importance of love, of loyalty. Perhaps one needed to be without it for so long to recognize its value. Henry had spent his time in jail. It had been her decision to steal, and she would pay the price for it.

She wasn't angry at herself for her decision, and she wasn't angry at her husband. He had a sickness—she understood that. Instead, she directed her anger at Mack: It was Mack who never asked her why she would do such a thing, Mack who had trusted and relied on her for so long yet so quickly assumed the worst about her, Mack who made the decision to press charges against her instead of giving her, his loyal assistant and confidante, a chance to explain, to beg his forgiveness, and to make plans to repay him. It was Mack who knew nothing about love, about sacrifice. She knew she was on shaky grounds in expecting his understanding, but nevertheless she had, and he had grievously disappointed her.

Agnes had always been the "good" girl, the eldest of three daughters whose mother died suddenly in Agnes' junior year of high school. All the girls were bright, but Agnes knew none of them would make it to college if one of them didn't assume the burden of supporting the others. She was the oldest and believed it was her responsibility to sacrifice herself so that her sisters could succeed.

Although at first Agnes regretted her own lack of a college education, her employers recognized and appreciated her intelligence, work ethic and common sense, and she continued to rise in each organization. Working as the personal assistant to the chief executive officer of a major corporation, with a salary exceeding that of any of her sisters, was an achievement she had never thought possible. It helped her to never regret the abnegation of her college aspirations. Agnes was used to sacrifice, and if she needed to sacrifice for her husband, she was prepared to do so.

The next day, Tony was back in the same claustrophobic interview room, Agnes once again sitting across the table from him.

"I don't have encouraging news for you," he said. "The assistant district attorney on your case is Tom Landers. I've known him a long time and he's not someone out to make a name for himself no matter who got destroyed in the process. He's usually pretty reasonable, but his heels are dug in on this."

"So are mine," Agnes said.

"I told him his case was shaky. The whole thing rests on an expert witness, and we'll bring in our own. I have someone who'll say it's not clear the same person who signed Mack's name on his letters also signed the contracts and payment authorizations."

Agnes's face brightened. "That's good. Maybe I won't be convicted."

"Not so fast. Tom told me his expert also examined the signatures of everyone else who had access to Mack's office and he's ruled them out as possible culprits. He's going to tell the jury you had the means, the opportunity, the motive, and your handwriting fits the profile. He feels pretty comfortable about this one, so he's not so anxious to offer a deal."

Agnes slumped back in her seat.

"It's not completely hopeless," Tony said. "You've never even had a traffic ticket before. You're as clean as they come. You're likely to come off as sympathetic to the jury, and jury nullification is not unheard of—although the chance of that is really remote."

"Is Mack pushing for a longer jail term?"

"No. I've interviewed him. He'd like this matter to go away. If we go to trial, Mr. Bryson won't be a strong witness for the prosecution." Tony reached over and took Agnes's hand. "Listen, Tom really believes you were set up by Henry. He's still offering the fifteen years concurrent for you, but if you testify against Henry, he'll work out a double plea agreement: five for you and ten for him, plus restitution, of course."

"Nothing for Henry. I've told you that over and over. I won't turn on him. Don't you understand loyalty?"

"I don't see it as loyalty, Agnes. I see you protecting a man who can't control his gambling and doesn't mind breaking the law to support it. I don't see him changing."

"You're wrong about Henry. He *is* changing. He's been going to Gamblers Anonymous."

Tony nodded. "OK, let's say he's changed. Fifteen years is still too much for you to do when I can get you much less."

"But I can turn down that deal. I can go to trial, can't I?"

"Sure. And no matter how sympathetic you are, you can be convicted and sentenced to twelve consecutive terms. Normally,

I like going to trial. And if I thought the plea deal was bad, I'd never suggest taking it to avoid risking a bad outcome at trial. But part of my job is to evaluate the risk of losing. I've got to tell you, Agnes, in your case that risk is sky-high."

Chapter 11

Winter had passed so quickly, and spring was just a blur; it hardly seemed possible that summer was just a moment away. Their family skis had been stored, and fly-fishing was now the order of the day. Tully was as excited as Cody as she packed his clothes for their first family weekend in Montana since she'd married Mack. Mack and Nick had already spent several weekends there in the spring, but now, mid-June, Mack had pronounced the rivers and creeks in Montana "fit for women and children." Both families were spending ten days at their respective ranches, although Nick's family had left the day before, and Tully found it hard to contain her excitement.

"I want my Clifford shirt and I want my blue shorts and I want my Bob the Builder hat," Cody said, pointing out each item of clothing he wanted her to pack in his suitcase, a miniature version of a pull-along bag.

Tully was always surprised at Cody's determination in choosing his outfit each day, demanding a favorite shirt or pants despite her protestations that they were too dirty or the day too warm or cold for the requested item. Of course, she recognized the importance of clothing as a statement but had assumed that urge wouldn't present itself until adolescence. Yet, at not quite four, Cody knew exactly what clothes he liked and what he didn't and was quite prepared to throw a temper tantrum if forced to wear something in the latter category.

Thank goodness for Lizzie and the Lenape Lane Ladies. Had Tully not had a group of mothers to assure her that Cody's behavior was typical—not only his persnickety streak when it came to clothing but *all* the behaviors that were foreign to her—having become a mother overnight, Tully would have spent each day in a constant state of panic. But with their experience to guide her, along with the innumerable books on parenting she'd devoured, she had eased into her role as Cody's mother relatively seamlessly.

Cody didn't need the help of others; he adapted to Tully's presence as if she had always been his mother and had just been late in finding her way home to him. From her first moment as Mack's wife, Cody had called her "Mommy." Tully knew it wasn't just an appellation but a reflection of the bond he felt with her. She was his mother, the mother he'd been waiting for as long as he could understand that other little boys had both fathers and mothers. From her first day in his house, Cody had told her he loved her, and Tully never doubted that he accepted as a fundamental truth that she loved him equally.

Tully did love Cody, as powerfully as if she'd pushed him through her own birth canal. Three mornings a week he attended a local nursery-school class, and although Tully enjoyed the quiet time for herself, she still felt a tug each day when the bus picked him up. Cody had taken to giving her a hug upon leaving and saying, "Don't be sad, Mommy. I'll be back soon."

Weekends with Mack and Cody were always fun, and Tully had high expectations for a full week and a half spent as a family, getting to better know the activities Mack held so dear. Although Rosetta had previously accompanied the family on their trips to the ranch, Tully had given her the time off. She didn't want to share Mack and Cody with anyone this week, not even Rosetta.

"Do you know how to fish?" Cody asked. "I do. Daddy taught me to fish, and I can teach you to fish. And I can show you how to put up a tent. Will you sleep with us in the tent? We have to be careful with our food when we sleep in the tent because bears can sniff our food if we bring it in the tent. Daddy ties our food up in a tree far away from our tent so the bears can't reach it. Are you afraid of bears? I'm not, because Daddy said if we don't bother them, they won't bother us."

"I don't know how to fish," Tully said. "My daddy never taught me, but I'd like you to teach me how. It sounds like fun. But would I have to put a worm on a hook?"

Cody giggled. "Girls don't like worms, but they won't hurt you, you know. We don't use worms when we fish at the ranch. We use a make-believe fly for bait."

Cody seemed so serious about the upcoming trip that Tully had to restrain the smile that kept pushing its way to her lips. Together, they finished packing his clothes, along with his favorite books and toys, and zipped up his suitcase. Cody placed it upright and grabbed the handle.

"I'm ready to go," he said.

Tully straightened up and gave a quick look around Cody's room to ensure that everything was in place. She had redecorated Cody's bedroom after she'd moved in, changing it from an austere, colorless space, the only evidence of its inhabitance by a toddler being the myriad toys strewn about, to an embracing room, with walls painted a sunflower yellow, a brightly colored wallpaper border along the top depicting different jungle animals, and the jungle theme continuing to his bedspread and curtains. A three-foot-high stuffed lion guarded one side of his door while a giraffe guarded the other, and a large wooden chest, also painted with pictures of animals, held his toys.

"Well, we all have to be ready to go, and I haven't packed for myself yet. Do you want to help me pack?"

"I'll help you, Mommy. I'm a good packer."

Tully and Cody began their packing of Tully's suitcase while Mack paced downstairs impatiently. Although Big Sky Communications owned a four-passenger single engine propeller plane that the senior executives used to shorten their travel time to meetings out of the state and which Mack and Nick used for their weekends in Montana, Mack never flew with his son in the plane, the only tinge of caution he ever displayed in his personal life. Instead, they were taking a United Airlines flight from the Denver airport, to Galletin Airport in Montana, about thirty miles from the ranch.

Mack kept a pickup truck at the ranch, and they would rent a car at the airport. Flying a commercial airliner meant adhering to its schedules and not his own, and the limousine had been waiting outside for fifteen minutes already while Tully decided what to bring.

"This isn't such a hard job, Tully," Mack called up to her. Just jeans and shorts and a bathing suit—that's all you need."

Easy for men, thought Tully. This was the first time she'd be vacationing with Mack since their honeymoon, at the place he held dearest, doing the activities he loved the most, all of them together as a family, and she wanted to make damn sure she looked her best. That meant picking out clothes that enhanced her attributes rather than buried them, a task that had been foreign to her before she'd married Mack.

Her new friends had helped her ease into her role as the wife of a wealthy businessman. They'd taken her to designer boutiques for casual clothes, to day spas for facials, manicures and pedicures, and to the "in" salon for a new hairstyle. They taught her how to wear makeup. Before her marriage to Mack, she hadn't been interested in shopping, in superficial changes to her appearance, and, in any event, didn't think it would make a difference in her appeal to men. Certainly, it wouldn't make her more interesting.

But the truth was, these outward changes did make a difference in how she felt about herself, and along with that change she also became more comfortable engaging in social chitchat. She no longer dreaded the social engagements that came with the territory of being Mrs. Mack Bryson.

Tully was under no illusion that this metamorphosis would make her more desirable to Mack. Although he apparently enjoyed her company, he didn't seem to want or need the emotional connection she now yearned for. Indeed, he was thrilled Cody had made that connection so quickly with her, but he kept a wall around himself, closing off any real intimacy. Still, Tully couldn't help but fancy that if she didn't push Mack, didn't pressure him, didn't make demands of him, perhaps one day he would want more from her. And she planned to do whatever she could to make that day happen.

"Put this in your suitcase, Mommy," Cody said as he pulled out from a drawer a bedraggled T-shirt adorned with a large red apple, a leftover from her days in New York City.

Tully knew she'd never finish packing with Cody helping her. "Why don't you go downstairs and help Daddy put the suitcases in the limousine?"

"But I want to help you."

"I know you do, and you've been a big help. But Daddy really needs your help, too." Tully breathed a sigh of relief as Cody reluctantly departed. She riffled through a stack of jeans and picked a pair of basic Levi's for camping and horseback riding and a pair each of 7 For All Mankind and Jean Paul Da'Mage jeans. It was amazing how jeans selling for hundreds of dollars fit so differently from standard off-the-rack jeans, accentuating her curves in ways she'd never thought possible. She'd always had a flat stomach, and the low-cut styles now popular added a sexiness that in the past she had been uncomfortable with. Of course, her twice-weekly workouts with a personal trainer in their home gym no doubt contributed to the way her shapely, well-defined buttocks caused men to turn their heads, but the truth was Levi's just didn't have the same effect as designer jeans.

She added some designer tops, capris, shorts, and a bathing suit and turned to her lingerie drawer. It was filled with silky bikini underwear, lacy uplifting bras, and sheer nightgowns that barely covered her pubis, all of which she'd purchased at the urging of her friends but had never worn.

Well, it can't hurt to throw some in the suitcase. After all, the worst that'll happen is they won't get used. Maybe, though, maybe the mood will strike him. Miracles can *happen, right? Better to have them with me than kick myself if I don't, if there's even an iota of possibility of wearing it.*

Tully quickly gathered up the remaining items to pack: toiletries, cosmetics, jewelry, shoes. She knew she was unprepared for outdoor activities, but Mack had suggested she wait until she saw the ranch and knew what she wanted to try. She could pick up any needed clothing, footwear, and supplies in Livingston.

She zipped her suitcase closed and wheeled it down the stairs. "I'm all set. We can get going now."

Mack glanced at her luggage, bulging at the seams. "It looks like you've packed for a month. We'll only be gone ten days."

"I know, I know, but I didn't know what I'd want to wear, so I just threw in everything. I can take things out if you think it's too heavy."

"No, it's late. Let's get going. I just don't understand why women need more than a pair of jeans. Well, maybe two pairs in case one gets dirty."

Tully smiled. Last year, one pair of jeans would have been all she packed. She had certainly changed in that year.

Chapter 12

Cody spent the short flight to Montana gazing intently out the window while Mack told Tully about his early visits to the state. "I first came to Montana with my father when I was around nine or ten. We'd spend the weekend, sometimes a whole week, fly-fishing, usually on the Yellowstone or the Madison. When Big Sky took off, my first significant purchase was the ranch."

"I can't wait to see it. Tell me what it's like."

"Well, it's a lot different now than when I first bought it. It's a 680-acre spread within walking distance of the Yellowstone River and miles of trails for horses. It came with a three-room log cabin, and compared to what I slept in when I came here as a child, that was luxurious. But as Big Sky grew, so did my plans for the property. First, I built a new stable for the horses and then, about five years ago, a new house. It's made of hand-peeled logs and native stone, and all the rooms downstairs have twelve-foot ceilings. There are three fireplaces—in the living room, kitchen and master bedroom—and a wrap-around deck that looks over the Gallatin and Absaroka mountain ranges. And you'll be happy to know, since you liked it so much in Chamonix, there's a hot tub large enough for eight people built into the deck."

"What happened to the original cabin?"

"Ben—he's the caretaker for the ranch—he lives there now. He takes care of the horses and watches over the main house."

"And Nick and Lizzie—where's their ranch?"

"Right next to mine. When the property came on the market, Nick jumped at it."

They stepped out of the plane at Gallatin Airport into bright sunshine, with nary a cloud overhead. The high peaks of the mountain range against the backdrop of the blue sky looked too beautiful to be real—it was as if an artist had painted them on a canvas. On the ride to the ranch in their rented Toyota Land Cruiser, Tully peered out the window, awed by the surrounding landscape.

"What's that?" she asked, pointing to a large bird soaring in the sky.

"It's a golden eagle," Mack said. "This area is home to a large population of them and some bald eagles as well, although you'll only see those in the winter and during the spring migration."

As they continued to drive, Tully said, "It seems like the land goes on forever and ever. It's so beautiful. Until our honeymoon, I'd only been in Florida or New York. Seeing pictures of this, even movies, doesn't do it justice."

Cody, who had been chattering throughout the drive, fell asleep in his car seat. The highway stretched out in front of them and they drove along in silence, with the comfort of long-married couples who no longer need to talk continuously. There were few other cars on the road, and the quiet filled Tully with a sense of well-being.

They stopped in Livingston to pick up some supplies. Tully delighted in the quaint shops and the old-town feel. "This is just what I pictured a Montana town would look like."

They made their purchases and continued on to the ranch, which was everything Tully had imagined and more. Lush meadows on rolling hills were framed by forests of aspen and spruce, with the stunning backdrop of two mountain ranges. A wide creek meandered through the property. In the distance, Tully could see the caretaker's log cabin, stables, and a corral. Three horses grazed in the fenced pasture.

Paradise Valley was aptly named, and Mack's ranch truly deserved its appellation: Eden Hollow Ranch.

"There's Chief," shouted Cody excitedly. "Can I ride him now, Daddy, please, please? Can we go for a ride now?"

"Whoa, cowboy. Settle down a bit. We just got here, and we should show Mommy around first, don't you think? Let's get set inside, have a bite to eat, and then we can go say hello to Chief. How about that?"

"OK, Daddy, but I missed Chief. Do you think he remembers me?"

"Of course he does. You're his pal, aren't you?"

Tully knew Cody had his own pony and even at the age of three, with Mack holding the reins, had gone riding. Horses were a foreign phenomenon to Tully. She'd never been on one. Mack had initially discouraged her from engaging in any of the activities he and Cody always shared at the ranch, shrugging his shoulders when Tully expressed an interest in tagging along.

"I don't expect you to enjoy the things I do. In fact, Lizzie never goes along when she's up here. There are plenty of boutiques to shop in and a couple of museums around. You can even take a drive over to Yellowstone National Park—it's real close. You and Lizzie could make a day of that."

"I see Lizzie all the time back in Denver. This is my chance to learn something new, and I think it would be good for Cody to see that women can enjoy these experiences, too."

"I'm not being chauvinistic, really I'm not, but we've always made a father-son thing of these excursions, Nick with his sons and, ever since he could walk, me with Cody. It's a special time we spend with them, teaching them about the things we love."

Tully kept pushing. She'd never hiked, never fished, never ridden a horse, but those were all things that Mack loved and she wanted to share them with him. Eventually, Mack promised he'd set aside a day to teach her fly-fishing and ask his caretaker, Ben, to give her riding lessons while he was off fishing with Cody.

"You can ride Joanna's horse, Paladine, while we're away. He's very gentle. And both families always spend one night at a camp-fire, women included. The men sleep out in tents that night, and if you want to join us, I'll set up an extra one for you, although Lizzie always chooses to sleep back at her ranch on a nice com-fortable mattress, with hot water and flush toilets. But you're welcome to join us that night if that's what you really want."

The week progressed with no opportunity for intimacy with Mack. Each morning, he and Cody joined up with Nick and his sons, fishing gear in hand, and headed off to a different creek, sometimes for the day, sometimes just the morning. Although Mack and Nick usually fished the Yellowstone on their solo weekends, they chose smaller waterways when they were with their sons, with fewer currents and less risk to the children's safety.

Sometimes in the afternoons they'd all go into town for lunch, and often in the evenings the two families would have dinner together, and Nick and Lizzie would join Mack and Tully for conversation, wine, and music after the children were in bed. But mostly Tully felt alone, isolated despite the company, and confused. *At least he's home at night. I don't think I could bear it if he was with a woman up here.*

There was so much about her new life that was satisfying, her love for Cody topping the list, but there was also so much that was *un*satisfying. Though she was part of a group of friends for the first time in her life, none were women she would have cho-sen as friends on her own, aside from Lizzie. She had the financial resources to buy anything she wanted, but how many pairs of jeans was it really necessary to own? She had the leisure time to indulge any of her interests, but what interests had she pursued? She felt stagnant, unmotivated to reach outside her daily routine in search of new endeavors.

She did enjoy working out, having a personal trainer to guide her, and was pleased with her newfound strength, toned muscles, improved endurance, and greater self-confidence, but she knew it wasn't enough. She needed more in her life and, against all reason, had yearned for that "more" to be Mack.

Tully spent her mornings learning to ride Paladine, an American Paint Horse with *tobiano* coloring, a sturdy, muscular body, and a gentle disposition, which made him willing to endure the mistakes of an inexperienced rider. Ben was a patient instructor, teaching her how to mount and dismount, how to hold the reins, how to move up and down with the horse.

"This here's the tack," he said, showing her the gear that goes on the horse. "You have the bridle, saddle, saddle pads, bit, cinches, lead ropes, halters, stirrup irons and stirrup leathers. Don't worry about how to put all those together on the horse. I'll do that for you. But you should know the names for it all."

"He's such a handsome horse," Tully said.

"That he is. The first Mrs. Bryson fell in love with Paladine for his coloring, but Mack knew he was a perfect horse for his wife to learn on and, as Cody grows older, for him to ride."

Tully learned that both horses and ponies are measured by "hands" and that Paladine was fifteen hands, which made him about average in size. By comparison, Mack's horse was sixteen and a half hands, and Cody's pony was almost thirteen hands. Mack's horse, Majesty, was a heavily muscled quarter horse who was speedy, easy to handle, and agile. Cody's pony was a quarter pony, similar in looks to Majesty but smaller, with a short, broad head, small ears, and kind eyes that seemed to look directly into Cody's face, brightening with Cody's smile and caressing touch. Tully was surprised to learn that Chief wasn't simply a young horse that would grow in time to the size of Majesty but a separate breed and had reached his mature height.

Ben taught Tully to jog—the western term for a slow trot—around the corral, but she didn't feel ready to join Mack on the trail rides he took those afternoons when fishing ended early. When not riding or spending time with Lizzie, she filled her days spread out on a hammock tied between two large oak trees, encased in the beauty of the valley, and caught up on her reading. As she devoured the pages, she thought again about her dream of writing. *I certainly have the time now, and I'll never know if I have it in me if I don't give it a try.* Yet whenever she thought about sitting down at her computer, she felt paralyzed. *I have everything I need except an idea for a story, and it's pretty damn hard to write without that.*

Tully had always been a hard worker, and it bothered her that she felt herself turning into a pampered housewife, her only responsibility the care and nurturing of Cody. Of course, she appreciated the importance of that role, but lately it hadn't seemed enough. She had hoped the ten days together as a family would reinvigorate her commitment to this life and jar her from the malaise she'd been experiencing. So far, three days before the end of their trip, it hadn't.

Tonight they were having their camp-out, and although Tully looked forward to it, it would be another evening spent with the Hanover family. Together, they'd all hike partway up a nearby mountain to a turquoise-blue lake and set up camp. Mack packed their gear in his backpack.

"Now, you're sure you want to sleep over?" Mack asked for the umpteenth time. "Nick is going to walk Lizzie back down to her car after dinner, so you really won't be putting anyone out if you'd prefer to sleep at home."

"Of course I want to stay. I've been looking forward to this all week."

"Well, then, camping means carrying your gear. I can put some of it in my backpack, but with the extra tent and sleeping bag, you're going to need to backpack some yourself."

"Hey, I'm not a weakling. I've really gotten stronger from the weight training."

"You're using different muscles for this. I'm just saying it's a lot easier climbing a mountain without twenty pounds on your back. If you go home with Lizzie tonight, you won't need to carry anything."

Tully certainly wasn't going to lose a chance to spend time

with Mack in his element, no matter how uncomfortable she might be. "Nope, I'm in for the whole experience."

Mack was right. Tully struggled up the mountain, lagging behind the others, and Mack often had to stop to wait for her while Cody ran on ahead with Nick's sons. But she made it to the lake, where she gladly plopped down her pack, exhausted.

Mack and Nick, along with Evan and Jack, Nick's eleven-year-old twin sons, began setting up the tents. When they were all up, including Tully's, Evan asked, "Can we go swimming now, Dad?" Nick nodded.

"Me, too, me, too," Cody said.

"You need to wait for me, Cody," Mack called over to him. "I just want to gather some wood first."

"I can take him," Tully said.

Mack laughed. "You don't realize how cold a mountain lake is. I don't think you really want to go in."

There he goes again. Always trying to dissuade me from becoming part of his family. I can do anything. Didn't I just prove it climbing up this god-awful mountain? "If it's not too cold for Cody, then I can stand it."

Mack smirked. "Why don't you first put your foot in the water and then tell me you want to go swimming."

Tully strolled over to the lake, confident that she'd prove Mack wrong. After taking off her boots, she proudly stomped into the water, screamed at the top of her lungs, and ran out as fast as she could. "Are you people nuts? No one can swim in this. You'd have to be a seal or a penguin."

Everyone laughed.

"You have to have testosterone to keep you warm," Nick said with a big grin on his face.

"Chauvinists," Tully muttered under her breath as she scrambled back to the campsite.

Despite the inauspicious beginning, Tully loved the whole experience. She'd found it exhausting climbing part of the mountain, but it was a good exhaustion, one that made her feel she'd accomplished something worthwhile. They gathered wood, explored, started a roaring campfire, and cooked their dinner over it. When the meal was finished, Nick walked Lizzie down the mountain to her car and returned alone to the campsite, the long summer day providing plenty of light.

"Let's play seek-and-hide," Nick said as the sun began to set.

"What's that?" Tully asked.

"It's the opposite of hide-and-seek," Evan said. "Instead of everyone hiding and one person trying to find everyone, one person hides and everyone tries to find that one person. When you do, you hide along with that person until only one person is left looking for everyone else."

"The only rules are, you can't go in the lake, you can't go more than ten feet off a trail, and you have only to the count of one hundred to hide, so you won't be able to go too far," Jack said.

Everyone had a flashlight, and Evan was the first to hide. Tully found the game fun, searching in the dark for shadowy figures, noting the disappearance of others as they discovered Evan's hiding place, stumbling across him herself almost by accident, and hiding with him until the last person joined the group. When it was Tully's turn to hide, she slipped into her tent and inside her sleeping bag, certain she would stump the others.

Mack was the first to find her and surprised Tully by climbing inside her sleeping bag alongside her, wrapping his arms around her in the confined space. "Cozy, isn't it?" he whispered. Tully held her breath, unsure of what to say, what to do. Her body tingled from the feel of Mack's body so close to hers, and she was disappointed when Jack quickly stuck his head into the tent and discovered her hiding spot as well.

After the game, they roasted marshmallows and made s'mores and then sang songs over the campfire. Each person picked a song for all to sing—"Home on the Range," "The Happy Wanderer," "This Old Man." When it was Mack's turn, he chose "This Land is Your Land." The boys knew the words, even Cody, and Tully felt the warm glow of the flames course through her body as she sang, "This land is your land, this land is my land, from California, to the New York Island, from the redwood forest, to

the Gulf Stream waters, this land was made for you and me." She
was happy she'd stayed, happy to be part of Mack's family, happy
to be experiencing the glorious country she lived in yet had seen
so little of until this year. Cody chose "If You're Happy and You
Know It," and Tully clapped her hands and stomped her feet
joyously as she joined in the song.

As they broke camp the next morning and hiked back to their
car, Tully was pleased she'd stayed the night, despite her soreness.
And so, when the next evening Mack tried to dissuade her from
his promised fishing lesson, she remained insistent.

"Are you sure you want to try fly-fishing?" he asked over dinner. It's not as easy as just dropping a line in the water. You might
want to try some simpler fishing first."

"No, you and Cody fly-fish, and that's what I want to learn."

"OK, we'll all go tomorrow morning. That means early, the
best fish are caught before the sun is too high in the sky."

Tully would get up in the middle of the night if that's what it
took to join Mack. "I'll be ready. But I don't understand—you've
been fishing all week, yet you've never brought any fish back to
cook. Does that mean they haven't been biting this week?"

Mack chuckled. "No, the fishing's great, but Nick and I
fish for sport, and when we catch one, we throw it back."

Tully was awake and dressed at dawn the next morning.
At Mack's suggestion, she had gone shopping at a fly-fishing
store in Livingston and picked up breathable Gore-Tex waders,
silk thermal bottoms, wading boots, a wide-brimmed hat, and
neoprene gloves. Although the day was expected to be sunny,
reaching a high of seventy-two degrees, Mack had warned her
that the water would be considerably colder and that she needed
to dress for it.

Ben, who also cooked for Mack and his family whenever they
were at the ranch, prepared a hearty breakfast of pancakes and
bacon, with warm fresh rolls and creamery butter and freshly
squeezed orange juice. Tully was too excited to eat, though.

"A good breakfast is as important as the clothes you're wearing
and the gear you're using," Mack said. "It may seem easy to just

stand in the water and throw out a line, but believe me, you're going to feel tired from it. You need the energy you get from a good breakfast."

Tully stuffed some pancakes into her mouth, gulped down the orange juice, and was ready to go. Mack had purchased the fishing gear she needed, and the three of them set off for Armstrong Spring Creek, just north of their ranch.

"This is a good creek to learn in," Mack said. "The water is usually flat, currents are pretty slow, and it's wide enough to cast without the line getting tangled in trees, but not too wide or too deep."

"What are we fishing for?"

"Mostly rainbows. Some browns and cutthroats, too."

They soon arrived at the creek, and Mack, after studying the water and the terrain, scouted out what he thought would be a good spot for them to start in. Before wading into the water, he gave Tully instructions. "First and foremost, when Cody is with us, you must always know where he is, what he's doing, and be within arm's reach of him. I never let him go in deeper than his knees. He understands the importance of being careful around water, but he's still a child, and I never take anything for granted with him."

"Of course, Mack. You don't need to tell me this."

"Now, fish are sensitive to movement, so you need to wade gingerly into the water. If the fish see vibrations, or ripples, in the water, they know a predator is nearby and they'll stay away. Also, if they see a shadow, that's a sign to them of predators, so always watch the sun and make sure you're not casting a shadow where you're fishing."

Tully nodded.

"The most important aspect of fly-fishing is the cast. Don't expect to catch on quickly. A great cast takes years of practice."

Mack spent a half-hour showing Tully how to cast, watching her practice flicking the rod forward and back, teaching her how to use her wrist to control the motion. "Your goal is to trick the fish into thinking this is a real fly, and to do that the line has to fall smoothly onto the water. Sometimes you'll cast a few times without actually hitting the water, so it appears there's a fly flittering over the water before it lands. Once your fly attracts a fish, you start reeling in the line while slightly raising the tip of the rod to hook the fish securely. Call me if you get one and I'll help you bring it in."

Mack, Cody and Tully waded into the creek, and the cold water was initially a shock to Tully, but it gradually became part of the background, no different from the feel of a breeze against her cheek. Mack stayed close to Tully and Cody, whispering pointers to her as she repeatedly cast her line into the rippling water. As she became more proficient, he moved slightly away, giving her and Cody greater space.

Cody fished with a seriousness Tully had often seen in him when he was absorbed in a task. Although now capable of being rambunctious, he remained more subdued than the children he played with. Tully didn't know whether this was a function of his personality or the result of being motherless for most of his life. She thought it unlikely her niece or nephew would be able to stay so quiet for hours and focus so intently. Some of it, Tully guessed, was his pleasure at being in his father's company and his recognition that to remain so required following his father's rules.

The morning progressed with each of them absorbed in a cocoon of silence and action, action and silence, casting the line into the water over and over, reeling in the line when a fish took the bait. The pristine beauty of the water, the mountains, the air they breathed—it was all intensified by the silence. Tully appreciated the lure of fishing, the meditative reverie that was induced by the stillness of the activity.

As the day passed by, her disappointment about the way the week had turned out, the paucity of time spent with Mack, seemed to lift and float away, borne aloft by the serenity she felt standing knee-deep in water but part of a family. If Mack didn't love her, Cody did, and that was more than she'd had before. She'd been too impatient, too unrealistic, in her hopes for a deeper relationship with Mack.

If it's to happen, and that's a big "if," it will be gradually, over years probably. I have to find my own happiness, with Cody, with my life, and I can't look to Mack to fill the void I feel. If Cody and the Lenape Lane Ladies aren't enough, then I have to figure out what I want, what I need. If I don't have an idea for a novel, then maybe I can write articles, maybe work on a short story. Maybe I can take a graduate writing class. Tully could feel the inertia that had blocked her for the past month drift away. She was excited about the prospect of starting something new, whatever that might be.

Cody startled her out of her trance. "Mommy, I'm tired now. I'm going to sit on the grass."

"I'll come with you, Cody."

"No, Mommy, you don't have to. Daddy lets me sit on the grass by myself when I'm tired."

Over the course of the morning, Mack had gradually inched farther away from them, and he was standing with his back to her at the moment. She knew not to call loudly to him.

"OK, Cody, but when you're ready to come in the water again, wait at the edge and I'll walk you in."

Tully walked Cody out of the creek, helped him get settled on the grass with a coloring book, and returned to her spot in the water. She hadn't caught a fish, but that didn't mar her enjoyment of the day. She quickly recovered the sense of peacefulness, absorbed into her pores like a sponge filled with water, and returned to her meandering thoughts. Her daydreaming was abruptly interrupted by a sharp tug on her line. Startled at first, she forgot everything Mack had told her and began screaming, "I've got a fish, I've got a fish."

Mack, who at that moment was reeling in his own trout, called back, "Hold on Tully, I'll be with you in a minute."

Cody began running toward the creek. "I'll help you, Mommy."

"No, Cody, stay back," Mack shouted.

But Cody ran into the water and, in what seemed like an instant, slipped on a rock. The slimy surface propelled him forward, his arms splayed overhead and his face disappeared under the water as the current pulled him away.

Paralyzed by fear, Tully screamed as she watched the water fill up inside his waders, saw the weight of it pull Cody under the swirling blue ripples. She remained frozen as he disappeared into the watery abyss.

Chapter 13

Mack threw down his rod and with giant strides rushed toward his disappearing son. He threw himself into the water when it became deep enough to swim, his long, even strokes propelling him forward. Tully watched Cody's head bob in and out of the water, saw Mack's strong strokes bring him closer but still far away. She tried to move but couldn't; she tried to scream but was choked by her silent sobs. *Please, God, please don't let him drown, please let Mack get to him before it's too late, it can't be too late.*

Cody flipped over, head down into the water, the weight of the water in his waders pulling him deeper, and then, miraculously, he resurfaced, his arms flailing helplessly. Tully felt a spasm of horror course through her body as his cries became fainter and he disappeared again under the frothy swirl. She stood transfixed.

And then, finally, Mack reached him. Reached into the water and grabbed Cody's waders and pulled Cody close to him, his large arm around Cody's small chest. He swam with him until they got closer to shore, picked him up when it was shallow enough to stand, and carried him to the grass. Cody's face was gray, but he was breathing, he was alive. Mack turned him onto his side and pounded him on his back to help him spit out the water he'd swallowed.

Tully stood beside them. "I'm sorry, I'm sorry," she cried, the tears rolling down her cheek. "It's my fault, it's all my fault, I should have stayed on the grass with him, I never should have let him stay alone."

Mack just stared at her silently as he continued to pound Cody's back. When Cody seemed sufficiently recovered, Mack said, "Let's get him to the hospital and have him checked out."

They drove to Livingston Memorial Hospital without talking, Cody lying in the front seat with his head in Tully's lap, his body wrapped in a blanket. The antiseptic building filled Tully with dread, the wait for Cody to be seen by the emergency-room doctor interminable. But the doctor, who seemed no more than Tully's age, was reassuring, although he wanted to keep Cody overnight for observation.

"He's fine, just shaken up. His lungs are clear, his breathing is normal. I'd like to watch him overnight to make sure there was no internal damage from the rocks knocking him around, but I'm just being precautious. You shouldn't worry at all."

After Cody got settled into his hospital room, Mack took Tully into the hallway. "You go home and get some rest. There's no reason for both of us to stay here with Cody."

Tears once again began running down Tully's cheeks as she tried to hold back sobs. "Please let me stay with him, too. I couldn't bear to go home and not know how he's feeling. I know I messed up, I know I'm responsible, but I love Cody, I would do anything for him. I shouldn't have left him alone. I don't understand why I froze."

Mack put his arms around her shoulders and gently pulled her close to him. "You're not responsible, Tully. I would have let Cody sit on the grass by himself, too. He does that all the time with me. He knows better than to run into the water, but I think he was so excited for you he simply forgot. And you froze from panic. Stop blaming yourself. I don't blame you, and Cody is fine. Now, take the truck, go home and get into dry clothes, bring back dry clothes for me, and we'll both spend the night here with Cody."

A flood of relief surged through Tully, and she erupted into a volcano of tears. "I swear, Mack, I'll never again let anything happen to Cody. Not ever, not if I have any ability to stop it. I promise you, I'll never panic again."

After Cody was released from the hospital with a clean bill of health, they returned to Denver a day early. "You'd be amazed at how resilient young children are," the young doctor told Mack and Tully. Tully was still shaken by the experience, as well as exhausted. She and Mack had slept on chairs in Cody's hospital room, and although Cody slept soundly through the night, Tully hardly closed her eyes, anxiously listening to the even sound of Cody's breathing, terrified that he'd been harmed by the ordeal. Mack had slept only slightly better, and they both dozed off on the flight home while Cody happily watched cartoons on his iPod in the seat between them.

Cody began summer camp the next week, five days a week, from ten until three, leaving each morning on a camp bus for the twenty-minute ride to the spacious grounds of the day camp. Tully had visited several in the area and chosen one that seemed to offer the most robust program for four-year-olds. Stepping Stones Day Camp provided everything a young child could want: daily swimming lessons in a large oval pool, sports geared to the nursery set, including pee-wee tennis, basketball, soccer, hockey and softball, a low ropes course, a petting zoo, an elaborate replica of a child-size village, playgrounds, kiddie karts, cooking, drama, music, nature, and, of course, arts and crafts.

Tully knew Cody would be happy there, and each day he bounded off the bus full of excitement, talking enthusiastically about the day's activities and the friends he'd made. Tully had rarely seen him so animated and was pleased he enjoyed camp so much, but the long days without him exacerbated her own sense of restlessness.

"I need to do something," she said to Ryan, her personal trainer, as she did her second set of leg presses.

The gym Mack had set up in the finished basement of his

house rivaled most commercial gyms. He had individual Cybex machines to work each muscle group, along with a full set of benches and free weights. In addition, he had a complete array of cardio equipment, including a treadmill, an elliptical trainer, and a stationary bicycle.

Tully had worked with Ryan for six months and savored her increased strength, as evidenced by the heavier weights she could lift and the new definition in her body. When she'd first started, she struggled through one set of leg presses at forty pounds, and now she easily pressed her own weight: 110 pounds. The progress on the other machines had been comparable.

"Cody is happy as could be, Mack is busy with Big Sky, and I feel like I'm floundering. How many shopping trips can one person make?"

"Funny, none of my other female clients think there can ever be too many shopping trips. Personally, I don't get it myself. I can't stand shopping—hate the crowds, hate the stuffiness, hate trying on clothes even more."

Tully nodded. "I always felt the same way. When I didn't have money to shop, it didn't bother me. Once in a while, I'd go into an expensive store and try on clothes I knew I'd never be able to buy, just for a lark. It was fun to see them on me and pretend I could own them. Now that I can afford to shop, it feels like I'm buying clothes just for the sake of spending money. It seems so pointless."

"Your workouts have been great. You're real consistent in your training. Why don't you set a goal for yourself—say, a 10K race or even a half-marathon?"

Tully shook her head. "I could never win a race. I'm not athletic. That was my sister's thing."

"Don't enter one of these races to win. Enter for the experience of running in it. Your competition is yourself, no one else. If you run five miles in fifty minutes, your goal may be to do it in forty-five minutes. Or your goal may be to complete a distance you've never run before."

"How long is a 10K?"

"Six-point-two miles."

"And a half-marathon?"

"Thirteen-point-one miles."

"Wow. Do you really think I could run that far?"

"Sure. You're already running three miles three times a week. I'll set up a training schedule that will have you ready to do a half-marathon by the fall. Littleton has its Autumn Classic race at the end of September. That one usually attracts a good crowd. I think you'd enjoy it. If you're interested, I'll work up a schedule for you and bring it to our next session."

"I *do* want to do it. I need something challenging." Tully was excited about the prospect of training to run such a long distance and finished her workout reenergized.

Three days later, Tully looked at the program Ryan had prepared. He had her running four days a week, increasing from twelve miles the first week to twenty-three miles the latter weeks, with two days for strength training and a rest day.

"I'm going to ease you back on the amount of weights while you're training," he said. "We'll do more repetitions at lower weights so I don't blow out your muscles for the running days. And I want you to start running outdoors unless the weather is bad. You can start out at the high school track, but after a few weeks go out on the roads. Take out your car and measure a course so you'll know the exact distance you're running. Make sure you pick a route that has some hills in it, both up and down."

Tully brushed back the wisp of hair that had fallen from her ponytail. "How fast should I run?"

"Don't worry about speed. The goal for this race is distance, not time. Just run at a comfortable pace for you. And make sure you do the stretching I've taught you. It's easy to get a stress injury when you start ramping up your miles."

Tully began her training the next morning after seeing Cody off on the camp bus. The sun was already high in the sky, but unlike the oppressive summer heat of Florida and the mugginess of New York City, the dry Colorado air made running outdoors pleasurable. She ran at a slow pace, no more than ten-minute

miles, an iPod strapped to her arm, the music of Pearl Jam urging
her on. To her surprise, as she ran she found ideas for a novel
swirling through her head.

The summer days quickly fell into a pattern. Tully would rise
with Cody, have breakfast with him before he left for camp, go
out for a run or to the basement gym for a weight workout, and
then, most days, spend a few hours writing at the computer until Cody returned from camp. At first halting, the words soon
flowed smoothly, and although she was unable to decide if what
she wrote was any good, she was nevertheless pleased with her
output. Although she always started the day with exercise, some
days she read by the pool, and she even occasionally joined the
Lenape Lane Ladies for their shopping forays or coffee klatches
instead of writing.

Mack, who always arose at dawn for an hour of exercise in
his gym, joined her for an outdoor run on weekends, slowing
his normally faster pace to keep her company and offer her encouragement. Mack and Tully had developed an easy rapport,
and with the writing to fill her time, Tully began to appreciate
what she did have with Mack rather than bemoan what she was
missing.

Cody, too, seemed happy. He seemed to have forgotten the
near-drowning in Montana. When Mack and Nick returned to
the ranch for solo fishing weekends and another with their sons,
Cody's enthusiasm for swimming and fishing was unabated.
Another weeklong family excursion was planned for the last week
of the summer, before the start of school.

"I want to thank you," Mack said to her on one Saturday-
morning jog. "You're wonderful with Cody. I don't think a real
mother could be more loving to him."

Tully stopped in her tracks, the sweat dripping down her face.
"I *am* his real mother."

"You know what I mean. You're his stepmother, not his natural mother, but Cody loves you as if you were."

"That's because I'm the only mother he's known. I don't
think of myself as his stepmother, and neither does Cody. I'm

wondering why you do. Are you concerned Cody is getting *too* attached to me?"

"Of course not. I'm happy about it. Why are you grilling me like this?"

"Well, I just think it's interesting that your son was hungry to make an emotional connection but *you're* still afraid of one."

Mack's face darkened as he started to speak and then stopped. He took a breath. "I'm not afraid of emotional connections. I've had them, and I certainly feel connected to Cody. I just don't want one with a wife now. Is that what this is about? You're not satisfied with our personal relationship?"

Tully wasn't satisfied, but she wasn't going to admit that to Mack. She understood that he wouldn't give more. "How could I be unsatisfied? Our relationship is exactly what you told me it would be. You've been incredibly generous, I have all the free time I want, I'm writing again for the first time in ages. I'd be a fool to complain."

"Tully, there's something going on here and I don't get it. I thought we were both happy with our arrangement."

"We are happy. Everything is just perfect. Now, can we get started running again before I get too stiff?"

Tully started her slow jog, and Mack quickly caught up to her. "Why do women always make things so complicated?"

Tully didn't respond, just kept her eyes focused on the road ahead as she ran at her steady pace.

"I guess we're not so different from other married couples," Mack said. "I think we've just had our first fight."

Tully awoke the morning of the Autumn Classic filled with anxiety. Her longest run had been the previous Sunday. At ten miles, it was more than three miles less than the distance she needed to run for the race. The past week had all been light runs, ending on Thursday. She'd eaten heaps of spaghetti, Cody's favorite meal, the evening before. The sky was overcast, although no rain was predicted, and the temperature a comfortable sixty degrees.

Perfect conditions for running. Why then am I feeling so jittery? Am I kidding myself, thinking I can run this? I'm going to run out of steam at five miles and everyone will laugh at me. Or I'll get leg cramps or stomach cramps or brain cramps, the way I'm making myself so crazy now.

"C'mon, Tully, we've got to get going," Mack said, jolting Tully from her fearful imaginings. "You want to get there early enough to stretch out, limber up, before the race starts."

Mack herded Tully and Cody into the car and they set off for Littleton High School, the site of the race's start.

"Mommy, do you get a prize if you win?" Cody asked.

"The winner will get a ribbon, I guess, but I'm not running the race to win it."

"Why not? Don't you want to win?"

"Sometimes winning doesn't mean being the fastest or the smartest or having the most, but it can mean doing the best that you can do and trying your hardest. And when you do that, you feel good about yourself, and that makes you a winner."

Tully thought about what she'd told Cody and realized that her nervousness was overblown. *I've run ten miles—that's something I never thought I could do. I've trained six days a week for three months, even on days when I was tired or didn't feel great. Whatever happens in the race, I've worked hard and I feel good about that.*

Tully arrived at the race start, picked up her number, and looked around at the throngs of people: men, women, children of every size, every color, every race. There were men and women who had the muscled bodies and obvious athleticism of Mack or Lauren and others who looked like everyday people, perhaps not the last to be picked for a team but certainly not the first, people like Tully. She knew that more than a thousand runners had registered for the race and saw markers near the start, with numbers five through ten, indicating the place to line up according to the pace of the runner. Tully joined three other women who appeared to be near her age at the ten-minute-mile sign and introduced herself as they all waited for the race to begin.

"Have you run a half-marathon before?" she asked one of the women.

"This is my third one. I keep saying I'm going to train for a full marathon, but it just takes so much time. I like this distance; it's a challenge without consuming all of my life to prepare for it."

Tully saw on the start clock that race time was approaching. "I'm a little nervous. I've never run any race before. Have any pointers for me?"

"The most important thing to remember is to start off slow. So many first-timers zoom out of the gate, and by the fifth mile they're exhausted. Take it nice and slow. If you're back here with us, you're not expecting to win, so don't worry about the time. Just get into a comfortable rhythm, relax, and enjoy yourself."

Another woman chimed in, "There's a long hill at mile ten, so you want to save yourself for that. And a nice easy downhill at mile twelve, so if you're still feeling good, that's when you can push towards the finish line."

The gun sounded and Tully set off with the pack, taking a full two minutes to cross the starting line because of the horde of people in front of her. After she crossed the start, the field spread out and she found enough space to run easily. Chatting comfortably with the women she started out with, she was surprised to pass the three-mile mark and the tables set up with water so quickly. Crowds of people lined the racecourse, cheering on the runners, motivating them onward. Mack and Cody would be waiting at the six-mile mark and, after she passed them, would drive to the finish line.

Taking the advice of her running companions and following their lead, Tully kept her pace at a steady ten-minute mile. She felt good, her breath even, her muscles limber, and as she approached the six-mile mark, she heard Cody call out, "Mommy, Mommy."

Tully diverged from her group and ran over to Cody, gave him a big hug and a smile, and returned to the pack. Mack beamed at her and shouted encouragement. The remainder of the race continued smoothly. She took the ten-mile hill strongly and surged at the end to cross the finish line in two hours and five minutes, slow for some people but amazing for Tully. Before meeting Mack, she had never done anything athletic. Now, at this moment, she had absolute certainty that she could do whatever she set her mind to, anything at all.

Chapter 14

Agnes's trial date was fast approaching. Henry sat in her baby-face lawyer's spartan office and waited to hear the prosecutor's latest offer.

"So you see, Henry," Tony said, "the prosecuting attorney is adamant. He won't offer Agnes anything less than fifteen years unless you take a piece of it, preferably the biggest piece. He's convinced you were behind the embezzlement. His witnesses will testify you were neck-deep in gambling debts and were into some pretty rough people who demanded payback. Agnes has been silent on you, just keeps saying, 'I take all responsibility,' and won't consider any plea involving you. If you really love your wife, I don't see how you can let this happen."

Henry sat quietly in the straight-back wooden chair, his eyes downcast. He'd fidgeted with his hands until Tony's last statement. "What the fuck do you know about how I love my wife? I've been a good husband to her, and I'd do anything for her, she knows that, but I can't do prison again. Besides, I didn't put her up to this. Yeah, I needed money, but getting it from Big Sky was her idea. She put it all together, not me. What she needs is a real lawyer, one who's not afraid to go to trial and get her off."

Tony slumped in his chair. "You know, Agnes never told me what happened, and that was good. If she wanted to take the stand to say she didn't sign those papers, I would have no way of knowing whether she committed perjury or not. Now I can't even put her on the stand if we go to trial, and without her denying that she forged Mack's signatures, we have nothing to give the jury."

"That's crap. Put her on the stand. The jury will see what a good woman she is."

"I can't do that now."

"And if she loses?"

"If we go to trial and lose, the judge has discretion to order consecutive sentences, effectively locking her up forever. In a battle of the expert witnesses, juries tend to side with the prosecution's witness, no matter how likable the defendant."

Unable to look Tony in the eye, Henry kept his head down. "I can't do time again," he said, his voice low. "Agnes understands."

"I hope she understands enough to take a plea on this case. If she doesn't, she may never come home again."

"Eight years straight, credit for time served, and restitution, but that really is my bottom line, and I need an answer today," Tom Landers said.

Tony had already discussed the possibilities with Agnes. She remained firm in her conviction that she was better-prepared to serve time in prison than Henry. She knew she would have books available to her, and although she'd be required to spend her days performing mind-numbing chores, she was ready to do so. They had agreed that her chance of conviction was sufficiently high that she should accept any offer of ten years or less.

"I can give you an answer now. She'll take it."

The days had settled back into a routine for Tully: exercise in the morning, writing in the afternoon, occasionally interrupted by get-togethers with the Lenape Lane Ladies. As she tucked Cody into bed one night after reading him a third children's book and answering his imploring cries for more with a firm "Time for bed," he asked, "What's your book about?"

"Hmm. It's hard to explain, Cody, because it's a book for grown-ups, not for children."

"Why don't you write a book for children?"

"I don't know. I've never thought about it. Would you like me to?"

Cody pushed back the covers, and jumped up and down on his bed. "Yes, yes, yes! Then my teacher could read your book to all my friends at school."

"Well, I'll see if I can think of a story your friends would like, OK? But only if you promise to go to sleep now."

"OK, Mommy. I love you."

"I love you, too, sweetheart."

The next morning, after her workout, Tully put aside her novel and began jotting down lines, in verse, for a children's book. Before Cody returned from nursery school, she had created a story about Pitty Pat Cat, named after her own childhood pet. At Cody's bedtime that night, after reading the obligatory three books, she said to him, "I have a surprise for you. I've written a story just for you. Would you like to hear it?"

"Yeah," shouted Cody. "My very own story."

"Now, there are no pictures for it yet, so you have to use your imagination, OK?"

"OK, Mommy."

Tully took out her pages and read to Cody:

Pitty Pat Cat Wears a Hat

Pitty Pat Cat liked to wear a hat
but not just any old this or that.
Oh no, when all was said and done,
it had to be a fancy one.

Perhaps with flowers, purple and pink,
or maybe feathers, what do you think?

One had birds on top who'd sing
and bells that went ding ding ding.

One hat she tied beneath her chin,
one she clipped with a yellow pin.

Hats, hats, hats in every drawer,
under her bed and on the floor.

So many hats from which to choose,
sometimes Pitty Pat felt confused,
so she'd just close her eyes and go,
"Eenie meenie minie mo."

When Pitty Pat Cat would go to town,
she'd wear her hat upside down.

When to the store Pitty Pat would go,
she'd wear her hat on her toe.

When Pitty Pat Cat got the mail,
she'd wear her hat on her tail.

When Pitty Pat Cat went out at night,
she'd wear a hat with an orange light

Now, I know you're going to laugh,
she'd even wear one in her bath.

Wherever Pitty Pat Cat would go,
the other cats were sure to know
something special would be on her head.
Why, she'd even wear her hat to bed.

Good night, Pitty Pat Cat

"I like that, Mommy. Read it again."

"Oh, no, mister. It's time for sleep."

"Can I bring it to class for my teacher to read?"

"Well, how about we wait and see if Daddy can find someone to draw pictures to go with it, and then you can bring it to school?"

"OK," Cody said and laid his head on his pillow.

Mack didn't return until Tully was asleep that night, ostensibly working late, but Tully understood that that was code for a rendezvous with some woman. The following evening, after dinner and before Mack retreated to his bedroom, she asked him if there were any artists on his staff who might enjoy drawing pictures for a children's story.

"That's really good, Tully," he said after she read her story to him. "I have an art director, and there are a number of people on his staff. Any one of them would probably be willing to draw a few pictures for the book if it's just for Cody and his classmates. But shouldn't you try to get it published?"

"Oh, no. I just did this because Cody asked me to. It's not good enough to be published."

"You're wrong. I've read enough books to Cody to appreciate what's out there, and I think children would like your book and parents would enjoy reading it to them. I can ask one of my people to draw illustrations to go along with the story, and then why don't you send it out to some publishers?"

The idea of attempting to have *Pitty Pat Cat Wears a Hat* published seemed laughable. She'd scribbled down the verse in a few hours, a throwaway effort to present a tale to Cody. As she continued to demur, Mack continued to encourage her.

"If I were really to send this out to publishers, then I wouldn't have it illustrated first," Tully said. "I worked for a publishing house and knew people in the children's division. Unless the author does her own illustrations, they prefer to receive only the text so they can adopt their own vision for the story with their own illustrator."

"I forgot you worked for a publisher. Why don't you send the story to them and see what they think?"

"I guess I could send it to my old boss. He's not in the children's division, but he would be honest with me. If he thought it had no merit he'd tell me."

Tully wrote a note to Sam Horowitz bringing him up to date on her life since she'd left Mangrove Publishing and enclosed a copy of *Pitty Pat Cat Wears a Hat*. She ended by asking him to be brutally honest with her: "I'm really sending this to appease my husband, so don't worry about hurting my feelings. I've finally started writing a novel and it's coming along slowly but steadily." Tully mailed the envelope and then promptly put it out of her mind.

Chapter 15

Clad only in black silk boxer shorts, he stepped into the darkened bedroom and silently moved toward the sleeping woman in the bed. Pulling back the covers, he slipped in beside her, wrapped his arms around her and pulled her toward him. Tully opened her eyes and smiled at the sight of Mack, his sinewy body glistening in the moonlight.

"Shhh!" he said as he rolled her onto her back, cupped her breasts in his hands and began slowly, delicately kissing her forehead, her nose, her lips, open and ready for him.

"I've been waiting for you," she said.

"We've both waited too long," he answered as he rolled his body on top of hers, ready to enter her.

Tully awoke with a start, her face flushed, her body aroused by her dream. Damn, she thought before drifting back asleep, I need to get laid.

Rebecca Armstrong sat opposite Mack's desk along with Oliver Nyberg, the senior vice president of marketing for Big Sky Communications. She had just run through the advertising campaign for the company's new channel launch: Movie World, a twenty-four-hour movie channel showcasing movies from around the world. The channel was a departure for Big Sky, targeting a demographic different from its other program services. Appealing to an urban, predominantly female population, the channel carried with it Mack's hopes to expand his subscriber base.

He had agreed with Oliver to hire a new agency, with a new perspective, to spearhead the launch. Rebecca was the young wunderkind from Chicago-based O'Donnell Advertising Ltd. assigned to Big Sky's account. After two months of meetings with Mack and his internal creative staff, Rebecca had prepared a campaign that was hip, contemporary, and, according to the focus groups, appealing to urban and suburban women in the coveted eighteen-to-forty-nine age group.

Rebecca placed several large poster boards on Mack's desk. "The last piece for us to discuss is the brand design. These are the branding choices we propose. I personally like this one best," she said, pointing to the first. "It has a thematic consistency with the brands for your other programming services while still imparting its unique identity."

Mack looked over at Oliver. "What do you think?"

"I agree with Rebecca. It's distinctive, memorable, and fits with our image. I'd go with that one."

"Then I'm fine with the first also. Thank you both," he said as he stood up, indicating that the meeting was at an end.

Mack asked Rebecca to wait a moment and closed the door behind Oliver as he left the office. Rebecca smiled as Mack approached her and, with his finger on her chin, lifted her face toward his and kissed her tenderly on her lips. "Tonight's our last night before you return to Chicago. I thought we'd do something special. There's a terrific restaurant in Boulder on top of a hill, with extraordinary views, the best food around, and a world-class wine cellar. I'm taking you there tonight."

"Something special could also be room service at my hotel, you know."

"Oh, we'll end up back there, no doubt about that." Mack had started seeing Rebecca almost immediately after she arrived in Denver to pitch her agency four months earlier. The decision to hire O'Donnell Advertising had been Oliver's, without input from Mack, but he had been pleased with the outcome, happy to extend their romance.

At thirty-three, with medium-brown hair falling in soft waves to her shoulders, a slim but shapely figure, and a sharp mind, she was both attractive and interesting. She had told Mack at the outset that she was untroubled by his marital status, in fact welcomed the idea of a fling without expectations for more. "I'm dedicated to my work," she'd said. "I'm thought of as a rising star there, and I'm not interested in anyone getting in the way of that right now. I can taste the vice presidency, it's that close, and I'll be damned if I'll let some man start thinking he can make demands on me now because I belong to him."

Rebecca had made numerous trips to Denver during the creation of the advertising campaign, but now, with the campaign coming to a close, they both knew that her reasons for being in Denver would be scant.

"I'll pick you up at your hotel at seven tonight," Mack said before opening the door for her to leave. As she walked out, Mack saw Nick standing in the doorway of his office. Nick caught Mack's eye and asked, "Can I talk to you for a minute?" Mack nodded, and as Nick entered, he closed the door behind him.

"I gather Rebecca is your latest paramour," Nick said.

"You gather correctly."

Nick shook his head. "You do realize how much she resembles Tully, don't you?"

"What are you talking about? She doesn't look at all like Tully. Her hair is lighter, she's taller, everything about her is different."

"Mack, she looks more like Tully than Tully's own sister. You don't see it because you don't want to."

"What are you getting at?"

"Look, I was Tully's biggest detractor when you told me about your wild scheme. I did everything I could to talk you out of it. You'd known her less than a week, the marriage was designed to be a sham, I didn't see any good coming out of it. But I was wrong. Tully is not only great for Cody but she's great for you. I haven't seen you this relaxed and happy since before Joanna died. I think you realize that as well and it scares you. And that's why you're sleeping with someone who looks like your wife, so you can transfer your hunger for Tully to her."

"Your imagination has gotten the better of you. Tully and I are both fine with our relationship. She's told me so herself, and I like Rebecca because there's a lot there to like, not because of anything to do with Tully."

"I'm not wrong, Mack. Maybe it's time for you to stop running away and think about what you have at home."

Later that evening, Mack knocked on the door of Rebecca's hotel room. He had pushed aside his conversation with Nick and immersed himself in the demands of running his business, and so he was startled to realize when Rebecca opened the door that Nick was right about her resemblance to Tully. *Funny I never saw that before. They're completely different people, though. Rebecca is aggressive, tough, ambitious, full of hard edges. Tully is softer, more malleable, more eager to please.* But Mack had to admit he had been drawn into an affair with Rebecca before he had spent much time with her, before he had gotten to know her personality. Frankly, he had been physically attracted to her at their first meeting.

"You look delicious," Mack said, looking up and down Rebecca's svelte body inside a clingy black knit dress, the low cut displaying her ample breasts.

"I'm glad you think so. I was hoping you'd have me for dessert."

"I'm salivating already. If we don't leave now, I'm going to want you for an appetizer."

"I always thought the appetizer was the best part of the meal."

Suddenly, Mack's arousal was so strong, so immediate, that he couldn't wait for the end of the romantic dinner he'd planned— he had to have Rebecca that very moment. They never made it to the restaurant that night.

♦ ♦ ♦

The Bryson family had Thanksgiving dinner at their country club, together with the Hanover family. Although it didn't have the intimacy of a home-cooked meal in a family home, their nannies/housekeepers were with their own families.

When they returned home, they finalized plans to return to Middleton for Christmas, which would be the first time Tully had seen her sister and her niece and nephew since the wedding. They had debated such a visit because of the logistical problem it presented: How would they explain to Mack's sister why they weren't sharing a bedroom? Tully had confessed that her sister knew of their arrangement and suggested they could sleep at her house, but Mack insisted his sister would be offended if he didn't stay with her. Eventually, they agreed to shorten their visit to only a few days and they would stay with their respective sisters. The frequent phone calls and e-mails Tully and Lauren shared over the past ten months had heightened Tully's wish to spend quality time alone with her sister, Mack explained to Molly.

With their holiday plans resolved, Mack said, "Your thirtieth birthday is coming soon. That's an important occasion, don't you think? We should do something special. Would you like a party?"

"Oh, no, definitely not. I don't like being the center of attention."

"How about dinner at the club with Nick and Lizzie?"

"If you'd like."

"What would *you* like?" Mack felt a tinge of annoyance at Tully's lack of assertiveness. She was always prepared to please him or Cody yet so rarely demanded anything for herself. "It's not my birthday, it's yours. I want to do what you'd like."

Hesitantly, as if afraid to even make the suggestion, Tully said quietly, "What I'd really like is for just the two of us to go out to dinner together, alone. We haven't done that since Chamonix."

"Then that's what we'll do. Do you have anyplace special in mind?"

"Lizzie told me about a restaurant in Boulder, Willow Creek Inn. I'd like to go there if that's OK with you."

Reluctantly, Mack agreed. Willow Creek Inn was the restaurant where he often took a lover. It was romantic and secluded, and he was unlikely to be seen by colleagues there. Mack wondered whether Lizzie had deliberately recommended it to Tully because she knew, through Nick, that it was his secret hideaway, but he supposed he was being paranoid.

Denver in December was cold like New York City, but unlike the Big Apple, the Mile High City felt charged with energy, the nearby mountains looking like outstretched arms inviting the multitudes to embrace their wildness, the clear crisp air abuzz with fevered excitement. On the morning of her thirtieth birthday, after Cody had left for nursery school, Tully headed down to the gym to run her daily four miles on the treadmill. Thirty-five minutes later Rosetta entered the room.

"There's a telephone call for you, from New York. He said it's important."

Almost finished anyway, Tully said she'd be right there and got off the treadmill. Still short of breath, she picked up the phone. "Hello?"

"Tully? It's Sam Horowitz. How are you?"

"Sam!" It's so good to hear from you. How is everyone?"

"Everyone's doing fine. Listen, I shouldn't be the one calling you, it's not my division, but it just really seemed right for me to give you the good news. Mangrove wants to publish your children's story."

Stunned by the news, Tully could barely utter a response.

"Tully, are you still there?"

"I'm here, Sam. I just can't believe it. I sent it off to you to as a lark, to appease Mack. I never thought it would be good enough to be published."

"It's not only good enough to be published, but they'd like to consider a series of Pitty Pat stories. Do you think you could do more?"

"Actually, my son was pestering me so much I've already written a second one."

"Wonderful. The editor you'll be working with is Elliot Langstrom. I don't know if you know him. He can send you out a contract or work with your agent if you have one. And if you don't, I'd be happy to recommend one."

"Let me talk to Mack. I suspect he'll have one of Big Sky's attorneys look over the contract."

"OK. In the meantime, why don't you send Elliot the second story."

"Sam, you've just given me the best birthday present."

"Hey, I didn't know today was your birthday. Now you have two reasons to go out and celebrate."

"You bet I will. Thanks for being the one to give me the good news. Bye, Sam."

Tully hung up, ran over to Rosetta, and gave her a huge bear hug. "I'm so excited I just have to hug someone," she said.

Rosetta laughingly squeezed her back. "*Me alegra por usted.* I'm happy for you. If anyone deserves something good, it's you. Why don't you call Mr. Bryson and tell him about this."

"Oh, I don't think so. He's so busy at work, and we're going out to dinner tonight anyway. I'll tell him then."

The truth was, Tully never telephoned Mack at the office. It wasn't that he'd discouraged her from doing so. Rather, it just seemed that part of the separation of their lives included refraining from the normal spousal communications that typically occurred during the course of a day. They spoke to each other at dinner, when Mack was home, sometimes at breakfast if she hadn't seen him the previous evening, but never at work.

Tully told Mack her good news as they drove to Boulder. He was as excited for her as she had been and, after being seated at their table, ordered a bottle of 1985 Dom Perignon.

After it arrived, Mack held his glass of Champagne up to Tully's. "To your first publication. May this be the beginning of many. And to your thirtieth birthday. Cheers."

"Thank you. I'm thrilled about the book, of course, but not sure I'm so thrilled about turning thirty."

"You know, even the best grapes need to mature to bring out the optimum flavor. I've always thought a woman doesn't reach that perfect stage of ripeness and flavor until she turns thirty."

Tully laughed. "I'm flying so high tonight I almost believe you."

"Well, I'd like you to believe this: I'm happy you agreed to my proposal, I'm happy you're my wife, and I hope you're happy, too. And as a small expression of my gratitude to you, I hope you enjoy this birthday present." Mack took a long slim box wrapped in gold paper from his inside jacket pocket and handed it to Tully. She opened it quickly and gasped on seeing a necklace with a large round diamond in a platinum setting on a white gold chain.

"Mack, it's exquisite. I don't know what to say. I didn't expect this at all."

"Just tell me you like it and I'll be pleased."

"I love it. I've never owned anything so beautiful."

"A beautiful woman deserves beautiful jewelry."

The remainder of the evening passed like a dream for Tully. The surrounding tables, the chatter of other diners, the quietly efficient movements of the waiters and the bus staff all receded into the background, an indistinct vapor. Mack ordered a different bottle of wine to accompany each of their four courses, and they finished with an after-dinner cognac. Throughout the meal, they talked, they laughed, they marveled at how well they got along. Tully's head was spinning by the time they left, and on the drive home she rested her head on Mack's shoulder, eventually falling asleep to the soporific hum of the engine. Mack gently shook her awake when they arrived home and, with his arm around her, helped her into the house.

"Happy birthday, Tully," Mack whispered to her as he walked her up the stairs. "I hope it was all you wanted it to be."

Suddenly, everything stood still for Tully as a war raged inside her head. *Tell him. No, don't be a fool. He should know. He'll want to end it all. Tell him—you want to. No. Yes. No. Yes.* Tully knew she should be silent, knew she should just thank Mack and go off to her bedroom, knew that saying anything more would be wrong. But the wine, the Champagne, the magic of the evening, the sleepiness she was still shaking off—all of it seemed to force her mouth open and pull the words from her lips as she stood aside in wonder at her courage, at her stupidity.

"Only one thing more would make it perfect," said the stranger inhabiting her body. As Mack looked quizzically at her, the stranger continued. "You thought of every contingency in our prenuptial agreement except one. You didn't cover the possibility that I would fall in love with you." Tully heard the words come from this stranger and pleaded, *Pull it back, take back the words, tell him you're joking.* But no, the stranger stood there mutely and watched Mack's face, his beautiful face, smiling before but now somber, wordless.

Mack looked at his wife standing expectantly before him, silent and still. "I can't, Tully," he said, his voice hoarse, his words stumbling, his body moving away from hers. "I'm sorry, I just can't. It's not you. I can't love anyone now. Maybe someday, I don't know." He watched the tears begin to stream down her face as she stood there quietly. "Please don't cry. I don't want things to change between us, I don't want you to leave, and I don't want you to be hurt. But I can't return your feelings. Can we talk this out?"

Tully heard his words through her trance, the stranger slowly leaving her body, letting her feel the full brunt of his rejection herself. "I should never have said anything to you," she said, the tears continuing unabated. "It wasn't fair to you. I know how you feel. I was just so happy tonight. I don't know what overcame me. It was too much wine, I suppose, but it's OK, I'm OK with my feelings. You don't have to return them. I'm not going to leave. I don't want to leave Cody."

Mack reached out for Tully's hand and held it in his own. "You're very important to me, you must know that. But I don't want you to think there's hope for us, that I'll change. I can't promise you that. I said at the start you should see other people, other men. Perhaps if you do you won't think of me in that way."

"Yes, yes, I'll do that. It'll be OK, really, I'll be OK. I'm tired now. It was a wonderful evening, and tomorrow we'll forget what I said tonight. Can you do that for me? Can you put it out of your mind? I can do that, and I want you to."

Mack leaned over and kissed her forehead. "It's already forgotten. Go to sleep."

Mack was true to his word. No further mention was made of Tully's admission. Mack continued to display the same warm yet distant demeanor as before. Gradually, Tully, too, was able to interact with Mack without feeling like a fool.

Mack sat with his sister at her kitchen table, the rest of her family already asleep. He knew Molly was thrilled to have him visiting for Christmas for the second year in a row. Growing up, she had idolized him, and he in turn had been her protector against the cruelties of prepubescent adolescents. She still revered him.

Being with Molly reminded Mack of those early years. Even at a young age, he was a magnet, attracting friends from every group: the athletes, the academics, the goths, the nerds. He was friendly to everyone, and everyone wanted to be his friend. A natural athlete, he shunned the team sports of baseball and basketball and opted instead for track-and-field events, making all-state in the long jump, the triple jump and the 440-meter hurdles.

With his natural charm, he attracted women easily. He had dated the cheerleading captain in high school and broke her heart when he left for Stanford and told her she shouldn't wait for him. He met Joanna at college, the first woman he'd known whom he had to fight for. It wasn't just Joanna's beauty that attracted so many suitors. She had a mysterious quality, a gauzy veil covering her essence that allowed only a peek into her psyche. Her elusiveness, rather than pushing men away, drew them to her like flies to a glowing light. Mack had pursued her since they'd met, him a junior and her a freshman. By his senior year, he knew he would be incapable of loving another woman, incapable of leaving Stanford without her. They married two months after Joanna's graduation.

"I still don't understand why Tully is sleeping at Lauren's," Molly said.

"I've told you, Tully rarely sees her sister now, and we're here for such a short time. There are always so many children around, it just seemed the only way they'd be able to really catch up would be with Tully staying at her house."

"Well, wherever she stays, I must say she's been good for you and Cody. Cody is like a new person. I've never seen him smile so much, and he's even playing with Max. And you! She must be doing something right, because you seem so much more relaxed than your visit last year."

Mack picked up his coffee mug and took a sip. "Things are going well with Tully and me, and our new channel launch has exceeded our projections. So, yes, I guess I have reason to be relaxed." He *was* happy. The incident with Tully seemed to have passed without causing too much damage. It had been awkward for the first few days afterward, but he maintained his steady manner and they gradually returned to their normal interactions.

Mack had been rattled when Tully said she loved him, terrified that the security they had created for Cody would disappear, returning Cody to his prior state of disquietude or leaving him in an even worse state, because he would remember Tully, remember what it felt like to have a mother. Even more horrifying, though, he had seen the perfect cocoon in which he'd wrapped his life begin to unravel at the edges, whispery strands of filament flying away, opening the sore he had worked so hard to bandage. It would have been easy to take Tully in his arms that night, whisper in her ear that he loved her, too. But it would have been wrong, would only have led to disappointment. "And Cody is madly in love with Tully. They suit each other like a sculptor with her clay."

As Mack sat conversing with his sister, so did Tully with her sister in Lauren's den, surrounded by her children's toys.

"It's been almost a year now. How are you doing?" Lauren asked, the concern apparent in her voice. "You always sound so upbeat on the telephone, but I don't know—I still worry about you. About your marriage."

Tully sighed. Once, she could discuss anything with Lauren, her most intimate concerns, her most joyous feelings. But she had struggled to bury her feelings, pull them back into her deepest recesses so she wouldn't experience the stabbing pain of rejection each time she looked at Mack. She had been successful in that effort, and talking honestly about her feelings to Lauren would simply open a wound that was healing, had healed, she told herself.

"It's better than I could have imagined last year. I feel like I'm Cody's natural mother, and he feels that way, too. It's inconceivable to me that I wasn't always his mother, it feels so right. I've made new friends, I'm busy. And, of course, I'm excited about my children's story being published."

"But what about Mack? How are things with Mack? Isn't it awkward living with a man who's supposed to be your husband but not being intimate with him?"

"No. It's been fine. Mack is very good to me, and we have a nice comfortable relationship."

"And that's enough for you? Comfortable?"

"It is for now. Maybe not forever, but yes, for now it's enough."

Chapter 16

Tully packed her bags for a trip to New York City. Haley had repeatedly invited her to visit and she'd finally relented. Now, as she got ready for the trip, Cody asked for the umpteenth time, "Why can't I go, too?"

"Because you have school and Daddy would be all alone with both of us gone."

"But you'll be alone if I don't go."

Tully could see the concern in Cody's eyes, mixed with fear. Wrapping her arms around him, she said, "I'll be back before you know it."

Tully felt uneasy leaving Cody, even though she couldn't say why. She would also be leaving Mack for a week, and although he didn't seem ruffled by their separation, that, too, left her uneasy. *I guess it's just change. Change always makes me uncomfortable. But nothing's going to change very much by my trip to New York. Really, just a short time away. Everything will be the same when I return. Won't it?*

Once in New York City, the winter felt different to Tully. When she'd left a year ago, a depressive pallor enveloped the towering skyscrapers. Now, the gray, wintry air conveyed a steely strength. The city's energy was palpable; the throngs of people on the sidewalks generated a thunderous heartbeat that made the steel buildings and the sidewalks appear to be alive. Even the squawking of the pigeons seemed to shout, "This is the center of the universe." Tully felt part of that energy.

Haley still worked at Mangrove Publishing—where Tully had first met her—and Tully was meeting her there for lunch. She took a last look around Haley's apartment before leaving, then locked the door behind her. She knew she could, and perhaps should, take a taxi to the mid-town office of Mangrove, but she wanted to feel like a New Yorker again, and so walked the three blocks to the subway station. She skipped down the steps to the cavernous maze. A musty odor hit her nostrils and she felt a rush of familiarity.

Once, the subways were a haven for the homeless, their respite from the rain or snow or bitter cold. Former Mayor Giuliani had long ago removed them from the dank platforms, and it was just a straggle of passengers who awaited the next train. She wondered where the homeless went now. Did sweeping away unpleasantries, removing them from visibility, make us forget they exist? She had strived to forget about her birthday dinner, her declaration to Mack, but it was a struggle seeing him every day. Perhaps her distance from him this week, his invisibility, would help her do so.

Tully purchased a MetroCard and pushed through the turnstile. She followed the signs for the "A" train, heading downtown. Although she was unfamiliar with the west side of Manhattan, where Haley lived, she had directions. "Take the 'A' train to Forty-second Street, then the shuttle to Grand Central Station, then walk over to Forty-fifth and Madison," Haley had written on the notepaper in Tully's hand. Once on the correct platform, she didn't have to wait long. Within minutes, the train arrived, and although the New York City subways were never empty, at that time of day she found a seat easily. The rumble of the train filled her head and displaced any lingering thoughts of Mack.

The gray clouds had disappeared and the sun shone brightly when Tully exited the subway station. She walked the few blocks to Mangrove Publishing and, before entering the building, momentarily stood outside its doors. For three years she arrived every morning at this spot. For three years she walked through those doors with the hope that someday she'd walk out an editor, perhaps even a writer. Now she *was* a writer, and a writer of children's books—something that had *never* been part of her imaginings. She walked inside, showed security her driver's license, and was given a stick-on badge with her name. She took the elevator to the seventy-first floor and walked over to the receptionist.

"Hi, Carolyn."

"Hey, Tully, nice to see you. It's been a long time. I heard you got married."

"That's right. I'm living in Colorado now. I'm just back for a few days to visit Haley."

"Go on back. I don't need to buzz her. Good seeing you again."

Tully walked down the familiar corridors to Haley's desk.

"I tried reaching you," Haley said when she saw Tully. "You must have already been in the subway, because I couldn't get you on your cell phone. A rush job just came up. I'm sorry but I won't be able to make lunch today."

"Don't worry about it. It's so nice outside I think I'll walk around, do some shopping."

"Sam's in his office if you want to say hi to him first."

The door to Sam's office was open and Tully knocked as she stepped inside. Sam looked up from his desk and a wide smile appeared on his face. He got up and walked over to Tully, wrapped his arms around her, and squeezed tight. "So my protégée is going to be a published author. I take all the credit for it."

Tully laughed. "Well, you should. You were always encouraging me, and I learned so much from you."

"Joking aside, give yourself all the credit. I think your little book is terrific. I bet your novel will be good as well. From the little pieces you'd shown me, I knew you were talented, if you only gave yourself a chance."

Tully thanked Sam as they sat down. Although only five years older than she and still a bachelor, Sam had always appeared more mature to her, with his straight hair slightly graying at the temples and a beginning paunch at his waist. Now he seemed to have aged even more, with fine lines crunched together from the corner of his eyes toward his hairline. Despite his plain appearance, Tully had always thought he would make a good husband for a woman who valued a keen intellect and a sweet temperament over superficial physical appeal.

"How are things going here for you? Have you published any more poems?"

Sam sighed. "It's been crazy here. Everyone is overworked, the pressure is enormous, and there doesn't seem to be enough time in the day to read everything that comes in to my desk, much less find time to write poetry. Do you know any rich women who might want to keep me?"

As soon as the words left his lips, Tully's body stiffened. Sam looked chagrined. "I'm sorry, Tully. That was a stupid thing for me to say. I would never suggest that you married Mack because he's wealthy. I know how happy you are—anyone could tell just by looking at you. I was just thinking about myself and being a jerk in the process. Please forgive me."

Of course Tully would forgive Sam. He would never hurt her intentionally. It was just coincidence that his words cut so close to the truth, like a knife carving away the fat for the hunk of meat inside. "It's OK, Sam. I do have a charmed life, I admit it. But don't wish for money so quickly. It's not a substitute for love."

"Of course not," he agreed. "But isn't it nice to have both?"

"I can't argue with that." *Yes, it would be nice to have both. And even nicer to have both with the same person.*

"Are you here to meet with Elliot?"

"No, I was supposed to have lunch with Haley, but she got tied down with something. I'm staying with her for a few days. Just a quick visit."

"Well, since you're here, let me take you upstairs to meet Elliot," Sam said. "I heard your contract is signed."

"Yes, that's all done, and I'd love to meet him."

Sam walked Tully up a flight of stairs and over to an office along the windowed wall, its door closed.

"Is he busy?" Sam asked the woman at the desk opposite the office.

"He has someone in there, but I'll buzz him."

Moments later the door opened and a middle-aged man with a receding hairline and wire-rimmed glasses stepped out. "What perfect timing. You must be Tully," he said as he shook her hand. "Come in, I have the illustrator of your book inside. We were just discussing it. Come meet Adam Landau."

Sitting on one of the two chairs in the small office was a youngish man with a mop of soft brown curls falling over his forehead, covering the tips of his ears. As he stood to greet her, extending his hand to shake hers, she noted that he was shorter than Mack, perhaps five foot ten or so, slim and lanky, with a delicacy to his bones. She felt an immediate connection to him, reinforced by his crooked smile and his first words to her: "I'm so pleased to meet you. I think *Pitty Pat Cat Wears a Hat* is adorable. Very whimsical. From my first reading, I immediately had pictures swirling through my head of what she would look like."

With his droopy eyes, dark bushy eyebrows, full lips and soft-spoken voice, Tully thought there was a dreamlike quality to Adam. "Thank you. I wrote it for my stepson and never dreamed it would be published."

"We were just heading out for lunch," Elliot said. "Why don't you two join us?"

Tully looked over at Sam, who nodded. "I'd love to," she said.

They left the building and headed for a Greek restaurant on the corner. Adam sat down at the table, his body relaxed in a slight slump. Over lunch, Tully learned that he was thirty-four, lived in a loft in the East Village, and had been drawing pictures since he was three years old. As he spoke about himself, Tully often had to strain to hear his words. His soft voice was not the result of shyness or disinterest; rather, the world in which he thrived was a visual one, not auditory, and verbal interaction had taken a backseat in his life.

"I think I drove my mother crazy," he said, "because if I got anywhere near a crayon, I'd draw on any surface around, whether it was a wall, a floor, a tablecloth. She bought me an easel when I was four and insisted I could only draw on that, but I was irrepressible. My mother would read me a children's story and I'd be more interested in the pictures than the story. At night, I'd climb out of bed and draw my own pictures of the story my mother had read. When I started school and we were assigned a book report, mine was always accompanied by pictures. I don't think I ever considered a career other than as an illustrator."

They chatted comfortably throughout lunch, and as they were leaving, Adam turned to Tully. "Hey, if you're not doing anything tonight, would you be interested in dinner? I'd like to get to know you better, know how you view the world of Pitty Pat Cat. That'll help me with the project."

Tully hesitated. She had enjoyed talking to Adam over lunch and liked the thought of seeing him again. "I'm having dinner with my girlfriend tonight, but I could do it tomorrow. Would that work for you?"

Adam nodded and flashed a warm smile. "Until tomorrow night, then."

With time on her hands, the sun peeking through the clouds and the temperature above freezing, Tully decided to walk along Fifth Avenue, now with the freedom to actually make purchases at the stores in which she had only been able to window-shop when she lived in New York. The Christmas tourists were gone, but the sidewalks still throbbed with masses of people rushing to their destination.

A year ago, the crowded streets had seemed to be squeezing Tully into herself, reducing her to a mere speck. Now she felt part of an enormous swell of mankind. Every stranger she passed was a secret conspirator, complicit in the knowledge of the City's magic, its majesty. Why hadn't she realized this before? *Has the City changed so much, or was I blind?*

She felt giddy with excitement as she walked along the sidewalks, browsed in any store that caught her eye, and made small purchases along the way. She stopped at FAO Schwarz on Fifty-eighth Street and bought Cody "Pappie, the Baby Orangutan," a stuffed replica of a real orangutan, with soft floppy arms and realistic features. The rest of the afternoon passed that way as she walked up Fifth Avenue toward Central Park and then cut through the park at Sixty-eighth Street to make her way to Haley's apartment. The sun was low in the sky as she passed joggers, bicyclers and roller-bladers along the paths, their bodies wrapped in layers of clothing and their faces reddened from the cool air. *I'm one of them. I'm a runner, I've run a race. I know the exhilaration of running along the streets, the wind in my face, the struggle up a long hill.*

She had always felt like an outsider, different from others, even as a child growing up in Middleton. Now, in the city of strangers, she felt she belonged in the world, accepted by Mack's world and by this towering metropolis, the most demanding of all. And then it hit her: She felt acceptable to herself. She wasn't Lauren's lesser sister, gangly and unathletic. She no longer felt tongue-tied and socially inept with groups of people. That's why New York City had changed. Because she had changed.

Chapter 17

Tully had agreed to meet Adam in his neighborhood, where they could go to his favorite restaurant. As she dressed for their meeting—that's what it was, a meeting, not a date, she told herself—she wondered why she felt so charged. Yes, he was cute, in a cuddly sort of way. Yes, he was unlike other men she'd known. He was at ease with himself, like Mack, yet not intense like Mack. She hadn't noticed a ring on his finger and wondered if he had a girlfriend. *Stop it. This is just a business meeting.* There was something about the way he'd looked at her at lunch, though, that made it feel unlike a business meeting, more personal. And she liked that feeling. She liked him, she had to admit.

Tully met Adam at the restaurant, a tiny room serving Thai food on St. Mark's Place, with dim lighting, candles on the table and a friendly wait staff. "I hope you like Thai food," he said.

"Actually, I've never tasted any. I lived in New York City for three years and the most exotic food I ever ate was Chinese. I've never even had Japanese food."

"Then let me order for you, if you don't mind." Tully nodded appreciatively, and Adam started them with appetizers of *tod mun pla*, fried fish cakes made with Thai spices, and *mee krob*, a mixture of noodles with baby shrimp, chicken and pork sautéed in a plum sauce, both of which they shared. They also shared entrees of roast duck curry and *nur yang num tok*, a barbecued beef dish in a hot and sour sauce, both ordered medium spicy, and finished with bowls of coconut and mango ice cream.

Throughout the meal, Adam spoke sparingly, but the conversation was never strained, the pauses never awkward. Adam asked her about her life, about her lifestyle, her interests and dreams. She asked Adam about his drawings, whether his interests were limited to illustrations or if he painted on larger canvases as well. She learned that Adam had grown up in Roslyn, on Long Island, the only son of an advertising executive and a guidance counselor. And she learned that he didn't have a girlfriend.

"My mother stopped trying to fix me up three years ago. I think she's given up hope of ever having a grandchild. I wouldn't mind marrying, it's just that the women I meet in New York seem to have different values from mine. Either they're looking for a well-paid executive or professional to support them in high style—something I'll never be able to do as an illustrator—or they're very focused on their own career and I'm too laid-back for them."

Tully knew there were many women in New York who would be thrilled to meet someone like Adam. She also knew how difficult it was to meet people in a city so large and so impersonal. Adam was as uncomfortable with the idea of going to a bar to meet other singles as she had been before she married Mack. "What do you like to do for fun?" she asked. "That's often a way to meet people."

"I spend so much time indoors, hunched over my drawing table, that when I do have free time I head for the country, to the mountains."

"So you'll go skiing?"

"No, I like hiking in the mountains. Just me and my two legs taking me to the top of the world, looking down on a valley or a lake or across at other mountains."

"But you don't hike in the winter. What do you do for fun now?"

Adam smiled. "I do hike in the winter. In fact, it's my favorite time to be in the mountains. I'm sure skiing is fine, but it's always seemed to me one goes skiing for the thrill. With hiking, especially in the winter, there are few hikers. It's so quiet and serene, so devoid of machines or commerce, that the overriding feeling is one of peacefulness. I prefer that to the adrenaline rush of downhill skiing. I feel rejuvenated when I return from the mountains."

Tully was still confused. "How do you hike through the snow? If I just walk through my backyard when the snow is deep it's exhausting."

"If there's a lot a snow, I use snowshoes. If there's ice, I use crampons. The movement uphill keeps the body warm, yet the air still feels brisk against your face. I bring along a thermos of hot coffee and stop at the top and just sit there, taking it all in." Suddenly, Adam's face brightened. "Say, the weather is supposed to be great tomorrow. Why don't I take a break from my drawing and we'll drive up to the Catskills. I'll show you what I've been talking about. There hasn't been any real snow yet, so you shouldn't need snowshoes, and the hiking won't be too difficult. I'll take you to an easy mountain."

She had come to New York to visit Haley, but the idea of spending another day with Adam was enticing. Besides, the emergency that had kept Haley from lunch the other day was still ongoing—she'd had to cancel the vacation days she'd planned on taking to be with Tully.

"I don't have boots here," she said. "I don't have appropriate clothes for hiking."

"You don't need any special clothing. Just dress in layers. I have an extra Gore-Tex jacket you can use as an outer layer and a sweatshirt you can wear, also a hat and gloves—they'll be a little big on you, but that shouldn't be a problem. The boots are an issue, though. I don't suppose you'd be willing to buy a pair? There's a hiking store on the way we could stop at in the morning. It's usually never a good idea to hike before breaking in the boots, but it won't be a long hike."

Why not? Mack would be impressed I went hiking in winter. Hell, he'd be impressed I went hiking any time. And I like Adam.

He's easy to be with, and if he's going to work on other books of mine, this will help build rapport. What Tully didn't think to herself, what she wouldn't admit to herself, was that she was more and more drawn to Adam—and that's why she agreed to go hiking with him the next day.

For once, the weather forecasters were correct. Friday morning was clear, just a few wispy clouds in the pale blue sky, the air invigorating but not frigid. Adam picked her up in his four-year-old Subaru Legacy at six in the morning to beat the rush-hour traffic out of Manhattan, and they scooted up the New York Thruway, stopping for breakfast at a rest stop on the highway. They got off in New Paltz to get Tully a pair of hiking boots, warm socks and liners and then continued up to Kingston, exited the highway and took winding roads the remainder of the way to their destination.

"The mountain I'm taking you to is called Bearpen. It doesn't have a marked trail, but even so, it's one of the easier mountains. There are rarely many hikers there, even in the summer, and in winter it's practically deserted."

When they arrived at the trailhead, Adam gave Tully a hiking pole. "This will make it easier for you going up and down the steeper parts." He put on a backpack. "You don't need to carry anything. I have everything we need in here." They set off along a woods road surrounded by tall trees, clumps of snow clinging to their branches, with several inches of snow underfoot. Stillness surrounded them; not even the whistle of a bird disturbed the quiet. They walked together, sometimes talking, sometimes in silence, along the gradual uphill. In the city, the roads and sidewalks were dry, but here inside the forest was a winter wonderland waiting to entrance them. Soon they arrived at a deserted structure and veered from the dirt road onto a narrow pathway, where the climb became steeper.

"How are you doing?" Adam asked as he watched Tully labor.

Despite the thirty-five-degree temperature, Tully was perspiring. "This is hard, but I love it."

"Let's stop and take a break." Adam brushed snow off a boulder for Tully to sit on and took a bottle of water from his backpack. They each sipped from the bottle, and after a few minutes Tully felt ready to continue. They walked through the snowy path for an hour and then Adam stopped. "We leave the path here."

Tully looked where he was pointing and saw nothing but trees, some deciduous, others coniferous. "There's nothing there. How do you know this is where we go?"

"There's a trail marker, but if there weren't, I'd be using a compass and my topographical map and that would tell me where to turn."

Tully looked at him quizzically. "What trail marker? There's nothing but trees here."

Adam pointed to a mound of rocks carefully piled to form a peak. "That's a cairn. It marks a turnoff for a trail. Someone placed it there as an aid to other hikers. Trust me, we won't get lost."

Tully followed Adam as he left the road and grimaced when she realized the grade had steepened considerably. She struggled up the hill, and as she neared the top, she turned a corner and entered a clearing, where spread out before her was a view of a wide creek, with farmlands beyond and mountains in the distance. The mountains didn't have the ruggedness of Colorado or Montana or the majesty of Chamonix, but she felt imbued with a sense of beauty. Adam took a thermos out of his backpack and two peanut butter and jelly sandwiches and they sat quietly, eating their lunch and drinking hot chocolate. Tully understood why Adam loved being in the mountains, away from the crowded ski slopes and clanging chairlifts. As they sat there, the solitude settled over them like a magical enchantment.

They talked about nothing and they talked about everything. They discussed the mild winter New York had been having, their favorite books, the scarcity of good rental apartments in Manhattan.

"You're very lucky, you know," Adam said. "You're doing something you love professionally and have a happy family life as well. It's so hard to have both."

Encased in the placidity of the forest, Tully knew she couldn't lie to Adam, knew that to do so would eviscerate the serenity of the idyll. "Marriages aren't always what they seem to outsiders."

"They rarely are."

"But mine especially."

"Aren't you happy? Your face glows when you speak about Cody and Mack."

"Oh, I love them both, love them deeply. And Cody loves me back. It's Mack …"

"Mack?"

"Mack didn't want a wife. He wanted a mother for Cody. He was honest about it from the beginning. Our relationship is platonic. He sleeps with other women, not with me. Never with me."

Adam's face showed his surprise, but he kept his voice controlled. "Why would you have agreed to that?"

"He asked me at a time in my life when I was recovering from the death of my fiancé. I didn't think I would ever be capable of loving again; I didn't *want* to fall in love again. I took to Cody instantly and I felt a connection with Mack. I liked the idea of living with a man who normally would never have noticed me. And I thought I could handle the charade. But I can't. I fell in love with him and it's so painful to know he doesn't love me." As Tully described her marriage to Adam, she was forced to acknowledge to herself the depth of her unhappiness.

Adam said nothing but took her gloved hand in his, and through the heavy fleece she could feel the warmth of his touch.

After a while, Tully began to get cold, and so they started their trek back down the mountain. They were almost to the car when Tully, her legs wobbly from fatigue and her concentration lax, stumbled on an icy patch and fell, turning her ankle under her foot as she hit the ground. Adam helped her up, and as she placed her legs on the path, her left knee buckled and she began to fall again. Adam caught her before she hit the ground. Gingerly, he helped her sit down.

"Let me take a look at your foot." Carefully, he tried moving her ankle, but she screamed in pain. "I think we need to go to an emergency room up here and see if your ankle is broken."

"Oh, Adam, I'm sure it's not. I can't believe I did this. The ground was completely flat. Now I've ruined the day for you."

"Don't be silly. Anyone can fall. When there's a covering of snow on the ground, it's hard to tell if it's icy underneath. Your ankle probably isn't broken, but you should have X-rays to make sure."

Tully was insistent. "I hate emergency rooms. The wait is interminable, and besides, who knows what kind of care they have here in the country? Let's just go back and I'm sure it will be fine tomorrow."

"I'm not so sure. If you won't go to the hospital, then let's stop and get some ice to put on it for the ride home. And if you don't mind coming back to my place, the guy next door to me is an emergency-room resident at Beth Israel Hospital. If he's around, maybe he'll take a look at it."

Tully agreed, and Adam supported her as she hopped and limped the short distance back to his car. Adam pushed the passenger seat as far back as it would go and propped Tully's leg on his backpack to keep it raised, and she iced her ankle on the drive back to Manhattan. They were in luck when they arrived at Adam's apartment—his neighbor, Dr. John Colonna, was home after his eighteen-hour shift at the hospital. He walked next door to examine Tully's foot. When he tried moving it in different directions, Tully forced herself to stifle cries of pain. When he asked her to try to stand on the foot, she couldn't.

"I don't think it's broken," he said after examining it, "but I suspect it's a grade two sprain, which means you've partially torn a ligament. I'd like you to have X-rays to make sure it's not broken, but it's fine to wait until tomorrow morning, and if you come by the emergency room then, I'll make sure you don't have to wait too long. In the meantime, I'll wrap it in an ACE bandage. Continue to ice it for fifteen minutes at a time every few hours, and keep your foot elevated. And try not to move around too much during the first forty-eight hours." He gave her a few anti-inflammatory pills and said he would see her in the morning.

Adam's loft apartment was a large open expanse with twenty-foot ceilings and circular wrought-iron steps leading to an upper floor, a third the size of the main floor, where he had a bedroom and bathroom. Decorated in bright colors, with furniture that looked thrown together rather than planned, his work space was separated from his living room with a series of folding Chinese panels. A large wood-burning fireplace was the focal point of the living area, with a thick flokati rug in front of it and a small kitchen and bath off to the side.

"Why don't you stay here tonight?" Adam said. "This way I'll be able to take you to Beth Israel first thing in the morning and you'll be off your ankle until then. The couch opens up, and I promise I'll behave myself."

Tully was grateful for the invitation and accepted readily. She called Haley to let her know while Adam scurried about to make her comfortable. He brought her pillows to elevate her foot, a blanket to wrap around her until the room warmed up, and a steaming cup of hot chocolate, and then he called a nearby restaurant to have dinner delivered.

"That's what I loved most about New York when I lived here," Tully said. "You can get any kind of food delivered at any time of the day or night."

They ate dinner to the strains of Brahms's First Symphony playing on the stereo, and when they finished, Tully made her nightly call to Cody to say good night. Later, Adam started a fire in the fireplace and they sat together on the couch, talking quietly, until Tully's eyes began to close. Adam helped her over to a chair and pulled out the couch to make a bed, got her settled, and kissed her good night on the forehead.

◆ ◆ ◆

At the hospital the next morning, Dr. Colonna came into the examination room with the X-rays taken of Tully's foot. "I was right, no broken bones, but given the amount of swelling and discoloration you still have, it is a grade two sprain. I'm going to put on an air splint to immobilize the ankle, and you'll need crutches for the next few days until you can put pressure on your foot without pain."

"I'm supposed to fly back to Denver tomorrow. Can I still go?"

Dr. Colonna frowned. "If you're able to stay here a few extra days, it would be preferable. Even with pressurized cabins, it's a long enough flight for there to be swelling in your foot, and I'd rather the swelling you have now has a chance to subside first."

As they left the hospital, Adam told Tully he hoped she would stay with him until she was ready to fly home. "I'm home during the day—I work from my apartment—so I can take care of you. I can drive up to your friend's apartment and bring your belongings down here. Please say yes."

Tully did say yes. Eagerly.

Chapter 18

Henry Woodman scanned the bar where he spent most of his evenings. The three-room apartment he'd moved into after he sold his house was too damn lonely to sit in night after night. He hadn't been much of a drinker after his high school car accident, but there didn't seem to be any reason not to get drunk every night. The finest woman in the world was sitting in prison because he was weak, a sniveling, cowardly drunk of a gambler.

Well, at least he'd stopped gambling. He had no money and no one was fronting him any, and good riddance to that vice. A third of his paycheck went to Big Sky Communications, required by the plea bargain Agnes had agreed to. He wanted her to go to trial—he was sure the jury would acquit her—but that wimp of a lawyer persuaded her to take the plea, that spineless no-talent gutless wonder.

Now Agnes was stuck in the Women's Correctional Facility, down in Cañon City, and it took him an hour and a half each way to visit her. He only got there once a week, and if his foreman needed him for a rush job on the weekend, sometimes it would be longer. Agnes always put on a cheerful face when she saw him, but he knew it was a pretense. Her skin had taken on a pasty pallor, her eyes had disappeared as if into a sinkhole, and he watched her drag her body to the visiting table as if she were pulling a leaden weight. But she would always smile when she saw him and tell him she was doing fine, teaching a word-processing class to other inmates, taking college-credit classes herself, finally able to read all the books she'd never had the time to before.

Her sisters hadn't been to see her until Henry got on the phone and called each of them. "Your sister needs you, she needs to see you, and your children, too," he said each time. When the first sister declined, saying how busy she was, how it would be too frightening for her children to see their aunt in prison, with criminals all around them, he exploded. "You selfish, lazy bastard. Your sister gave everything she had for you, there was nothing she wouldn't do for you, and this is how you repay her? If you're not there at least once a month, then I'm gonna drag your sorry ass out of your fucking house and take you there. Just see how your kids will like that."

By the time he called the other sisters, they'd already heard about Henry's outburst and knew not to challenge him. They readily agreed to begin visiting their sister.

Henry was just starting to get a buzz after his ninth beer. He seemed to need more of the suds lately to bring about that agreeable state of numbness, that feeling where the negative vibes could no longer penetrate his mind. If he allowed himself to think, to feel, he could barely control the tidal wave of rage that always threatened to erupt.

Was he angry at himself? At his bookies, who wouldn't give him more time to come up with the money? No. He was angry at Mack. Mack was the son of a bitch who had turned his back on a friend, who cared more about money than friendship. Mack, who had more money than he could count, who wouldn't even notice a missing million dollars, had taken away his beloved wife. Henry knew about Mack's private plane, knew about his fancy house—Agnes had told him all about it—knew about his spread up in Montana. That bastard!

Henry had been thinking lately about his father. Brick Woodman was just like his nickname, a solid hunk of man who'd worked as a lumberjack during the day and drank himself unconscious every night. He never hit Henry or his mom when he was drunk—that much Henry could be thankful for, but that was about all. He rarely spoke to Henry, and when he did it was to complain about his noise, his clutter, his existence.

It was Henry's mother, Mary, who'd provided any love he received, and she'd worked so hard cleaning homes that she was often too tired to show Henry how important he was to her. Henry knew, though, knew his mother worshipped him, knew she was proud of his good grades, the money he always had in his pocket. He never told her it came from gambling. Instead it came from extra work he was doing, getting double pay for overtime. His father disappeared when Henry was twelve, and good riddance to him. His mother lived long enough to see her beloved son go to jail and died before he was released.

Alone now, with no mother, no wife, he'd been wondering if his father was still alive. He wondered what had happened to him. The rare pleasant memory of his father kept popping into his head—the baseball glove he bought him for his tenth birthday, the catch they'd played in the street that same day, never to be repeated. He remembered the day his father took him to work—Henry couldn't have been more than eight or nine—and Brick had actually bragged to his friends about how smart Henry was. The good memories were few, and Henry latched on to them, replaying them in his mind over and over. Had his father died alone, his liver shriveled to a peanut from years of drinking? Is that how Henry would end up? He no longer cared.

Henry looked up and saw Julio enter the bar. Julio, a two-bit bookie and high school dropout half Henry's age, was dressed in black cowboy boots, tight black leather pants, and a leather jacket draped over his short, rounded body. His black hair was slicked back, and with his pencil-thin mustache and carefully trimmed goatee, he looked like a bad imitation of a pimp.

He strutted to Henry's table and surveyed the empty bottles. "Hey, Henry. You sure been packing them away here."

"What's your point?"

"No point. Just looks like you can use some company. OK if I sit down?" He slid into the booth opposite Henry.

Henry shrugged. "It's a free world." He picked up his bottle and took a chug, doing his best to ignore Julio. Seeing his former bookie aroused feelings in him he'd tried to bury: the exhilaration of the bet, of the prospect that the next race was going to change his life.

Julio looked Henry up and down. "How's your old lady doing?"

"She's not my 'old lady.' Her name is Agnes."

"I know, I know her name. I was just asking. Don't be an asshole."

Henry stared silently at his bottle, his lips trembling.

"I read about her old boss in the paper today. His company went public, sold their first shares yesterday. I bet you didn't know I read the business section." Julio laughed. "Hell, I bet you think I don't even read. You know, I'm a businessman myself. I gotta keep up on these things. They say he's worth over a billion dollars now, can you fucking believe that? And that's just for now. If it goes up, he'll be worth even more."

Henry just shook his head and mumbled, "Son of a bitch, son of a bitch."

"His old lady—now, *she's* sitting pretty. My girlfriend, she's a nanny for one of her friends. They all live in the same fancy-dancy development in their big-bucks houses. She told me the women all get together at each other's homes and bring their nannies along to watch the kids, so she's been in his house. She says your wife's old boss has the biggest one of them all."

Henry waved over the waiter to bring him another beer. "He thinks his shit don't stink? He's gonna get his someday. Nobody treats my Agnes that way and gets away with it. I don't care how rich he is."

Adam doted on Tully. He cooked her meals with exotic flavors, bought her books to read when she finished the ones she'd brought from home, and rented movies for her to watch on his DVD player. Each night Tully called home to say good night to Cody and, during those calls, felt increasingly guilty about her enjoyment of Adam's company.

Tully's flight was scheduled to leave LaGuardia Airport at 3 p.m. Tuesday, and at noon that day winter arrived in New York City with a vengeance. Heavy snow began falling and didn't stop until the next afternoon, leaving the city buried under eighteen inches of snow. The airports closed down at one o'clock on Tuesday and didn't reopen until Thursday morning, with a backup of stranded passengers clamoring to get on flights. When she learned that her flight had been canceled, Tully was pleased that she would be spending more time with Adam. She enjoyed his company and recognized a growing affection for him. It wasn't the heart-thumping, stomach-churning, knees-quivering sensation she'd felt with Mack, but it was a satisfying warmth, a feeling of being cared for, and that felt good.

They stayed indoors all day Tuesday and continued to learn about each other. "Tell me about your family," Tully said.

"Everyone thinks I inherited my creative genes from my father, him being in advertising, but really it's my mother who's the true artist. She never studied formally and only dabbles in it, but she's remarkably talented. So many of my friends grew up with dysfunctional families, but I've always felt my parents were abnormally normal. They were always loving without being overindulgent. They support my career choice even though I don't have a steady salary. They have such a good relationship, I think I've always been afraid I wouldn't be able to duplicate that with someone."

"You're lucky to have them."

"How about your family? What are they like?"

"My father died when I was five and I barely remember him. When he died, my mother worked two jobs to support us, and Lauren and I always worked when we were old enough for after-school jobs."

"I envy you having a sister. I was an only child."

"Lauren always looked out for me." Tully chuckled. "It's funny how some things stick with you. I still remember climbing into Lauren's bed at night when I'd wake up from a nightmare. If I went to my mother, she'd pull back the covers and mumble, 'Only for a half-hour.' I'd be so afraid of extending my time limit that I'd lie awake for the whole time while my mother slept. Lauren was never cross from having her sleep interrupted. She always made room for me next to her.

"As I got older, I understood the burden my mother shouldered working two jobs to support us, and I loved her for her sacrifice, but it was always Lauren I felt closest to. I miss my mother, though. I miss her a lot. She died just before I came to New York."

"Does Lauren know about your relationship with Mack?"

"Yes, I couldn't hide it from her. But she doesn't know how unhappy I am." Tully smiled wistfully. "In fact, you're the only one I've told, and you're practically a stranger. But don't think it's all bad. Cody makes everything worthwhile. I sometimes find it hard myself to take in how close I feel to Cody. I may not be his biological mother, but I can't imagine loving my own child any more deeply."

They continued to confide in each other throughout the afternoon, openly discussing their lives, their feelings. Tully didn't talk about Mack, though. She didn't want his presence to intrude on her shared intimacies with Adam.

By Wednesday, as the snow tapered off, Tully and Adam were both stir crazy. Tully was able to put weight on her foot by then and they ventured out to the streets, still pristinely white before the snowplows arrived and the fumes turned everything gray and dingy. Adam held on to her tightly so she wouldn't risk a spill, and they walked around letting the snow fall on their cheeks, sticking out their tongues to catch the flakes, throwing snowballs at each other. When they returned, Tully sat on the couch wrapped in a warm shawl and sipped wine. A fire burned in the fireplace while Adam drew sketches of her. After a while, he brought his sketches over to the couch and showed them to Tully.

"Adam, these are so good. They're very realistic, not at all like your illustrations."

"I like this one best," he said, pointing to the last picture of her. "You have such a great smile and I think this captures it. What do you think?"

"I think everything about you is wonderful," she said and then kissed him, not on the cheek or the forehead but on the lips, pulling herself close to him, feeling his body against hers. They made love, not because of the wine or the warm glow from the fireplace or because he was a substitute for Mack but because Tully wanted to, wanted to feel Adam beside her, feel his smooth body next to her, inside her. They made love again that night and then again before she left for the airport on Thursday.

She had come to New York on the heels of Mack's rejection of her, eager for the next step in her career but confused by her emotions. She left New York more confused than ever.

Chapter 19

"Eat your cereal, the school bus will be here soon," Mack said as Cody dawdled over his breakfast.

"I miss Mommy. When will she be home?"

"Soon. Before you know it." Mack shared his son's dismay at Tully's absence. The house seemed so still without her. He hadn't realized how much her mere presence filled their home with light.

"But she was supposed to be here a long time ago."

"Mommy told you—she hurt her ankle and then the plane wouldn't fly in the snow."

"We have snow here, too. Will the plane have to wait until the snow's all gone?"

"No, it's OK if the snow's on the ground."

"Maybe Mommy doesn't want to come home. Maybe she's angry at me."

"Why would Mommy be angry at you? She loves you. I promise, she'll be home tomorrow."

Rosetta had been gone for two days. Her absence had been long planned—she'd promised to help her mother for a few days after a surgical procedure. Tully expected to be home before then, and now suddenly Mack found himself caring for his son alone. Even with Cody having extended nursery-school hours, Mack didn't understand how women managed to get everything done without going crazy. At work, he could order an employee to act at his command. Not so with his son. Cody moved at his own pace, sometimes as slow as sap dripping from a sugar maple tree, at other times like a whirlwind blowing up during a storm. It looked so easy watching Tully. She never seemed rattled, always got Cody where he needed to be at the right time. Mack needed her to be home, not stuck in New York.

But, he admitted reluctantly, it wasn't just for Cody's sake that he wanted Tully back. Over the past year, gradually, imperceptibly, he had come to look forward to his time with Tully, had come to feel more complete when he was in her presence.

The sound of Cody's school bus pulling into the driveway broke Mack's reverie.

"Dammit, Cody, I told you it was late." Mack immediately regretted his shortness. How could he teach his son not to curse if he couldn't control himself? "Are you still hungry? Do you want to finish eating?"

Cody pushed his cereal bowl away from him and jumped out of his seat. "I'm not eating until Mommy comes home."

Mack knew that wasn't true. He put on Cody's jacket, hat and gloves and shoved a glazed doughnut into his fist. "Here, eat this on the bus." Once he got to school, it'd be the teacher's problem to get food into him. He knew she would, somehow. At least he hoped she would. Mack walked Cody outside, smiled warmly at the bus driver, an assistant teacher at the nursery school. She was young and pretty, with short black hair and multiple earrings in her lobes. She smiled back flirtatiously. "How's it going, Mr. B.? You handling being on your own?"

"I'm managing, thanks."

"Well, you need any extra help, I'm available. I mean at night, after work. Even if you'd just like some company." Not long ago, Mack would have flirted back with her, but something had changed. He still had his dalliances, but less and less often. He no longer felt the same compulsion to move from affair to affair. Was it because of Tully? He'd been comfortable with her from the start, but it was more than comfort now. He needed her. The sweet, shy young woman he'd met in Florida had morphed into an attractive, vibrant partner. As the school bus pulled away and Mack walked back into his house, he shook his head. *Dammit, Tully. This was supposed to be simple with us, a straight bargain. How did you become so essential to me?*

Mack hadn't wanted to feel dependent on a woman again, yet he didn't mind his growing need for Tully. What he couldn't live with, though, was a woman's becoming dependent on him. And so despite her increasing desirability, he kept Tully at arm's length, kept an invisible barrier around him that he wouldn't let her penetrate, much as he'd sometimes like her to when he was lying alone in his bedroom, knowing she was but a few steps away, knowing she wanted him to come to her.

Mack drove faster to the office than his usual excessive speed. He'd been getting in late and leaving early to be home for Cody the past two days, and work was piling up. The launch of Movie World had gone well—four million subscribers were already signed up. An important meeting was scheduled for that afternoon with FiberConnect, a major cable operator. They were close on an agreement that would add another two million subscribers and help push Movie World into the black earlier than the projected three-year timetable. Brian Montgomery, Mack's vice president of programming, had handled the negotiations until this point, and Mack was stepping in today to close the deal. A preparatory meeting with his internal staff was scheduled for ten o'clock, and he was close to being late. It didn't matter to him that he was the boss—Mack liked to lead by example.

Flashing lights and a blaring siren signaled the presence of a police car behind him. Mack pulled onto the shoulder of the highway and sat in his car as the policeman approached.

"License and registration, please."

Mack looked up at the young man, a wool navy jacket over his starched blue uniform, with a Denver Police badge on its lapel. He couldn't have been more than twenty-five. Everywhere he turned it seemed people were getting younger and younger while he felt the years adding up. "Was I going too fast?" Mack asked with a sheepish look on his face.

"You were going ninety in a sixty-five zone, sir."

"I'm sorry, officer. My wife's away and I got harried getting my son off to school. I guess I was distracted. Can we forget about it this time? I assure you it won't happen again."

The young officer hesitated, his pad in hand. Mack saw the mixture of envy and admiration in his eyes as they took in the expensively dressed executive in his well-shined Porsche. "Sorry, you were going too fast for me to ignore," the officer said and began writing. "Be careful all the time, not just when you're caught." He handed Mack the ticket. "I know your type. You think you can get everything just the way you want it. That you're entitled to it. But you're no different than anyone else. You speed, you pay. Have a nice day," he said with a smirk and walked back to his cruiser.

Mack was already in a bad mood when he walked into his office, and it didn't get better when Brian told him FiberConnect had postponed the meeting. "They claim it was just a mix-up with scheduling, but I have a feeling they're going to play hardball with us, and canceling the meeting is their first shot." Mack knew the two companies would eventually reach an agreement, but price and distribution were key. FiberConnect balked at the per-subscriber fee Big Sky had set for Movie World. More troubling, they were resisting packaging it with other movie services. Packaging was the key to driving subscriber growth; Big Sky could give a little on the price but needed to stay firm on how the service was sold.

Deep in concentration over the financial analysis of the impact of different packaging scenarios Brian had put together, Mack was startled to suddenly see Nick standing over his desk. "How long have you been here?"

"A few minutes. You look lost to the world."

"I've been staring at these numbers, but nothing's getting through to me today. I can't seem to concentrate on anything."

"Well, this should get your mind off numbers. We got served with the Hawkins lawsuit today."

"Well, why not? Everything else today is going wrong." Mack had expected the lawsuit, a sexual-harassment claim against one of his vice presidents that Nick had attempted to settle before it reached this stage.

Nick looked at him quizzically. "Something you want to talk about?"

"No, it's nothing. What's our exposure on this suit?"

"Well, as you know, Daniels is adamant that he did nothing wrong. A couple of the employees we interviewed described Hawkins as a provocative dresser who often talked suggestively to the men in the office, as though she wanted to entice them. Daniels says that's true, but he always resisted. Faithful to his wife, he says."

"What evidence does she have?"

"Well, she tells a good story, with a lot of details, but so far hasn't come up with any definitive proof. Her lawyer says he's saving it for trial, where it'll make a bigger splash in the media. Now that she's filed a complaint, we'll be able to get discovery, see what she really has."

Mack liked Daniels. He'd been a solid worker, producing consistent results during his five years with the company. Mack had met his wife and teenage children at the company's annual picnics. A public trial would be embarrassing not only for Blue Sky but also for Daniels and his family. "What was our last offer?"

"Fifty grand just for it to go away. We started at ten."

"And no interest? How much do you think it'll take?"

"Her lawyer claims nothing less than a million."

Mack's face reddened. "That's practically extortion! What's her salary here? Thirty, forty thousand a year? Even if her claims were true, how could she think she's entitled to a million dollars?"

"Emotional distress," Nick said. "She says she's so upset by his groping her that she hasn't been able to sleep at night or look for another job."

As a large company, Big Sky had had its share of lawsuits over the years, and Nick and Mack agreed that it was better to fight the baseless ones, even if legal fees far exceeded the claimed damages, pay when they were in the wrong, and try to settle the questionable ones. Neither Mack nor Nick thought the Hawkins claim was questionable. They believed Daniels's denials and wanted to stand by him. The strain on the man's marriage from fighting it out in court, though, might be difficult to survive. But giving in to extortion was not an option. "I wonder if she's done this before," mused Mack. "Have you checked into her background?"

"We've done a Lexis search. Haven't come up with any other cases in which she's a plaintiff."

"But what if she settled the others? What if she's used other names? Has Vince checked her out?"

"Just preliminarily. He still has some good contacts with the Denver police. I'll have him dig further to see if she's used any other names."

"Good. See what you can find. And if she comes up with anything damaging—something concrete—during discovery, then I'll go up to three hundred thousand. But make sure her attorney understands that if anything is leaked to the press before trial, negotiations are off the table. I don't want Daniels's marriage ruined by her if he did nothing wrong."

Nick nodded but didn't turn to leave. "So, feel like talking now? What else has been going wrong for you?"

Mack pushed back the papers on his desk and motioned for Nick to sit down. "Usual stuff. Cody couldn't get going this morning and was giving me a hard time. Then I got a speeding ticket on the way in."

"And that's it? Nothing else bothering you?"

"What are you getting at?"

"You've been on edge ever since Tully left for New York. I think you miss her."

"Of course I miss her. She's my wife, maybe not in the usual sense, but you know."

"No, I don't know. You say you don't love her, yet you lose a beat when she's not around. Is it just because the household doesn't run as smoothly? Because Cody's not the same?"

"Yes ... No ... I don't know what it is." Mack slumped in his chair. Since Tully's birthday declaration, he'd battled a swirl of conflicting emotions. Desire mixed with fear; affection mixed with steely resolve. Her absence had intensified those feelings. "I only know this: Nothing seems right without her."

Chapter 20

"It's good to have you back," Mack said over dinner her first night home. "We missed you. How's your ankle?"

"Much better, thanks. The rest really helped." Tully had thought about Adam most of the flight home. She had been happy staying with him, being cared for by him, making love to him. Now back in Stonington Village, she wondered whether the week had been a mirage, a fleeting romance nurtured by the circumstances, destined to fade into a pleasant memory.

She looked at Mack anew, with changed eyes. Before she'd left for New York, she was desperately in love with her husband, something that in most marriages would augur well for a lifetime commitment. Now, after spending a week with Adam, after being intimate with him both physically and emotionally, did she feel differently toward Mack? She wished she would. It would make her life so much easier to bear. She had to admit, though, that it was still Mack she wanted, still Mack who made her heart race. *Why is the unattainable always so much more alluring? Why is it so difficult to be content with what we have?*

"I stopped into Sam's office to say hello and he brought me upstairs to meet the editor of *Pitty Pat Cat*."

"What's his name?"

"Elliot."

"Did he tell you when it might be published?"

"Oh, it takes longer than you'd think. Probably not until next year. And I happened to run into the guy who's going to illustrate the book."

"Did you get to see his work?"

"I did. I think he'll be great for the book." Tully told him about Adam's work and background. Mack brought her up to date on Cody's latest doings, how the launch of Movie World was proceeding, and the other bits and pieces that make up the routine of any household.

As they continued with their dinner, the conversation flowing easily between them as if they were an old married couple, Tully remembered her sister's warning: "You think he'll change after you're married, that he'll love you, but he won't. I know about men like him." *I should have listened to her. I didn't expect to fall in love; I didn't know it would hurt so much if I did. And I thought making love to Adam would make it easier being with Mack. It hasn't.*

Mack sat before Agnes in the visiting room of the Colorado Women's Correctional Facility. "I wanted to visit you earlier, I wanted to explain, but Nick wouldn't let me. He said it would look like interference."

"I've never known you to let Nick make decisions for you."

"Agnes, you have the right to be angry at me. It kills me to see you here. But we were becoming a public company. If I just let it slide, I could have been investigated for wasting shareholder assets. The Justice Department could have prosecuted me even though I knew nothing about what you'd done."

Agnes had cared about Mack for so long that being angry at him exhausted her. She saw the look of anguish on his face and knew his remorse was genuine.

"You let me down, Mack. I know what I did was wrong, but it wasn't against you personally. I felt I had no choice. You reported it to the police without even coming to me and asking me to explain. Maybe I could have found a way to pay you back. You didn't know and didn't seem to care."

Mack took her hands in his. "Is it too late? I can't do anything about your prison term, but when you get out, I promise I'll be there for you. You can have your job back if you want it, and I'll pay the rest of the restitution out of my own pocket. If you don't want to work, I'll set up a pension fund for you. You won't have to worry about money."

"Help me now. Give Henry the money instead of me. He has to pay the restitution now as part of my plea bargain. If you want to help me, pay it for him."

Mack's back stiffened, his face clouded. "Why, so he can gamble it away? I can't do that."

"He's a good man. You don't really know him."

"He's letting his wife sit in prison for eight years when he could have gotten her out."

"This was my decision."

"I can't do that, Agnes. Ask me anything else, but I can't help Henry. I blame myself for not stopping your marriage in the first place."

"You wouldn't have been able to. I love him, and he's been good to me."

Agnes was grateful for Mack's generosity and appreciative of his continuing concern for her. She needed his friendship. She only wished she could make him understand her need for Henry's love as well.

Henry hadn't wanted Agnes to accept the plea offer. "You can win at trial, I know you can," he'd said. Agnes knew it was a long shot, and Henry was the gambler, not her. When he couldn't dissuade her, he turned his fury on Mack, and at each visit, he unleashed on Agnes his vitriol toward her former boss. Each visit, she would attempt to defend Mack, but her attempts were always futile.

And so Agnes was caught between the two men she cared most about. Mack didn't want to hear that Henry had cherished her and would wait loyally for her release from prison. Henry didn't want to hear that Mack had been caught in a regulatory vise, pushed to press charges by outside forces. She didn't even attempt to tell Henry about Mack's financial promise regarding her future. She knew it would inflame him further that Mack would not help now, when Henry needed it the most.

Agnes dragged herself from the prison library after returning the latest book she'd borrowed and choosing another. She disliked crime novels, of which there seemed to be so many, and gravitated toward the classics: Jane Austen, Charles Dickens, the Bronte sisters, and Mark Twain, whom she'd read in high school but was enjoying all over again.

She had been disappointed that, rather than being sent to the Denver Women's Correctional Facility, she was sent to the women's prison in Cañon City, the lockup for more hardened criminals. She wasn't a risk to anyone, had never hurt a soul in her life, yet here she was with murderers, drug dealers, and arsonists. They were kind to her, though, treating her like a mother figure. Most of their mothers had been absent during their growing-up years, emotionally if not physically. They instinctively recognized Agnes's capacity for nurturing and gravitated toward her, offering protection against the roughest inmates, the sociopaths who were beyond the need of a mother's attention.

She wondered why she felt so tired. Her prison job in the laundry was not physically demanding. The college psychology class she took was mentally challenging but not physically draining. The afternoon walks in the prison yard provided needed fresh air with minimal exertion. Yet she felt tired most of the time. Lately, she'd felt some fluttering in her heart, but it would go away after a minute or so. *Nerves. It's being in prison, knowing I'll be here for eight years—that's what's doing it. Probably why I feel so tired as well. All nerves, I'm sure.*

Agnes worried about Henry. He hadn't been looking well himself during his visits to her. She noticed his bloodshot eyes, his increased irritability when describing his work, his carelessness with his appearance. He assured her he was fine, just working hard, but she was concerned nevertheless. She had seen her parents drink to excess every night and feared that Henry had fallen into that liquid abyss. But mostly she was alarmed at the vehemence of his anger toward Mack.

Agnes made her way back to her cell, her home for the next eight years, the six-by-eight box with narrow bunk beds, a single overhead bulb, and a small table and chair she shared with Sonia, a twenty-year-old former junkie who had been shuffled from foster home to foster home since the age of three. A high school dropout, Sonia was barely literate and yet had a sweet nature, a yearning to be liked. Agnes was teaching her to read, teaching her to appreciate herself, and Sonia idolized Agnes in return.

It was the end of the day, the time when prisoners had un-structured time. Cell doors on the block were open, and the women could mingle until the doors were shut again, when the loud click of the lock would signal their confinement for the night. Sonia hadn't returned to the cell yet, and Agnes settled herself on the chair to begin her new book, *Great Expectations.* She liked the longer books, liked being drawn into another world for weeks at a time, losing her thoughts about herself, where she was, what she had become.

She barely noticed the palpitations when they began, not un-til they became louder, harder, like a hammer pounding on her chest. She stood up, placed her hand on her chest, as if the touch of her fingers contained a healing power, and collapsed.

Henry was in a state of shock, unable to comprehend the words spoken over the telephone.

"It was very sudden, Mr. Woodman. She didn't feel any pain, didn't suffer at all. If someone else had been with her, seen her collapse, perhaps she could have been saved. But she was alone, and no one found her until it was too late. We're terribly sorry, Mr. Woodman."

Henry sat down and wept. How could this be? How could Agnes be gone? What would he do without her, without the hope of being with her again? They said it was ventricular fibrillation; it caused a sudden heart attack. They had no idea she'd had any heart disease. She had never complained of chest pains, dizziness, shortness of breath. It happened sometimes, unexpectedly, just instant death. If a doctor had gotten to her within a few minutes, she might have survived, but she was alone, with no one to help her. She died in a six-by-eight prison cell all by herself.

Chapter 21

Mack paid Agnes's funeral expenses. Henry made the arrangements, made all the decisions, but Mack, devastated when he heard the news, paid the bill. Tully kept telling him that it wasn't his fault, that he wasn't responsible for her death, but he did blame himself. If she hadn't been incarcerated, perhaps she could have gotten medical attention quickly, gotten CPR to restart her heart, gotten someone to care about her. Agnes's sisters told Mack their mother had also died suddenly. It probably wouldn't have mattered where Agnes was. It was just her personal time bomb, ticking away inside her.

None of their words mattered. He'd been a coldhearted businessman, and his friend of more than fifteen years was dead.

The turnout at the church was large, with many of Agnes's former colleagues from Big Sky in attendance. They had turned their backs on Agnes after she'd been fired, after she'd been charged with stealing money from the company, after she'd been sent to prison. Now, though, they all came to say good-bye to her, to walk past her casket and whisper how sorry they were to have abandoned her, to absolve their consciences.

Henry and Mack didn't speak to each other at the funeral. Each blamed the other; each accepted the blame himself. Mack recognized it was something he would have to live with. Henry vowed to avenge his wife's death. He would take his time, he would plan it carefully, but he would have his revenge.

Mack returned to his office after the funeral, his overcoat buttoned up on the uncharacteristically cold late-March day. Snow was forecast for that evening, and the leaden skies, which seemed to confirm the prediction, settled like a shroud over Mack as he walked into his building. He sat at his desk, unable to clear his mind of the image of Agnes lying in her coffin, her face masklike. He needed to be with someone, a woman, to lose himself in her soft, perfumed body. If he went home, the urge to take Tully into his arms, to have her caress him, would be intense, his resistance excruciating.

After fiddling with paperwork, pushing it around on his desk without achieving any results, he picked up the phone and telephoned Rebecca. Mack hadn't seen Rebecca in months, although they spoke occasionally on the phone. It was always ostensibly for business reasons, but it was clear the physical attraction was still there, the flirtatiousness underlying all their conversations.

"I realize this is last-minute, but how about hopping on a plane and coming here today. I still owe you that romantic dinner."

Rebecca hesitated only for a moment. "Let me see if I can get a flight. I'll call you right back."

A few minutes later, Mack's secretary buzzed him and put Rebecca's call through. "I've booked a seat on a United flight to Denver, arriving at five o'clock."

"I'll pick you up. And thanks."

"For what?"

"For coming so quickly, for not asking questions. Why can't all women be like you?"

"Because other women have different goals. My goal is the executive suite, not bagging a husband. You know, despite the window dressing on equal rights, a woman still has to be twice as good as a man to be offered the same opportunities."

"Well, I hope it's not that way in my company. I'd like to think we ignore gender when we hire and promote."

"You have a lot of women working for you, including in

middle management, and that's good, but you have thousands of employees and I'm only aware of one woman in senior management. You don't even have any women on your board of directors."

Mack was taken aback by her observation, unaware of the imbalance within his own company.

"Besides, men have another advantage," Rebecca said.

"What's that?"

"They can have a wife at home to keep the kids happy and the meals ready, give them support in their career. That's an enormous benefit. It's a rare man who's willing to do the same for a woman. Even men who accept a working wife, a career woman, expect her career to take a backseat to theirs."

Mack realized she was right. Since Tully had moved into his home, he felt less stress. Comfortable with the knowledge that Cody was well cared for, he was better able to focus his energies on Big Sky.

"Maybe later, maybe after I've gotten what I want in business, I'll look for that rare man who's secure enough to appreciate me and not try to stifle my drive. You have potential, you know, except you're already married, and I hope I would pass on an obvious philanderer anyway. In the meantime, we have fun together and that's all I'm looking for now."

At five o'clock, Mack picked Rebecca up at the airport, and they drove to her hotel. "You look beautiful. I've missed you," he said. He felt a gnawing ache in his gut, a hunger that needed to be satisfied immediately. They checked into the hotel and, with barely a word spoken between them, tore back the covers on the bed and fell into it, voracious in their need for each other.

Afterward, as they lay limply on the bed, Rebecca's head lying in the crook of his arm, Mack thought about Agnes. *I failed her. I thought making love to Rebecca would obliterate that fact, erase the knowledge that I didn't try to understand her, help her, but it hasn't.* He wanted to cry, wanted to plead for forgiveness, but it wasn't in his nature to cry, and it wouldn't matter anyway. There was no one to forgive him. Instead, he pulled Rebecca tight against his body and they made love a second time.

Later, they drove to Boulder, to his special restaurant, where the headwaiter always smiled when Mack arrived with a pretty woman on his arm and was always discreet. They lingered over the meal, and as they enjoyed the vintage wines from the restaurant's superb wine cellar, the alcohol gradually relaxed Mack. The tension that had kept his muscles tied in knots all day eased. By the time they left, it had begun snowing heavily and the roads were slick with ice. Mack drove slowly, mindful that his first wife, Joanna, had died on such an evening. When they reached Rebecca's hotel, she urged him to stay the night rather than attempt a treacherous drive to his suburban home.

"I think I can make it. I'll be careful driving. It's too late now for me to call Tully, and I don't want to worry her."

"If it's too late to call her, then she won't know the difference. She'll be sound asleep. Leave early in the morning, when the roads have been cleared. You can be home before she wakes up."

Mack recognized the practicality of Rebecca's suggestion and also realized that he wasn't ready to return to his solitary bed in his separate room. He left his car with the valet and accompanied Rebecca to her room. They made love again, this time slowly, exploring each other's bodies, finding new spots to elicit cries of arousal. They fell asleep in each other's arms.

Waking up in the darkened room, it took Mack several moments to remember where he was. The glowing numerals on the bedside clock said it was 3:10 a.m. He stepped out of bed, pulled open the heavy drapes covering the window, and saw that the snow had stopped. Even through the thick glass, he could hear the whirr of the snowplows pushing snow off the streets, sanding the icy roadways. Quietly, he put on his clothes, sat down in a chair to lace his shoes, tiptoed to the bed and gently kissed Rebecca's forehead. She opened her eyes. "What time is it?"

"It's the middle of the night. Go back to sleep. I'm going to leave now."

Rebecca sat up and looked around, saw the time on the clock, the darkness of the room. "Don't go now, it's too early. Stay and have breakfast with me in the morning. You can call your wife then and tell her you stayed in town overnight because of the weather."

Mack shook his head. "I want to be there in the morning to have breakfast with Cody."

That was true. He relished his breakfasts with Cody, listening to his son's nonstop chatter. Cody had become a different person in the year since he'd given him a mother. Although he could still hardly be called an extrovert, his quietness and easygoing temperament seemed to fit him now. He was no longer painfully shy.

Yes, having breakfast with Cody gave Mack the start to his day that helped carry him through the long hours at the office. But it wasn't just Cody he wanted to see. It was also Tully's pretty face. Her words consoled him when he needed it and soothed him when his temper arose over some imbroglio that she always managed to keep in perspective.

"I'll call you," Mack said and kissed Rebecca good-bye, both of them understanding that this meant their rendezvous was over for now. It was back to their professional relationship: client and vendor.

Ever since her return from New York City, after reading to Cody at bedtime and cuddling him until he'd fallen asleep and Mack had retired to his bedroom, Tully would retreat to her own bedroom to talk to Adam on the phone. The first night, he'd called to see how the flight went, how her ankle felt. They stayed on the phone for over an hour, talking aimlessly, the way new lovers often do. He called again a few nights later, and then again the next night, and the next, until it was clear that neither would go to sleep without hearing the voice of the other. Sometimes they'd speak for just a few minutes, other times for hours.

It was easy talking to Adam. They were so much alike, much more than she and Mack. They were both quiet, reflective, easygoing. Both had been a little unsure of themselves growing up, yet both gained confidence as they found something that they loved and that inspired them. For Adam, it was the drawings he'd done since childhood, a crayon or paintbrush almost an appendage to his hands. For Tully, it was being Cody's mother, being loved by Cody—that had allowed her to begin to value herself. Her writing, her running, her openness to new activities were all outgrowths of her realization that she could be good at something, that she was already good at something.

Their conversations were always open and honest, sometimes painfully so. Tully talked to Adam about Mack, about still desiring him, knowing that it was hurtful to Adam yet also knowing that Adam didn't want to be lied to. Tully cared about Adam as well, cared more and more deeply for him as they became more intimate and their connection to each other strengthened. If Mack weren't in the picture, if Cody wouldn't be lost to her forever, she could imagine herself living with Adam, loving him fully and truly.

On this night, Tully stayed up talking to Adam later than usual, knowing Mack would be home late. "I'm worried about him," she said. "He was so distraught about the death of his former assistant. He holds himself responsible, although, really, there was nothing else he could have done. He had to go to the police."

"Attending a funeral is always depressing, especially when the person is still relatively young. Give him time. He'll come around."

They stayed on the phone, talking as best friends would, talking as lovers would, unsure of which they were. It was past midnight when Tully hung up, and Mack still wasn't home. At least six inches of snow had already fallen. The streets were no doubt slippery. She knew she wouldn't fall asleep until she was sure Mack was safe, and so she padded down the carpeted stairs to the family room, popped a DVD into the player, and got herself settled on the couch. Despite her anxiety about the roads and

Mack's mental state, she fell asleep on the couch before the movie was over.

She was still there when Mack quietly entered the house shortly before four. He saw the bright light from the television before he noticed Tully asleep on the sofa, her head on a cushion and her legs curled up close to her body. She looked like an innocent child, her long hair falling over her face, her breathing even, her chest moving up and down. *Have I been unfair to you? Are you happy here? You've made my life so much better, but have I made yours better? Or have I taken advantage of you? Have I kept you from finding happiness with someone else?* He took a blanket out of the closet and covered her and kissed her forehead. "I do love you, you know," he whispered, knowing he couldn't be heard, surprising himself with the admission he'd struggled so hard to deny.

Chapter 22

Spring arrived early in Denver that year, and April 5, opening day for the Colorado Rockies, dawned with rain-free skies and temperatures hovering near sixty-five. Mack and Nick continued their tradition of attending the home opener at Coors Field with their sons, regardless of what was going on at work or school. They settled into company seats four rows up from the field, between home and first base. This was Cody's second year at the event, and he was as caught up in the excitement as Nick's older boys.

It was a day the two friends looked forward to each year, but Mack had been fidgety throughout the afternoon. Nick tried to engage him in their usual sports banter, to no avail.

"What's going on with you today?" he finally asked.

As the boys munched on popcorn, drank soda, and shouted cheers with each base hit and home run by the Rockies, Mack turned to Nick. "I think Tully is seeing someone," he said quietly.

Nick reached over and grabbed some popcorn from his son's bag, taking a moment to respond. "I'm not surprised. She's young and attractive and your arrangement makes it OK."

"I know it's part of our agreement, but I expected she would have flings. You know, affairs. She's on the phone every night to the same person, sometimes for hours. I've checked the phone bills; it's a call to New York. She must have met him when she was there for her book. Maybe her illustrator, or maybe her editor, I don't know."

"Why are you bothered by it? This keeps her happy and you free to carry on as you want. It's your bizarre plan borne out to fruition," Nick said in an airy tone.

"It was most certainly not my plan that she fall in love with someone else! This has been going on for almost three months. What if she wants to leave me for him?" Mack's voice rose.

"Well then, buddy, I guess you're going to have to decide whether you want a housemate or a wife. If it were me, it'd be an easy choice."

While the men were at the ballgame, Tully spent the afternoon with Lizzie. It had been a while since they had just hung out together, without the larger group of women, let alone any children. Lizzie always made Tully feel welcome, had from the first time they'd met, and Tully appreciated her friendship. They had just finished a leisurely lunch in the sunroom at Lizzie's home, a spacious glass enclosure with a view of the distant mountains, when Tully asked, "Do you ever miss working?"

Lizzie thought for a moment before answering. "You have to understand, my father was a named partner in a top New York City law firm. My mother was a socialite from old money whose career was making my father comfortable. From a young age, I got mixed signals: Achieve, but your husband comes first. My father was proud that I graduated from Yale Law School, and my mother was proud that I snagged Nick in the process."

"What did *you* want?"

"Both. I was offered jobs at top New York firms, the best in the country, but turned them down to work in San Francisco so I could be close to Nick. We were already engaged by that time."

"Nick is so wonderful. I would have done the same."

"And I loved my firm. It was much more collegial than the

backbiting that goes on in Wall Street firms. I got to work on big deals, too, sooner than I would have in New York. I did corporate law. I never minded the long hours. I even had fun staying up all night at the printer to make sure a prospectus I'd worked on got done by the deadline."

"Yet you left when Nick came out here."

"Sure. He's my husband. I got another job with a Denver firm and then stopped altogether when the twins were born."

"And no regrets?"

"I loved the work while I was doing it, and I knew I was good at it, too. But from the moment I held the boys in my arms, I never had any doubt that I wanted to be home with them."

Tully admired Lizzie's certainty about herself and her choices. "I always thought I would have a career and have children also. Now it seems so hard to do both without feeling that one is being shortchanged. I love working on my novel but feel guilty when I leave Cody with Rosetta. And when I don't work on my novel, I feel restless."

"Is this really about Cody? Because you've been incredible with him. I've never seen such a transformation in a child." Lizzie hesitated. "I know about your arrangement with Mack. Nick drafted the agreement, and we don't have any secrets. Is that what's disturbing you?"

Nodding, Tully began to cry, her cheeks splotched with wet drops. "I thought it would be easier. I knew from the beginning Mack didn't love me, and that was fine. I didn't want to be loved. I thought this strange arrangement would be OK. I even thought it would be good. And it has been in so many ways. But now I've fallen in love with him, and it hurts so much. I ache, I physically ache from it, as if I have a twenty-four-hour flu that I can't shake. I keep telling myself to accept it, and most days I can, but it's always there in the background, my longing for him."

Lizzie walked over to Tully and put her arms around her. "Well, it was inevitable you would fall in love with him. You share his life so completely. I expected you'd either end up loving him or hating him. Don't give up on him, though. I haven't seen him this happy in years. He cares about you more than either of you realizes. Have you told him how you feel?"

Tully wiped the tears from her cheek. "Yes. It was awful. Oh, he tried to be gentle, but rejection always hurts. I know he cares about me. He just doesn't love me. He doesn't even want to make love to me. I know I'm not beautiful like Joanna, and I know how devastated he was by her death. I don't think he'll ever let anyone replace her."

"Don't be so sure. You really don't know anything about Joanna or about her relationship with Mack. You've only heard the superficial stories, what the Lenape Lane Ladies have told you. But Joanna was very good at creating a façade. Mack was certainly affected by her death, but not in the way you think."

"How then? Tell me."

"I shouldn't have said this much. I shouldn't even know about it, but Mack has always treated Nick as his confidant. Give Mack time. He'll wake up eventually."

"Lizzie, this is important to me. What on earth are you talking about? What is it about Joanna I should know?"

Lizzie shook her head. "You need to ask Mack about her. But carefully, ask him carefully."

Cody bounded into the house charged from his day at the ballgame, his day with his dad. "The Rockies won, the Rockies won," he shouted upon seeing Tully. "Rosario and Gonzalez hit home runs, and once when the bases were loaded. And Daddy bought me a hot dog and french fries, and I had popcorn and ice cream, too." He was wearing a Rockies cap, another purchase obviously made that day.

Tully laughed as she picked up Cody and gave him a hug. "Well, I guess you're not going to be very hungry for dinner tonight."

"I'll be hungry. I promised Daddy I'd eat my dinner tonight even if he bought me ice cream."

Instead of eating dinner, though, Cody fell asleep still dressed in his clothes, exhausted from the day's game. Mack and Tully had dinner alone, together, both quiet. Tully thought perhaps Mack had been worn out by the outing as well.

Tully kept thinking about Lizzie's comments about Joanna and giving Mack more time. Everyone had told her that Mack had put Joanna on a pedestal. Hearing their description of Joanna, of their relationship, knowing how she herself had reacted to Scott's death, she assumed Mack didn't want anyone to come between him and his memory of his true, great love. Could she have been wrong? Was there another reason that stopped Mack from loving again, from loving her? Lizzie had said to ask Mack carefully. She wanted to know about Joanna. She wanted to understand the hurt Mack carried in him.

"What was Joanna like?" Tully asked casually.

Mack looked up from his dinner plate abruptly. "Why do you ask?" Tully could see his body stiffen.

"Well, she's Cody's biological mother. I'm sure he inherited some traits from her. I think it would help me understand Cody better if I knew what she was like." Tully hoped her explanation sounded plausible but knew it was a feeble attempt to seem innocuous.

"Cody is nothing like Joanna. He's his own person. It wouldn't help you to know what she was like."

"I think it *would* help me. Cody is just starting to develop his personality."

"I said it's not important for you to know." Mack's voice rose, his face reddened. He looked back at his plate as if he could physically withdraw from her question.

"Mack," Tully said gently, "I know speaking about Joanna is painful for you, but she's here, between us. She's the elephant in the room that shapes our relationship. I never thought I could put Scott's death in the background, but living with you and Cody has helped me do that. Let me try to do the same for you. Please. We talk to each other about everything else. Why can't we talk about her?"

"Do we talk about everything else? I know about your phone

calls to New York. Do we talk about your boyfriend there? Do we talk about how you feel about him?"

Tully put her fork down and folded her arms. "Well, dear, you encouraged me to see other men. I'm just following your advice."

"Hmph! I told you to sleep with other men. It's a simple biological act. Can't you women understand that without trying to turn every relationship into something more?"

His words hung in the air. Tully's icy stare widened the gulf between them.

"You're right," she said. "I guess there are things we don't share with each other. If you'll excuse me, I'm finished with dinner."

She got up from the table, went to her room, and made her nightly call to Adam.

Chapter 23

Still working on construction jobs, Henry went through each day robotically. His only thoughts concerned how to hurt Mackenzie Bryson. "You destroyed someone I loved and I will destroy someone you love" was the theme that ran through his mind day after day, hour upon hour. He hated Mack with a venom that seared his soul. He thought about killing Mack's wife. That would provide symmetry. But he knew there was someone Mack loved more than his wife and Henry began to design his scheme for retribution around that person.

Revenge required careful planning and a lot of patience, and Henry was capable of both. He had let his wife sit in prison because he was too cowardly to return there himself. Now he planned an act so daring, so outrageous, that if caught he would be locked behind bars forever. He no longer cared. His world had ended with Agnes's death.

But he didn't think he would be caught. He believed that if he were careful and thought through each step, he could walk away with enough money to disappear. Money was not the primary objective for Henry, though. The obligation to repay the embezzled money had died with Agnes. And he was used to living modestly. But he would need help to carry out his plan, Julio's

help, and a large sum of money would be an incentive for his
friend.

Henry had stopped drinking after Agnes's death. Not even
alcohol could dull his pain. Oscar's Tavern was a safe place to
meet Julio, convenient for each to get to but not a bar that either
had frequented in the past. They were strangers to the staff and
patrons, and Henry wanted that anonymity. Once again, as in
the past, Julio sat opposite Henry in a booth, nursing a beer.

"What's the big deal you wanted to talk about," Julio said,
"and why couldn't you tell me on the phone? My old lady is
waiting for me tonight, so make it quick."

Henry leaned over the table. "I got a proposition. It's high-
risk, but high-reward, too."

Julio shrugged. "So spill it."

Henry knew he had to proceed carefully. Julio was no model
citizen and didn't mind bending the rules to make a buck, but
so far he'd steered clear of the law, whether by dumb luck or
knowing how to travel under the radar. Either way, Henry was
ready to offer him a chance at a big score, but he needed to
make sure Julio wouldn't turn on him and notify the police
instead. "What if I told you I had a plan for us to split six
million dollars?"

Julio laughed. "I'd say you have shit for brains and leave me
out of it."

"I'm serious. I'm not gonna kid you. It's risky, but I got it all
planned out. I've covered every angle except one, and I need you
for that. But if you're not interested, tell me now and I'll forget
we even spoke."

"How can I be interested? I don't know what the fuck you're
talking about."

Henry watched Julio's body language, his facial tics, looked to
see if he seemed nervous about being brought into a score. He
didn't. He was relaxed, waiting to hear why his friend had called
him to this tavern.

"This is a big job, Julio, bigger than anything you've been
in before. If you want to play it safe with booking bets, always

scraping for money, then tell me to shove off and we'll still be friends. But if you want to take early retirement, maybe on a beach somewhere, some island, I can tell you how we can do it."

"I'm interested. Let me hear it."

Henry bent his head closer to Julio's and laid out his plan.

Relations had been strained between Mack and Tully ever since she'd asked about Joanna, ever since Mack had alluded to Adam. They remained cordial with each other, but there was an unmistakable barrier, translucent, untouchable, but there nevertheless. She couldn't understand his reaction to her phone calls. After all, he'd pushed her toward that ever since they married.

It was clear he saw other women. She didn't believe for a moment that he'd stayed in the city all night because of snowy conditions two weeks ago. He'd driven home in far worse, the adventurer in him fearless even when it came to treacherous driving. What, then, had upset him so?

It never occurred to Tully that it could be jealousy, that Mack could feel threatened by her interest in Adam. Instead, her thoughts dwelled on Joanna. *Why won't Mack talk to me about her? Does he feel he's betrayed her by bringing me into their home, allowing me to raise her child?* Despite Lizzie's assurances, it seemed futile that Mack would ever want her as his true wife. No, Joanna must be firmly rooted in his mind as his one true love.

Tully thought some distance between her and Mack was needed and decided to visit Adam. When told she was going to New York City for a few days, Mack asked if she would stay with Haley.

"I'm staying with another friend," Tully said. "You can reach me on my cell phone."

Mack hadn't asked the name of the friend. Perhaps he didn't want to know.

Eager to see Adam for the first time since January, Tully hastily packed her bags, said her good-byes to Cody and Mack, and left for the airport. In the limousine ride and on the airplane,

she kept thinking about Adam. Their nightly phone calls and
frank conversations had intensified her feelings. Was that true for
him as well? It seemed that way, but long-distance relationships
sometimes fell apart when the couple reunited.

She needn't have been concerned. Adam met her at the airport, and as soon as she saw him, she knew the bond between
them was strong.

"God, I've missed you so much," Adam said upon first seeing
her, pulling her close to him, and burying his face in her hair.

Tully realized she'd missed him, too, missed having his body
next to hers. She missed watching him at his drawing desk, leaning intently over his sketch pad. She missed his crooked smile.

They spent her few days in New York City absorbed in each
other. Adam took her hiking in the Catskills again, this time a
beautiful spring hike, with the flowers in bloom, lush foliage surrounding the trail, the reward of a spectacular view at the sum-
mit, and, thankfully, no broken bones at the end. They visited the
Bronx Zoo and the South Street Seaport and spent one day going
from museum to museum: the Metropolitan, the Guggenheim,
the Frick, the Museum of Modern Art.

One evening they went to a movie at the Angelika theater and
laughed when the rumble of the subway underneath their seats
drowned out a love scene. Another evening Adam lighted a fire
in the fireplace, took out his guitar, and serenaded her with folk
songs.

At night they made love, hungrily, trying to compensate for
the time they'd spent apart, dreading the time when Tully would
return home.

As the time for her to leave drew closer, Adam became more
and more agitated.

"What's going on with you?" she asked the morning of her
departure.

"Nothing."

"You've been sulking around the apartment since we got up."

"I don't see why you can't stay longer."

"Whenever I leave it'll be hard for us, whether it's today or next week. I care about you, I do, but the best we can expect is a long-distance relationship."

Adam walked up to Tully and put his arms around her. "That doesn't have to be."

"What are you saying?"

He stroked her hair. "Stay here," he whispered in her ear. "I love you. I want to marry you."

Mack awaited Tully's arrival home from New York City with trepidation. He was certain she'd spent the time with her paramour, the voice at the other end of her long-distance phone calls. He was afraid she'd made a fateful decision while she was away from home, away from Cody. He'd been distracted at work for the past few days, knowing the peaceful existence they'd had for the last year and a half could come to an abrupt end.

Also haunted by thoughts of Joanna during these few days, thoughts he had successfully buried long ago, he wrestled with his longing to keep those memories buried—and the recognition that to do so could destroy his future. Tully had asked such a simple question—"What was Joanna like?"—but how could he tell her? How could he tell anyone? He had started out deeply, profoundly in love with Joanna, but it had ended so differently.

Their last conversation was seared into his memory. They had just returned from a visit to Joanna's family in California for Christmas. Her siblings had gathered at their parents' home: her younger sister and her husband with their two children, and her older brother, Derek, back from a year in Australia. Mack had just gotten Cody to sleep when he walked into their bedroom. "I've had it, Joanna," he said. "You've had enough time to adjust to being a mother. My God, Cody's over a year old and he barely knows you exist. And me! I can't keep going on like this. We may share a bed, but that's about all."

Joanna just stared at him.

"You need to see a psychiatrist. He can help you deal with your depression."

"I'm fine. Nothing's wrong." She lay on the bed and turned away from Mack.

"You're not fine. You're a different person since Cody was born."

She turned back to him and smiled wanly. "You're exaggerating."

"Talk to me, dammit! Are you having an affair? Is that what this is about?"

"Why would you think that?"

"Because you say you're not depressed, yet you no longer seem to want me. Because you've withdrawn from me. Because you don't seem to care about me, or even Cody, frankly."

She didn't respond.

"Do you still love me? Do you love someone else?"

She sat up, leaned back on the pillows, and put her hands over her eyes. She remained like that without speaking at first and then removed her hands and looked straight at Mack. "I love my brother."

"I don't mean that way. Do you love me as a husband?"

"I love my brother," she repeated.

Mack didn't understand and then slowly it dawned on him, the secret glances they'd exchanged, the affectionate hand-holding, the hours they'd gone off on their own. He felt as if a bolt of lightning had gone through his body, seared his organs, bludgeoned his brains. How could this be? It was unnatural, perverse, sick.

He could barely speak. He slumped into a chair. "When?" he asked in little more than a whisper.

Joanna lay down again, her back to Mack. Quietly, she began to speak. "When I was fourteen. My body had already matured and the boys in my school flocked to me. I could have had my pick of any of them, but they were laughable. So awkward, so pimply, so different than my brother. Derek was handsome, athletic, charming. Every girl in school envied me because he was my brother. His body was perfect, his smile was radiant. All my friends wanted him. I wanted him. And so when his girlfriend left him and he was miserable, I consoled him. I sat on his lap,

I stroked his arm, I told him she wasn't right for him. And then I pressed my body close to his and kissed him. That's how it started. That night we became lovers."

Mack forced himself to ask the next question. "Are you still?"

"He stopped it when I became pregnant with Cody."

Mack couldn't believe what he'd heard. He couldn't believe how he'd been so deceived for years. He was disgusted. "I want you to leave. Go back to your brother," he said, his voice icily cold.

"He doesn't want me anymore," she cried.

"I don't want you either."

Joanna packed her bags that night and got into her car despite Mack's protests that she should wait until the morning. It was snowing outside and the roads were slippery.

"No, I have to leave now. There's nothing here for me any longer," she said. Those were the last words she ever spoke to him. Before she could even get to the highway, she crashed into a tree, dying instantly. Was it an accident or a suicide? The police report was inconclusive. Out of courtesy to the grieving husband, it was ruled an accident.

Mack never told anyone why Joanna left him that night, not even Nick. Instead, he only told Nick that she had admitted to an affair, they'd fought over it, and he'd thrown her out of their house.

It was a secret he would take with him to his grave, tormented by the knowledge that he had failed his wife. He'd failed to appreciate that she was sick, that she needed help, his help. He had been incapable of putting his own hurt behind him, of understanding that she needed him more than ever.

He had been successful his whole life, but he realized he was a fraud. He couldn't be counted on when he was needed the most. He hated himself for a year after Joanna's death, and then gradually, day by day, that hatred receded into the background. He decided he would never allow himself to love another the way he had Joanna, never allow himself to fail someone he loved, as he had failed his wife.

He knew that he hadn't changed, that he wasn't capable of changing—hadn't he failed Agnes, failed to recognize she'd acted out of desperation? He knew he would be lost, could never recover, if he allowed himself to love again, deeply and intensely, and then once more failed his wife when she needed him.

Now his determination was being put to the test as he struggled with his conflicted feelings for Tully. He yearned to hold her close to him, to love her fully, yet was terrified that if he did, the cocoon he'd spun to shield him from his hatred of himself would disintegrate around him. Could he risk loving her? Could he risk losing her? Was it already too late?

Chapter 24

Adam's proposal sent tremors through Tully's body. The silence in the room seemed to last an eternity. She hadn't expected this from Adam, hadn't realized he felt so strongly about her. Although she was drawn to him, felt truly herself with him, and, yes, loved him, she didn't know if she was in love with him. Would it matter if she was?

She looked around the room, with its haphazard furnishings, its carefree style so different from her impeccably furnished home in Colorado. She looked at Adam, wearing his faded chinos and wrinkled T-shirt, his hair a disheveled mess of curls, so different from Mack's polished attire. She knew that Adam was a kindred spirit, his surroundings familiar to her, the connection between them genuine.

"Adam," she whispered, "oh, Adam."

She sat on the couch and rubbed her temples. "If only we had met earlier, before I married Mack. I know I could be happy with you, I *am* happy with you. But it's too late now. I can't leave Mack."

Tully could see the pain on Adam's face.

"Why? You don't have a husband waiting for you at home. He's just a companion, a meal ticket."

"A meal ticket? You know that's not important to me. You make it sound like I'm a gold digger." Tully got up from the couch and walked away from Adam and then spun around and came back. "How can I leave Cody?" she asked, glaring at him. "Just tell me, how could I do that?"

"I know you love Cody, but you're his stepmother, not his biological mother. We can have children together, you and I, and you'll be a wonderful mother to them. Cody is young, he'll adjust. Maybe Mack will marry someone else. You can't deny your own happiness because you feel beholden to him."

"Beholden? You don't understand. I love him. Cody makes me feel whole."

Adam wrapped his arms around Tully and held her tight. "You *are* whole. I don't know what you were like before, but you don't need a child to make you feel good about yourself, not anymore."

Tully wished she could make Adam understand how she felt. Adam was comfortable, safe, secure, lovely to look at and lovely to be with. Adam was the life she had expected for herself when, a lifetime ago, she had allowed herself to dream.

Mack offered her no future, no passion. Yet as Cody's mother she had blossomed, emerged from her self-imposed exile and allowed herself to cherish Scott's memory as a sweet reminder of what might have been without letting it hold her back. As Mack's wife, she'd learned to ski, run a race, written two children's books, and was well into her novel.

When she was with Adam she felt happy. When she was with Mack, especially of late, she felt hurt. Yet until their recent flareup, Mack had been so thoughtful, so generous, so kind to her since they'd returned from Chamonix, always considerate of her feelings, always fun to be around.

Was that enough for her? She once thought she could live the rest of her life without passion. Was that still true? How could she explain her decision to Adam when she couldn't explain it to herself?

"You're right, Adam, everything you say makes sense, but I

can't leave him now, I just can't. I'm sorry, more than you realize, and maybe things will change, but not now, not yet."

"I'm glad you're home. I've missed you," Mack said when he returned from work and found Tully on the floor with Cody, helping him put together a puzzle. He strode into the living room and sat on the floor beside her, kissed her on the cheek, and opened his arms for Cody, who began climbing on him, planting kisses all over his face.

"Daddy, look at the puzzle Mommy bought me. I can put it together almost all by myself!"

"Hey, you're a real pro. I bet you're glad Mommy's home."

Cody became very serious. "I am. I told Mommy she shouldn't ever go away again."

Mack looked Tully over. Did she seem different, altered by her few days away? He realized how changed she was from the woman he'd first met at his sister's home in Florida. *She's not a woman I would have pursued when we first met, not someone I would have wanted to take to bed. I was drawn to her because of her warmth and because of her attention to Cody. Now, everything about her seems right, seems to fit so well with what I want, with what I need.*

That night, after Cody had fallen fast asleep, Mack said to Tully, "I have a business trip next week, to Paris and I thought you might like to join me. We can spend a few extra days and I'll show you the city. It's really a special place."

Tully's face lighted up. "Paris! I've always dreamed of going there."

"Then it's settled. We'll leave next Tuesday and stay through Sunday. The weekend will be just for us."

Left unspoken was the cause of the rift between them the previous month: Tully's curiosity about Joanna.

At Lizzie's house the next day, Tully confided her excitement about visiting Paris and her confusion about Mack's invitation.

"It's been uncomfortable between us ever since I asked him about Joanna. Then I come back from New York and suddenly he's changed. Warmer. It's like our rift never happened."

"I told you Mack cared about you," Lizzie said.

"And Paris? He's never invited me on a business trip before, and now he's taking me to Paris? I can't imagine a more romantic city. I just don't understand it."

"You're more important to him than you realize. Maybe your trips to New York are making him afraid you don't think he's important to you."

Tully sighed. "If I'm important to him, it's only as Cody's mother. It's not as his wife. But he needn't worry. I wouldn't do anything to hurt Cody."

"No, Tully, it's not just about Cody. He wouldn't take you to Paris if that's all it was about. He and Joanna honeymooned there. He's always loved that city, always considered it special. Trust me, it's not Cody's mother he's taking there, it's you. Even if he's not ready for a full relationship yet, he knows you're special and he wants you to stay a part of his life."

Tully wondered why Lizzie would say this, why she thought Mack might be concerned. Surely he couldn't know that Adam wanted her to leave Mack and marry him. Or did he?

It was unimaginable that Mack had arranged for an investigator to follow her and Jean-Luc on their honeymoon, yet he had. Could he have arranged for an investigator to follow her in New York? *That's impossible. Mack was so contrite after Chamonix. Surely he wouldn't have done that again.*

Although she dismissed her paranoid thoughts as foolish, a kernel of doubt remained.

The day before Tully and Mack were set to leave on their trip, it was Tully's turn to host the weekly luncheon for the Lenape Lane Ladies. As usual, their nannies arrived along with them and were consigned to the playroom with the children while their mistresses dined alfresco in Tully's backyard, on the terrazzo patio with a view of the jagged mountains. As they picked over the perfectly ripened melon pieces served for dessert, they gave Tully advice on her upcoming trip.

"You absolutely must go shopping while in Paris. There's no place like it in the world. Even New York doesn't compare," Angie Johansen said. "While Mack is at his business meetings, you can hit the shops. He won't mind."

"Ooh, you have to go to Jean Paul Gaultier, very haute-couture," Karen Harding chipped in. "And Alberta Ferretti. The dresses there make any woman irresistible."

"Don't forget Zadig and Voltaire. Their clothes are just plain fun," Angie said. "And there are adorable clothes for Cody at Bonpoint."

The women were clearly excited at the prospect of a shopping foray in Paris, and they deluged Tully with suggestions, giving her addresses and shopping tips as well as restaurant recommendations.

"The food is incredible in Paris. Even at the most unimposing storefront restaurant, everything is delicious," Susie Howard said. "It's worth going to Paris for a weekend just to eat there."

"You may go for the food, but never leave without shopping," Angie said, and they all joined in the laughter.

"Where are you staying?" Lizzie asked.

"At the Four Seasons Hotel George V."

"Of course. Mack always stays there. It's the best hotel in Paris. You'll love it."

Tully wasn't so sure. Although excited about the trip, it was the first she was taking alone with Mack since their honeymoon. She was afraid that, as in Chamonix, he would leave her on her own while he pursued his own "personal" interests. She suspected Mack had a woman waiting for him in every city he frequented, and the thought of being abandoned in such a romantic city while Mack escorted another woman dampened her enthusiasm. Still, it was Paris, and she was determined to enjoy herself no matter how Mack behaved.

♦ ♦ ♦

They left Denver on Tuesday afternoon. The flight to Paris, which arrived the next morning, was similar to the flight to Chamonix—first class all the way. Everything else about the trip was different. Their limousine brought them to the Four Seasons just before eleven and they were immediately taken to their deluxe suite. They walked from the large entry foyer into a lavishly decorated living room, furnished in Louis XVI style, with exquisite antiques and neoclassic paintings on the walls. The bedroom, furnished similarly, contained a king-size bed and led to a marble bathroom with a deep soaking tub and separate shower. A large balcony overlooked the Eiffel Tower.

After the bellman left, Tully said, "Does the couch open up into a bed?"

Mack smiled. "I don't know. I didn't ask."

Tully, still sleepy from the overnight flight, was confused. "I don't understand."

Mack walked over to her, drew her close to him, and lifted her face toward his. "Darling, I've been so stupid. I thought we could be married and live together and keep emotions at bay, but I was wrong. Incredibly wrong. Please tell me it's not too late for us. Tell me you still want me, because I want us to be truly husband and wife. I love you, Tully."

Tully could feel her body tremble as she took in Mack's declaration. She was awash with happiness, ecstatic that Mack loved her, and the lingering doubts she'd had about leaving Adam dissipated instantly. It had always been Mack she wanted, always Mack she loved.

Still silent, she lifted her lips to his and he returned her kiss, tenderly, deeply, then passionately. As he led Tully to the bed, they heard a knock at the door.

"Bonjour, monsieur," said the bellhop, who held a basket of fruit. "The manager wished to give you this with the hotel's compliments. May I set it down for you?"

"Yes, of course."

Tully went out onto the balcony. She couldn't stay in the same room with Mack and not touch him, her desire was so strong.

She looked down over the city, saw lovers walking hand in hand along the Seine, the spires of the Eiffel Tower beyond. *Hurry, Mack, hurry up with the bellhop. I can't wait a moment longer.*

She heard the heavy door of the suite close behind her and went back into the room. Mack came to her and led her to the bedroom. Slowly, he unbuttoned her blouse, unhooked her bra. He cupped her breasts in his hands and bent down to kiss them. "So beautiful," he murmured and ran his tongue over her nipples.

He threw the multiple pillows piled high on the bed onto the floor and tossed off the quilt.

Suddenly, Tully began to laugh. "You wouldn't believe the amount of sexy lingerie I've bought since we married. I kept hoping someday I'd be able to wear it for you. I even took it with me to the ranch. I finally accepted that I was kidding myself, and now it's all there, in my drawer at home."

"You don't need sexy lingerie to arouse me, can't you tell?"

They undressed each other and fell onto the bed. Mack was the most beautiful man Tully had ever seen, his sinewy body perfect in every way. They took turns exploring each other's bodies with their hands, with their tongues. Mack nibbled on her ear, whispered into it, "I love you so much," and Tully felt as if it were a dream. She'd never been so happy, never felt so aroused. Afterward, they both fell asleep, exhausted from the jet lag and the fervor of their lovemaking.

After awakening, they had a quick lunch and Mack left for his business meeting. On her own, Tully walked for hours, enthralled by the streets of Paris. She knew she'd be a disappointment to her friends, for she did no shopping. Instead, she just absorbed the ambience of the city. She stopped at a sidewalk café for a glass of wine and sat for a half-hour watching French couples, arm in arm, stroll by. Young or old, in haute couture or hippie garb, everyone seemed to be in love. Her head still spun from Mack's embrace of their marriage. She had been resigned to a platonic relationship. She'd been certain Mack's feelings would never change, and she was too committed to Cody to think of leaving him. Now her life had changed again, and this time she felt as if she had landed in a fairy tale, her childhood fantasy come true.

They ate at the hotel restaurant that night, Le Cinq, too exhausted to venture far and too impatient to get back to their suite to once again fall into each other's arms and discover each other's bodies. "This is our real honeymoon," Mack said over Dom Perignon, "the real start of our marriage. I want to make up to you for all the time we lost, make you happy beyond your expectations."

Tully took Mack's hand and smiled. "You've already made me happier than I could have imagined. I think I'd explode if I were any happier."

"Just wait and see. This is only the beginning for us."

Mack was at meetings from the next morning until dinnertime. Before he left, they jogged together along the Seine. Tully spent the rest of the day indulging herself at the hotel's spa. There were so many places she wanted to visit, but she wanted to see them with Mack. They would have the next three days free from business commitments to do so.

When Mack returned, he gave her the bad news: A crisis had come up at the Denver office that required his presence. They would have to cut their trip short and leave early the next morning. "I promise I'll make this up to you. We'll come back to Paris again, just to visit, no business at all."

Tully was perfectly content to go home. It didn't matter where she was. She was so happy Mack loved her that she could have been living in an igloo in Alaska in the dead of winter and it would have seemed like heaven. Nevertheless, Mack wanted to make her last night in Paris memorable. Despite the last-minute request, the hotel concierge had managed a reservation for them at Guy Savoy restaurant, "an epicurean experience not to be missed," Mack promised.

He was right. Tully had never eaten food like it before, a savory fusion of tastes that seemed almost melodic in its perfection. When they weren't eating, Mack held her hand under the table. She slipped her shoe off and ran it up his leg, eliciting a smile from Mack as it rose higher. After dinner, they took a cruise boat along the Seine, the city aglow along its shores, the Eiffel Tower standing grandly at one end, lighted up like a Christmas tree. Mack wrapped his arms around Tully as they stood along the railing, his chin resting on her hair.

"Hmm. Your hair smells like a garden. How come I never noticed that before?"

"You never noticed a lot before. You didn't want to, remember?"

"Ah. That was in my idiot phase. Thankfully I've come out of it."

Tully turned around to look at Mack. "It's hard for me to believe this is real. I've loved you for so long."

"When? When did you realize you loved me?"

"It happened gradually, over months. Watching you with Cody, being part of a family, I began to want more from you. But the day we took Cody to the hospital, after his accident, you put your arms around me and told me it wasn't my fault. That's the moment I knew I was in love with you."

They returned to their suite and, after making love, fell asleep in each other's arms. Tully awoke during the night, the room dark but for a thin beam of moonlight peeking through the edge of the heavy drapes, and watched her husband sleeping peacefully next to her, his muscled chest rhythmically rising and falling. She hadn't asked about Joanna again, wouldn't ask about Joanna again, would do nothing to risk shattering the joy she felt because Mack loved her.

When they arrived at the Denver airport the next afternoon, Mack told Tully he needed to head straight to the office but would see her at home that night. "I think we should have another wedding, this time a real one, with all our friends and family," he said before leaving. "We'll tell them we want to renew our vows. What do you think?"

If she'd had any doubts, Tully knew at that moment that Mack's commitment to her was real. "I'm going to love you forever," she told him.

Chapter 25

As Tully's limousine took her home from the airport, Henry and Julio drove up to the gate of Belle Vista Estates in an indistinct white van newly painted on each side with the name "Ames Carpet Cleaning."

"I'm here for Mrs. Bryson, 24 Lenape Lane," Henry said to the gate attendant.

The attendant checked his roster, saw that the service men were expected, noted the Ames logo on the men's uniform shirts, and lifted the gate for them to pass through.

Julio's girlfriend, Anna Fuccella, the nanny for Angie Johansen's children, had given them the Brysons' address and arranged for their entrance to the secure community. It was a simple burglary, Julio had assured her. No one would be hurt. It was almost 4:30 p.m., a time when they could be certain Cody would be home with his nanny. Henry had waited for the right time. He knew that his plan required precision. He had been patient and it had paid off with the ideal circumstances for executing his plan, with Mack and his wife still away on their trip. He drove through the streets slowly, following Anna's directions to Lenape Lane, and pulled into the driveway of Mack's palatial home.

"Fucking pig," Henry muttered under his breath when he saw the size of the house. This was it, the day everything was going to

change for him. No longer a loser, no longer a coward, no longer
the scapegoat of Mack Bryson's greed, he'd reverse all that today.
Today, Mack Bryson would know what it felt like to lose someone he loved. Today would be the beginning of Henry's never
worrying about money again.

"Let's go," Henry said to Julio and grabbed a toolbox as he
opened the van door.

With wigs on their heads underneath caps emblazoned with
the logo of Ames Carpet Cleaning, pasted-on mustaches, beards,
bushy eyebrows, and dark sunglasses, they had changed their appearance sufficiently to make it difficult for an accurate description. Walking to the front door, they took a last glance at each
other and nodded, confirming their commitment to take this
last step, knowing that once inside, their course was irreversible.
They rang the doorbell and waited, listening for the footsteps
that would make their plan a reality.

The door opened slightly and Henry saw a middle-aged woman wearing an apron over her dress and holding a large spoon in
her hand.

"Can I help you?" Rosetta asked.

In an instant, Henry pushed the door open, stepped inside
and swung his big hairy arm around Rosetta's neck. He pulled
her close to him and clamped his other hand over her mouth.
Shutting the door behind them, Julio drew a small 9-millime-
ter Beretta from his pocket and hit the back of her head with
the butt, knocking her unconscious. He knew just how to conk
someone out without causing any real damage, a task he occasionally performed as a warning to scofflaw gamblers.

Henry opened the toolbox, took a roll of tape from it, and
placed a strand over Rosetta's mouth. With a heavy rope also
taken from the toolbox, he tied her hands behind her back and
then her feet and threw her limp body inside the hall closet.

Both men slipped gloves onto their hands, and each took a
rag, and wiped down the front door and the knob of the closet.
Quietly, Henry and Julio made their way through the house.
In the kitchen, a pot of water boiled and meat sauce simmered

in a pan. Henry turned off the flames. As he walked back into the foyer, he thought of his earlier years, burglarizing homes to pay his gambling debts. He would have hit pay dirt with this home—the latest electronic equipment, rare art and antiques in every room, Persian rugs, no doubt drawers filled with expensive jewelry, perhaps even fur coats in the closet.

Petty stuff. Today I cross over to the big time.

But despite Henry's resolve over the past few months, despite his continued hatred of Mack Bryson, still lingering in the back of his mind was the question of whether he had it in him to carry through to the end. Not the logistics—he knew he had planned it well. But he wanted to take the life of someone Mack Bryson loved just as Mack had taken his beloved Agnes's life. Would he be able to do it?

He felt as if he were being tested, being pushed to prove he was worthy of Agnes by avenging her death. But although he was fueled by his hatred, there was still a germ of humanity inside him that he struggled to suppress. He *had* to suppress it, to obliterate it completely, in order to kidnap and murder Mack's son.

Henry hadn't told Julio that his ultimate plan was to murder Cody. Instead, Julio believed that this was solely a kidnapping, that the ransom demanded would be six million dollars, half for Henry, the rest divided as Julio wished between him and Anna— Henry didn't care or even want to know their arrangement.

Silently, they walked through the first-floor rooms and then up the carpeted stairs, along the hallway past the master bedroom, past three other bedrooms, to a large open room where toys were strewn over the floor. His back facing them, Cody didn't hear them when they entered the room and was too startled to scream when Henry grabbed him off the floor. Before he had a chance to open his mouth, Julio slapped tape over it. Cody wriggled in Henry's arms, but he was small and easy to control. There was no need to knock him unconscious.

♦ ♦ ♦

As they made their way out of the playroom toward the stairs, Tully's limousine pulled up to the entrance to Belle Vista Estates and she gave the driver her access pass to insert into the automatic gate reserved for homeowners. When she got to her house, she hardly noticed the white van in her driveway. She assumed Rosetta had called the carpet cleaners, perhaps to clean up a spill on one of their expensive rugs. The driver carried her bags to the front door, but they were light, easy to handle, since she'd expected to be away for only a few days, and so Tully sent him on his way while she searched her bag for her keys. She knew she could ring the bell for Rosetta but hated to bother her if she was playing with Cody or preparing dinner.

When she finally opened the door and stepped inside, the first thing she noticed was the silence.

"Cody, Rosetta, I'm back," she called out. She peeked into the kitchen and then started toward the stairs, and that's when she saw them: two men, facial hair covering their features, walking down the steps. The bigger man held Cody, whose mouth was taped closed, and pointed a gun at his head.

"Don't scream, don't run. If you do, I'll shoot your son," he said, his voice icily cold, his eyes dead.

Instantaneously, Tully understood what was happening. Instinctively, she knew she had but moments before they reached her.

"Take me with you," she said, her voice even. "My son is frightened. He won't stop crying. It will make it easier for you if I'm with him. And my husband will give you more money for both of us."

Julio looked at Henry. "She's right, let's take her. She can control the kid."

Henry shook his head.

"C'mon," Julio urged. "She's seen us—she's had a better look than the nanny. Take her. She'll keep the kid quiet. Otherwise, we have to off her and I'm not in this for murder."

"We're going to walk out to the van," Henry said, with the gun still pointed at Cody. "I'm gonna carry your kid—the gun is gonna be pointed right at his stomach. You act natural, like nothing's wrong. We check to make sure nobody's looking and then you and the kid are going into the back of the van, along with Julio. You understand? If you try anything funny, the kid is dead. I'm not playing games."

"Please, take the tape off his mouth and let me carry him. I promise we'll do whatever you say."

Henry hesitated. He'd be better able to use his gun, if necessary, if he weren't carrying the kid. "Just make sure he doesn't make a sound. One word from either of you and ..." Henry just waved the gun at them.

Nodding, Tully took Cody from Henry's arms and carefully removed the tape from his mouth. She held her son close to her body and whispered in his ear, "Don't worry, sweetheart. Everything will be OK. Mommy will take care of you."

Cody's eyes were wide with fear, but he didn't say a word. As they left the house, Tully walked between the two men to the van. The smaller man opened the door to the back of the van and climbed in. He reached for Cody and brought him inside, and Tully climbed in behind him. After the door slammed shut, Julio took out pieces of rope to tie their hands with.

"Why do you need to do that? I'm not going to do anything to jeopardize my son."

"Because I don't want any surprises, that's why. And if you keep asking questions, I'll tape your mouth shut, too. Only reason I'm not is so you can keep your son calm."

No one stopped the van as it drove out of the development. The job of the security guard was to check vehicles entering, not leaving.

Tully shivered despite the heat. She had promised Mack she would never let anything happen to Cody. She would do everything she could to keep that promise, even if she died trying.

Chapter 26

Henry drove out the gate of Belle Vista Estates calmly, careful to draw no attention to himself or his van. He wasn't happy a second hostage had been taken, but otherwise the kidnapping had gone just as planned. He drove down the side streets onto U.S. 25, headed north toward Boulder and then west on Highway 270 to Highway 93, then north to Highway 170. He kept pace with the flow of cars. He didn't want to attract the highway patrol.

His years in prison had been a nightmare for him, but even in an inferno, one needed friendship. Isaac Micklin, a mild mannered accountant serving his tenth year in prison for murdering his wife, had latched on to him, talking his ear off whenever they were in the yard together. He had snapped one night over dinner, one ordinary night when his wife once again droned on about her ruined life, ruined by her choice of him. Isaac stood up from the dinner table, his steak knife still in his hand, walked over to his wife and dispassonionately stabbed her almost forty times. He pled temporary insanity at his trial but the jury didn't buy it, and after their guilty verdict he was sentenced to twenty-five years to life.

Isaac's favorite topic of conversation was his log cabin in Marblehead Springs, forty-five minutes northwest of Denver. Deep in the woods, it was his haven away from his wife's incessant harping. He loved the quietness, walking alone through the woods, breathing the country air. The closest public road was a mile away, with a narrow dirt track through the woods leading to his cabin. No other homes were within sight, no other people to disrupt his tranquility.

Isaac had described its location to Henry, told him where the key was hidden, and invited Henry to use it now and again when he was released from prison. Henry had used it once or twice when Agnes was alive, taken her away to the country for a special treat. With two bedrooms, a living room with a wood-burning fireplace, and a medium-sized kitchen, it was the perfect spot for holding the Brysons while the ransom was being collected. It was the perfect spot for committing murder, for hiding bodies in a remote wilderness where they could remain undiscovered for years.

Henry had prepared the cabin in advance. He nailed boards over the two windows in the smaller bedroom, as well as the bathroom window. He thought it unlikely any stray hikers would pass by, but as a precaution, nailed the boards on the inside of the windows, over the curtains, so the boards wouldn't be seen from the outside. He had left Agnes's four year old silver Honda Accord in the driveway. It was the perfect nondescript vehicle to drive into Denver to make a ransom demand.

As Henry drove steadily toward Isaac's log cabin, Tully held a frightened Cody close to her in the back of the van. "Don't be scared, sweetie," she cooed to him softly. "Mommy will take care of you. These men aren't going to hurt us. We just have to listen to whatever they want us to do and soon we'll be back home with Daddy."

Cody continued to whimper, his eyes wide, his mouth in a tight grimace. His body shivered despite the clammy warmth in their unventilated enclosure.

Tully told herself repeatedly she must remain calm, must remain in control of her senses, observe everything she could, remember everything she saw. She had acted instinctively in asking the men to take her as well but knew that was the right move. She knew she couldn't live with herself if something had happened to Cody and if there was the slightest chance she could have prevented it. She had frozen once before when he was in danger, when she had stood motionless as the river current pulled Cody away. She wouldn't allow herself to fail him again.

There was no window in the back of the van, nothing to give her a hint of where they were headed. It seemed certain they were on a highway for most of the trip. About fifteen minutes after leaving the uninterrupted flow of highway traffic, the van slowed to a crawl and began driving over a rough, bumpy surface. A few minutes later it came to a stop.

The back doors opened and Henry said, "Get out."

Julio descended first, and with his gun pointed at her, Tully climbed out, followed by Cody.

"Inside," Henry ordered as he pointed them to the log cabin.

Tully looked around at the dense forest. Nothing but trees in sight as far as she could see. She and Cody walked toward the cabin, Henry in front and Julio at the rear, the gun still in his hand. Henry led them into a small, airless bedroom and she looked around the room. One double bed, a chair, a small braided rug on the floor, an overhead light. That was the extent of the furnishings. No television, no radio, no books or magazines. Two pillows and a thin blanket were on the bed.

Henry turned his back on them as he headed for the door. "Wait," Tully called out. "Please don't leave us tied up. Lock us in, but untie us. I'll co-operate with you, do anything you want. We're not going to try to escape. At least let me hold Cody, please."

Henry hesitated. It would be easier for him to leave them untied. He wouldn't need to untie them each time he brought them food, each time they needed to relieve themselves. He had installed a secure lock on the door and one of them would always be present at the cabin. "OK," he said, and began removing the ropes, "but try anything just once and you'll regret it."

◆ ◆ ◆

It was almost nine o'clock when Mack arrived home, after resolving the crisis that had brought him back to his office prematurely. He hadn't had a chance to telephone Tully to let her know he was caught up in meetings, but that wasn't unusual. He often just showed up at home after the others had eaten dinner. These weren't usual times though. He and Tully were different now, both changed by their trip to Paris. He thought of calling her on his ride home but didn't want to chance hearing disappointment in her voice. Rather, he would just show up and hope she understood.

It was still dusk when he arrived home. Although the outside lights went on automatically at night, he felt no alarm that the inside of the house seemed dark. Cody was surely asleep already and, given her jet lag, Tully might be as well. He forgot that she was to move her belongings into the master bedroom, and so he should have seen a lamp burning in that front room. Instead, he opened the front door, walked into the darkened foyer, and immediately heard a loud thumping come from the hall closet. Quickly opening the door, he found Rosetta bound and gagged, lying on her side.

"My God! Are you OK? What happened? Where's Tully and Cody?" he asked, trying to control his mounting feeling of dread as he pulled the tape off her mouth and bent down to untie the ropes.

"Oh Mr. Bryson," she cried. "They came to the door and pushed it open, and then everything went black, and then I woke up, here in the closet, and I couldn't scream and my hands were all tied up. Is Cody OK, did they do anything to him?"

Mack's face drained of color, his heart beat loudly in his chest. "I don't know Rosetta, I just walked in."

He jumped up and called out for Cody, for Tully, and heard only silence in return. He ran up the stairs and went first to Cody's bedroom. The bed was empty, still perfectly made from the morning. He ran into Tully's bedroom, to the master bedroom, to the playroom, all empty, with no sign of a struggle, no sign of his family.

He ran back downstairs to Rosetta and as he finished untying the ropes binding her hands and legs he asked her to describe again what happened.

"It's just what I told you Mr. Bryson, I don't know. I was making dinner for Cody. He was upstairs in the playroom. Two men rang the bell and I just opened it a little, not too far, but they pushed it in and it startled me, and then one man grabbed me and I saw the other man take something from his pocket, it may have been a gun, but I don't know, it was so quick, and maybe he hit me with it, because then I don't remember anything after that, and my head hurts, right here," she said, putting Mack's hand over a large bump on the back of her head.

Mack, normally calm in all circumstances, tried to control a growing hysteria. "What did they look like? Did you see them?"

Rosetta thought for a moment. "*Si*. Just for a second, when I opened the door. They were wearing uniforms. They had funny hair, it was black and maybe it wasn't real, because it was stringy, and both were the same, and they had mustaches and beards. Oh, and they had caps on their head, you know, like baseball caps."

"Was there any writing on the cap? A name, maybe?"

"Si, there was a name."

"Can you remember it? It's important, try to picture it."

"It was a carpet cleaning company, I remember thinking we didn't need our rugs cleaned. And it started with an "A," maybe Adams, no Ames, Ames Carpet Cleaning."

Mack ran to the phone book and hastily turned the pages to find a listing for Ames Carpet Cleaning. There was none. "Are you sure of the name?" he asked Rosetta.

"*Si*, very sure."

"Who was here when they came, had Tully come home yet?"

"No, Mr. Bryson, just Cody and me."

Mack went through the house looking for a note, a message from the men who had entered his home. He checked to see if anything valuable was missing. Nothing had been left for him, nothing had been taken from his home: only his son.

He often worried about Cody but never dreamed he was at

risk of being kidnapped. Now, it seemed likely that had occurred. But where was Tully? Rosetta said she hadn't arrived home before the intruders came. Was it possible Cody was OK, that Tully had taken him somewhere, oblivious to the unconscious Rosetta in the closet? Perhaps she had startled the intruders in the midst of a burglary, and they had escaped out the back door without her becoming aware of their presence. Mack realized his hopeful scenario was unlikely. Certainly Tully would have called him if she'd arrived home and Rosetta was missing, Cody all alone.

He sat down on a chair in his living room, and massaged his throbbing temples. *I've got to be careful. If it's a kidnapping, they may insist I don't involve the authorities. If the police, the FBI, get involved, will it be riskier for Cody? I don't give a damn about money, they can have anything. I just want my son and wife back.*

Mack willed himself to remain calm, willed himself to believe his son and his wife would walk through the door unharmed. Mack thought about what he should do and realized he couldn't handle this on his own. He couldn't just wait for the phone call, the letter, the communication from the men who had his son.

He stood up, went to the phone and dialed the police first, and then called Nick. He needed his best friend with him, needed someone besides the police, besides the FBI, to make him feel his life had not just ended.

Chapter 27

More than twenty-four hours had passed since the kidnapping and still no communication had been received from the kidnappers. Nor had Tully been heard from, and her husband assumed she had been taken as well, but Agent Rick Lanzone of the FBI wasn't so sure.

Harry Collins, the Stonington Village police chief, had called him in shortly after Mack Bryson reported the disappearance, and he had arrived at the Bryson home Friday night with his partner, Tom Jennings. Lanzone appreciated that Collins stayed in the background while he and Jennings questioned Bryson and the nanny, Rosetta. The Stonington Village police department handled routine matters—traffic accidents, lost pets, even complaints of identity theft. Collins hadn't tried to hold on to the case, unlike what happened in some of the larger cities where the feds asserted jurisdiction.

Three more FBI agents soon arrived. They dusted for fingerprints, examined every inch of the house and grounds, and set up a communication network in the dining room that looked like a Pentagon meeting room. As the electronic specialists waited by their monitoring equipment in the Brysons' home, Lanzone and his partner began interviewing potential witnesses, gathering information. Their first stop was the security gate. "Were you on duty today, around four-thirty?" Lanzone asked.

"I was," said the attendant, John Williams. "I usually do the eight-to-four shift, but I've been pulling double duty yesterday and today since one of our guys is out sick. What's this about?"

When told about the kidnapping, Williams became distraught. He said he knew Tully and Cody well—she always made a point of stopping to chat with him on the way back from her runs, asking him about his wife and how his two sons were doing in college, bringing him muffins and cookies baked by Rosetta.

"Of course I remember the van, but I didn't think there was anything unusual about it," he said. "The driver was wearing a cap and shirt with the insignia of the company, and the company's name was painted on the van. I checked the roster and they were listed."

"Are records kept of calls from homeowners when they tell you they're expecting a visitor?" Agent Jennings asked.

"Sure, we write down the name of the visitor, who called it in, the date, and time. I took Mrs. Bryson's call to say she was expecting the carpet cleaners to come on Friday. She gave me the name and said they'd be arriving sometime in the afternoon."

"Is it possible someone else called and said they were Mrs. Bryson?"

John shook his head. "Each home has a special phone with a direct line to my booth. When they call, my phone shows the home they're calling from, so I can be sure the authorization is coming from the right house. There was nothing about the voice that made me think it wasn't Mrs. Bryson, and the call definitely came from her house."

The agents asked for the roster, and John handed it over. "We'll have to hold on to this for a while."

They looked at the entry for Ames Cleaning, noted the date and time of the phone call authorizing their entrance. The call had been made the day before the Brysons left for Paris, at one-fifteen in the afternoon. They saw Mrs. Bryson's name listed under the column "Authorized By."

Lanzone and Jennings returned to the Bryson house and questioned Rosetta. She had been taken to the emergency room to be checked over after the FBI had arrived and was released a few hours later, apparently unharmed by the blow to her head. Rosetta recounted that Mrs. Bryson had hosted a luncheon that afternoon for a group of women. She had prepared the meal and split her time between serving and keeping an eye on Cody in the playroom with the other children and their nannies. Mrs. Bryson had filled in with serving when Rosetta was away from the kitchen.

"We're going to have to question each of the women there that day," Lanzone said to Jennings. "See if they heard or saw Mrs. Bryson call in the authorization."

They got a list of names and addresses from Rosetta. Early Saturday morning they began a round of interviews of women who attended the luncheon at the Bryson home. None had seen or heard Mrs. Bryson phone the gatehouse, but they all acknowledged that she had left the outdoor dining table to return to the kitchen a number of times.

"But it was always to bring us something, once for more punch, another time for coffee and dessert, that kind of thing," Susie Howard said.

Only Lizzie Hanover was adamant: "Tully couldn't possibly have phoned in the name of the kidnappers. John must be mistaken."

Each of the women expressed shock at the turn of events.

At each of the homes, the men also spoke to the nannies, and again they found that no one had noticed anyone phoning the gatehouse. The agents had no reason to disbelieve any of the women.

Next, Lanzone and Jennings knocked on the doors of neighboring homes, hoping someone might have gotten a better look at the kidnappers. They struck out at the homes on either side of the Bryson house but had better luck with MaryLou Robinson, who lived in the home directly across the street. A sixty-six-year-old widow left wealthy by her husband, who had been twenty years her senior, Mrs. Robinson still had a trim figure and short, smartly coiffed hair kept a natural-looking honey blond. She said she tried to keep herself busy since her husband died two years earlier, but never having worked, and with no young children to care for, she often had hours of time to fill. She volunteered at the local hospital one afternoon a week and attended gatherings of a knitting group another afternoon, but much of her time was spent reading in her favorite cushioned armchair, right next to a window looking out on the street.

"I did see the van pull into the Bryson driveway," she said. "I happened to note it because I need to have my own rugs cleaned and thought I'd ask Tully if they did a good job. I saw them take only a toolbox from the van, which was surprising. I'd have expected them to take their steam-cleaning machines."

Agent Lanzone asked if she had noticed the license-plate number. She hadn't.

"Did you see them enter the house?"

"No. I went back to my book and didn't notice anything again until Tully's limousine pulled into the driveway. A few minutes after she got home, I heard a door slam. They were leaving the house, all of them—Tully and Cody, too. Oh, I like her so much. I do hope they're not harmed."

"Yes, ma'am. What did you see next?"

"Well, they walked to the back of the van, just normally, you know. Tully was carrying Cody in her arms. The smaller man opened the back doors, put his toolbox inside, then climbed in himself, and then Tully handed Cody to him and got in. The big man got in the driver's seat and drove away. I thought it seemed strange, Tully and Cody riding in the back like that, and I meant to call John, our man at the gate, but just then my daughter called. My grandson had fallen off his bike and broken his leg, and Alice—that's my daughter—she was so upset. I needed to console her. When I got off the phone, I kept thinking there was something I was going to do, but I just couldn't remember what."

"Could you tell if Mrs. Bryson looked frightened?"

"Well, of course I'm across the street, not that close, but she didn't seem frightened to me. She was just walking casually, talk-ing to Cody, smiling at him. I didn't understand why they were getting in the van, or riding in the back for that matter. That did seem peculiar to me. Oh, I wish I'd remembered to call John. If something happens to them I'll feel responsible."

"You haven't done anything wrong, ma'am. Do you remember what the men looked like?"

"I'm sorry, I couldn't see them very clearly. Just that one was big, kind of burly, and the other was smaller, thinner. It looked like they were wearing some kind of uniform, and I remember thinking it curious that they looked so similar except for their size."

Agent Lanzone thanked Mrs. Robinson for her information and promised to relay her good wishes to Mr. Bryson. "Please tell him I'm praying for the safe return of his family," she'd said.

The information the agents had collected suggested Mrs. Bryson was complicit in the kidnapping, a development not unexpected by the men.

"What do you think?" Jennings asked his partner as they walked back across the street.

"It could be a custody dispute." Lanzone knew that of the approximately eight hundred thousand reports of missing chil-dren each year in the United States, less than 8 percent were attributable to non-family abductions, and of that number, a study done by the U.S. Department of Justice showed a scant 115 that involved "stereotypical kidnappings," the kind seen on the TV cop shows, with a child taken by force and missing for more than twenty-four hours. It was much more common for missing-child cases to involve a family abduction. "It wouldn't be the first time a wife who wants out uses hired help to grab the kid. We need to find out more about their marriage. Could be it's a shambles and Mr. Bryson threatened to get custody, keep the kid away from her."

"Well, for Cody's sake I hope that's the case."

In the rare non-family kidnapping, forty percent of the chil-dren were killed and another four percent were never recovered.

Nearly half the children were sexually assaulted. "Bryson's chances of seeing his son again are far greater if Cody's been taken by his mother," Lanzone said.

"No ransom demand yet also points to Mrs. Bryson. On the other hand, it's still early enough for a demand to be coming."

"Maybe the kidnappers think the longer they wait to call, the more Bryson will worry about Cody's safety. Then he'll be more willing to do whatever they say."

"Either way, whether a custody dispute or a kidnapping by a stranger, we need to probe Bryson about his relationship with his wife."

Chapter 28

"Mr. Bryson, we need to ask you some questions about your marriage," Lanzone said after returning to Mack's house. "We appreciate that this is a difficult time for you, but it's important you be completely frank with us if we hope to get your son back."

Mack looked at the men quizzically. The agents were sitting across from Mack at his dining-room table. Nick had insisted on joining them and he sat next to Mack. Mack didn't understand what his marriage had to do with getting his son and wife home safely.

"Were you having any problems with your marriage?"

"Problems? Just the reverse. We've recently strengthened our relationship. In fact, we were talking about having a second wedding ceremony, one that all our friends and family could attend."

"So there's been a recent change then. Things weren't so good before?"

"No, no, things were fine. It's just that it's gotten better," Mack said, still confused by the questions.

Nick glanced at his friend, started to speak, and then stopped. Lanzone picked up on it. "Is there something you can tell us, Mr. Hanover?"

"Mack, I think you need to let them know about the nature of your marriage, about your prenuptial agreement."

The agents looked at each other. "Mr. Bryson, we'd like to look at that agreement."

Mack became indignant. He hadn't slept, hadn't eaten, had been consumed with worry about his son and wife. His terror during the past eighteen hours had taken its toll, and he erupted in an outburst of anger. "My wife and child have been kidnapped and you're asking me about my marriage? Are you guys nuts? My wife is in danger, my son is in danger—what the hell does it matter what a piece of paper says will happen if we divorce? We're not divorcing, we're very happy. Just find out who has my wife and son, OK?"

"Mr. Bryson, our investigation has revealed that your wife called in the authorization for Ames Carpet to gain entry to your house and was seen walking calmly out of the house, carrying Cody, alongside two men," Lanzone said, his voice steady. "We don't know what this means yet, but we have to consider the possibility that she was involved with the men who knocked out your nanny and took your son."

A nuclear bomb exploding in his living room couldn't have stunned Mack more than Lanzone's words did. Speechless, he leaned back in his chair.

"It can't be, it can't be, you must be wrong." Yet, lingering was the memory of their estrangement before the Paris trip, her nightly phone calls to New York, his fear that she'd met someone else. "I'll get you a copy of the agreement, but first I need to explain to you the circumstances."

Over the next ten minutes, Mack told the agents about his "contract marriage," the arrangement Tully had agreed to with him, the growing feelings they had for each other, the fulfillment of those feelings just a few days ago. He described the nightly phone calls to New York that had begun after her first meeting with her publisher, and his fears that she had fallen in love with another man.

"I know this is difficult for you," Lanzone said. "We don't yet know what all of this means, but your information is crucial if we hope to get your family back. Do you have any of your phone bills around? We need to track down the person your wife's been speaking to."

Mack nodded and numbly walked upstairs to his bedroom office. He quickly retrieved a copy of the prenuptial agreement from a file drawer in his desk and then sorted through a stack of bills and pulled out one from the telephone company. Walking down the hardwood stairs, his steps echoed as if he were living in a catacomb.

After reading the prenuptial agreement, Lanzone said, "Mr. Bryson, if your wife was in love with someone else and wanted to leave you, she wouldn't get any money under this agreement. She also wouldn't have any rights with respect to your son. Either of those circumstances could have motivated her to take some drastic action if she felt she was entitled to more."

Mack couldn't believe what they said, couldn't believe Tully's passion in Paris was concocted, her commitment to Cody a sham. Yet hadn't Joanna deceived him, led him to believe she loved him, only him? Hadn't he believed that to be true until the end, until their final confrontation? He wanted to scream, he wanted to cry, he wanted to turn back the clock on the incredible hubris that had allowed him to think he could take a stranger into his home and use her to make his life easier, to be so oblivious to the consequences that could occur.

Faintly, through the dense fog enshrouding his mind, he heard Nick say, "Don't assume the worst, Mack. I know it looks bad, but you know Tully, I know Tully. I think the world of her. I don't believe she would do anything to hurt Cody."

One hour later, FBI agent Bob Sommers from the New York office, along with his partner, Tim Josephs, buzzed a random apartment to be let into Adam's building. Sommers proceeded on the assumption that Adam was a possible accomplice in Tully's scheme to abduct Cody, perhaps to extort money from her husband, rather than a potential witness, and planned to treat him accordingly. As was often the case in New York City, the apartment's occupant didn't bother to ask for identification. The return buzzer unlocked the building door, and the agents proceeded to Adam's apartment. Moments after Sommers knocked, the front door opened.

"Mr. Landau? FBI." The agents flashed their badges.

"What's this about?" Adam asked.

"We're investigating the kidnapping of Natalie and Cody Bryson."

Adam's face blanched, his mouth dropped open, and his eyes watered.

"Oh, God. No. That can't be."

"Tell us about your relationship with Mrs. Bryson," Sommers said.

"When did this happen?" Adam asked. "Has there been a ransom demand? Has anyone heard from them? Do you know if they're OK?"

"Mr. Landau, we need you to answer our questions."

His voice hoarse, barely able to speak, Adam said, "I was illustrating her book, her children's book. I was hired by the publisher."

Sommers asked a few more innocuous questions and then bore down on him. "If you were just her illustrator, how come the two of you talked on the phone each night, sometimes for hours, the past five months?"

Adam hesitated. "We became friends, good friends. She was comfortable talking to me."

"Good enough friends to plan a kidnapping of her stepson with her? Maybe a little extortion from her husband?" asked Josephs.

Adam froze, his eyes widened. "My God, you don't think Tully is involved with this? That's beyond insane. It simply isn't possible."

"It's not only possible, but so far the evidence is pointing to it being probable," Sommers said. "The only question we have is your role in it."

Adam's voice rose. "My role? There is no role. She hasn't

planned anything. She's a victim. Tully would never put Cody in danger. She loves him, and frankly, she loves her husband, too, although he doesn't return those feelings. My only role was falling in love with her, wanting her to leave them and marry me, but she wouldn't. She said leaving them would hurt Cody, and she didn't want to do that. And if you're off on some half-baked notion that Tully kidnapped her son, then you're not focusing on the real kidnappers, and that's just wasting time. It's not going to get Tully back."

Sommers questioned him for a few more minutes but determined that they weren't likely to get anything more from him. They left his apartment and Sommers called in his report to Lanzone. "I don't think he knew anything about the kidnapping, but he and Mrs. Bryson are lovers, have been so since January. He proposed to Mrs. Bryson a few weeks ago and she supposedly turned him down. Maybe she got to thinking it over and decided she did want to leave her husband but didn't want to leave her stepson behind, maybe wanted a nest egg to take with her. On the other hand, Mr. Landau seemed real convinced she would never do anything to harm the kid, not just physically but mentally, too. And a kidnapping, taking him away from his father, sure as heck can mess up the kid's mind."

"Yeah. A lot of people made a point of Mrs. Bryson's devotion to Cody, including her husband. Either she's a very good actor or the evidence isn't what it seems. I don't know yet which it is. Put a tap on Landau's phone and post a man 24/7 on him while we wait to hear from the kidnappers."

The wait was excruciating for Mack. He'd barely slept and was exhausted. He tried to block out thoughts of his son helpless and frightened, but they kept returning, the image in his mind devastating. He already knew he would do whatever was asked and was impatient to receive the kidnappers' demands.

He'd never been comfortable doing nothing, always too restless to sit still. Now he had no choice. He couldn't leave the house, couldn't concentrate on anything else, could only hope that his son was unharmed, that there was time to save him. Stuck in a hellish nightmare, he couldn't stop his obsessive thoughts about Tully's possible involvement in the kidnapping.

He didn't want to believe she had betrayed him, couldn't believe she was capable of such duplicity. Yet why would she have told the gate man to let the carpet cleaners through on Friday? Why would she have walked out of the house with the kidnappers? After years of self-flagellation, of burying himself in work and meaningless affairs, he had allowed himself to love again. How could he have been so obtuse?

He thought back over the year and a half of their marriage and looked for clues. *Was it the pictures I had taken of her on our honeymoon? Was that the beginning of her desire to get back at me, to hurt me? It can't be. She knew I regretted it. We moved on from that. Is it my money? Was she always planning this? From the start? Was her declaration of love part of her scheme? No, it can't be. I couldn't have been fooled so easily. She* does *care about me, she* does *love Cody, I know she does.* His mind raced back and forth between absolute certainty that the agents were wrong and acknowledgment of the fact that there was no logical explanation for Tully's behavior.

With these thoughts swirling through his mind, Mack reminded Agent Lanzone that he and Tully hadn't expected to be back from Paris on Friday. "She called in the name of Ames Carpet on Monday, before we left for Paris, and told John they'd be coming on Friday. At that time she thought we wouldn't return home until Sunday night. If she was part of this plan, if she expected to go with them, why would she have done that?"

"Perhaps she wanted to be out of the country when the kidnapping took place and that's why it was arranged for Friday. But when the trip was cut short, she ended up walking in during the middle of it. If the kidnapping was going to proceed without placing suspicion on her, she had to make it seem as if she was kidnapped as well."

"Couldn't she have had them knock her out, like they did Rosetta?"

"Yes, that's a possibility. Maybe she thought she would be blamed if they'd taken Cody while she was home. Maybe she thought she could get more money if she was taken, too. I don't know. But she made a point of telling the limo driver she didn't need his help taking her bags inside the house. Once she saw the van in the driveway, she didn't want anyone going in the house with her."

Mack thought back to that News Year's Eve a year and a half ago when he'd impulsively proposed to Tully. He had viewed it then as a business proposition and he'd always trusted his business judgment. It was his judgment on matters of the heart that he'd doubted. Slowly, he'd come to realize how important Tully was to him, how much he wanted her in his life. He'd finally allowed himself to take a chance and love another woman. Now, he wasn't certain he could trust his judgment about anything.

Chapter 29

Henry and Julio settled in for the long wait. They didn't want to call Mack too quickly. They wanted him to sweat it out, to be so worried by the time they called that he would give them whatever they asked for. Henry had thought through the ways kidnappings went wrong, the ways kidnappers got caught, and believed his plan had all the bases covered.

The first step was securing the hideaway. The next was planning the transfer of the ransom. He had met a couple of kidnappers in the joint, and what always tripped them up was the drop or the marked bills. Never mattered that the target was always warned not to bring marked bills. The police and the FBI usually got their way on that. And no matter how many times a kidnapper warned that his victim would be killed if the authorities turned up at the drop, inevitably they were there, hidden in place, ready to pounce. Henry had considered those problems and planned for them. If there were no drop, there would be no marked bills, no feds.

The first call came at 11:08 Sunday morning. Mack had been instructed to demand confirmation that his son was alive and to keep the person on the other end of the line talking for as long as possible. The agents hadn't told him that 74 percent of abducted children who were murdered died within the first three hours of the kidnapping. When the phone rang, its clear tone cut through the silence in the house like a siren. The screen on Mack's caller ID read "Name Unknown," and he felt in his gut that this was the call he'd anxiously awaited. He looked for the nod from the FBI agent and then picked up the receiver.

"Hello," he said, his voice dull.

The voice he heard was garbled, as if the person were a freak in a carnival sideshow. The man spoke quickly. "Mr. Bryson, this phone call will end in sixty seconds, so I suggest you don't talk. I have your son and your wife. If you want them to live, this is what you're gonna do. Have six million dollars ready and waiting in a bank. I'll call you in two days and tell you what kind of bills I want, how many of each. Tell the bank they'll only have fifteen minutes to count it out and place it in gym bags. They should have as many as five bags on hand. If they mark the bills, I'll know, and you'll never see—"

Mack broke in, afraid the call would end before he could ask about Cody. "My son, is he OK?"

"I assume you've already notified the police. They're not going to help you. If you follow my instructions, your son and wife will be returned to you. If you don't, I'll kill them. I'll call you in two days with your next steps."

"But my son—"

"He's fine now, but if you don't follow my instructions he won't be."

Mack steeled himself to keep his voice calm. "I need proof he's OK. I need to know you have him and he's still alive."

The kidnapper chuckled. "This time you're not top dog. You don't get to call the shots. I'll speak to you in two days." The line went dead.

"We caught a break," said the agent monitoring the electronic equipment. "He's using a cell phone. He's in downtown Denver, on Mallory Street, nineteen-hundred block, and he's heading west."

Lanzone was already on another phone, dispatching agents nearer the location of the cell phone. The information would take them only to the location of the phone, and unless the perpetrator kept the phone on, they would have to go by the vague description given by the witnesses to stop and question nearby men. The constitutional guidelines were strict. They couldn't just stop anyone on the street, much less demand to see his cell phone, without a reasonable basis. But this was a kidnapping in progress and Lanzone didn't mind stretching the the rules if it meant getting a little boy back alive. The likelihood that either of the men was still wearing the same disguise of a black wig and black facial hair was slim. The only feature they were sure of was that one man was Caucasian, and the other was probably Hispanic, which meant they could be stopping a lot of innocent men on the block for questioning.

The agent monitoring the electronic equipment looked up from his monitor. "Looks like the perp has stopped. The phone hasn't moved for the last few minutes." The agent looked at the map on his screen. "It's a coffee shop. He must have stopped in there."

When the field agents arrived at the scene, the signal from the phone was still coming from the coffee shop. While one agent stationed himself at the back door, two agents walked in from the front and surveyed the premises. Just opposite the door was a cash register monitored by a heavyset middle-aged woman with bleached-blond hair pulled back in a ponytail.

In the square midsize room, customers were seated at eight of the twelve white Formica tables, rimmed in chrome and yellow with age, in straight-back chrome chairs with cushioned vinyl seats, some with tufts of stuffing peeking through the ripped fabric. Three of the tables had young children, two had only women, one had two couples, one had two men, and one had a sole male diner. All seemed to be at some stage of ordering, eating or digesting Sunday brunch. Two young men were standing over two of the tables, one taking an order and the other clearing dirty dishes. A narrow hallway led back to the kitchen and the restrooms.

The lead agent flashed his badge and announced loudly, "FBI. This is an investigation and we need your cooperation. Please remain in your seats." A hum arose in the room, different from the clamor of conversations that had been going on when they arrived. This was softer, more even, a harmonious undercurrent of whispering. One agent stayed by the front door while the second, Timothy Brunelli, approached the table with the lone diner, a middle-aged man of husky build with medium-brown hair and a goatee.

"Sir, do you have a cell phone on you?"

The man looked up from his coffee. "Sure. What's going on?"

"May I see your phone, sir?" The diner handed his phone to the agent. He scrolled through the list of calls sent. It hadn't been used to make the ransom demand. "Would you empty your pockets please?" The man complied, took out a wallet, a set of keys, a wad of bills, and some loose change.

"Thank you, sir," Brunelli said as he moved to the next table, where two men were seated on either side. He followed the same drill, and again no luck. At the fifth table, two elderly women were seated, both with silver-white hair, wrinkled faces, and knobby hands, both frightened by the intrusion into their weekly get-together. A purse was on the floor next to one, an open tote bag next to the other.

"Ma'am, do either of you have cell phones?"

One of the women quickly answered in a quavering voice. "Oh, my, no, they're much too intrusive, I hate it when people sit in a public place and talk loudly on the phone. Don't you find it rude?" she asked with a scolding tone.

He smiled. "Yes, ma'am, I do. Would you open up your bags, please?"

Both women reached for their bags, placed them on the table

and opened them. He reached for the tote bag first, spread it open, and reached in with his hand. Along the side, he felt a small hard object and pulled out a cell phone. "Is this yours, ma'am?"

The woman looked confused. "No, young man, I told you I don't have a portable phone. I don't know how that got in there."

Once again, he scrolled down to see the calls that had been sent. It was the phone used to call Mr. Bryson. "Damn," he muttered under his breath. "I assume you don't mind if I take this, ma'am."

"Of course not. I told you it's not mine."

Brunelli gathered the rest of the agents. "The bastard must have dropped his phone in her bag after his call. He knew we'd follow the GPS signal and knew we'd think he was still here while he got away. Shit!" He called Lanzone with the results of their search. "He's playing games with us. We got nothing."

"I'm sorry, Mr. Bryson, we weren't able to locate him. He stashed his phone in some lady's bag to throw us off."

Lanzone listened to the tape of the phone call again and then once more. He had a look of consternation on his face as he listened. He rubbed his temple with his forefinger and then suddenly thrust his hand out as if he'd just realized what he heard.

"Mr. Bryson, the kidnapper said, '*This time* you're not top dog.' Why would he say 'this time'? It suggests there were other times when you were on top and he wasn't, that there was a history between the two of you rather than a random pick. Can you think of anyone who would have a vendetta against you? Someone who resented you for being 'top dog'?"

Before even thinking about Lanzone's question, a flood of relief swept through Mack's body. *Then it's not Tully. If it's someone who wants to hurt me, then Tully's not involved. Thank God. I knew she wouldn't do this to me.* Despite the ever-present fear for his family's safety, the tension in his body eased imperceptibly. He thought about his business dealings, his personal relationships, and the people with whom he'd been in a position of authority and could think of no one who would want to hurt him, to jeopardize his son and his wife. "I'm sorry," he said. "I just can't think of anyone."

"Well, take your time. It may come to you. Or 'this time' could mean nothing, just a turn of phrase. It's just a thought. At this time, our primary suspect is still your wife."

Chapter 30

Henry brought lunch into the small bedroom for Mrs. Bryson and the kid. He had spoken to her husband an hour earlier, and hearing his voice again ignited Henry's fury once more. Staring coldly at Tully, furious at her youth, her attractiveness, her loyalty to that slime bucket Mack, he wanted to scream at her, tell her what a bastard her husband was, tell her she had thrown away her life for someone undeserving. She just sat still, docile. He put the lunch tray down and left the room.

Mack had sounded appropriately subdued. Henry had considered his request to hear his son's voice before paying for his return and decided Mack was bluffing. Too risky to travel with the boy to a spot where it was safe to call. He would trust his gut that Mack would pay no matter what. And if he didn't, it might matter to Julio but not to him. Still, Julio expected his payoff, and some of the proceeds were going to certain contacts who had provided needed services for the kidnapping. He would keep them alive until after he had the money. If pushed hard, maybe he'd let the boy speak to his father. Either way, when this was over the kid and his mother were dead.

◆   ◆   ◆

The minutes felt like hours, the hours like days. Fear and bore-
dom made the wait excruciating for Tully. In the small bare
room, with meals the only intrusion into the tedium, she tried
not to think of the kidnappers, especially the bigger one, the
one whose eyes seemed as black as his hair, as cold as icicles. The
one who emanated a malevolence that terrified her, a terror she
suppressed, needed to keep at bay, so as not to alarm her son.
There was something familiar about him but she couldn't place it,
couldn't reach in and pull out the memory that his face triggered.

She tried to sing to Cody, to tell him familiar stories from
books she'd read him over and over before bedtime. Then they
made up stories together as they'd done the first time they met.
How long ago that was. How different everything was now. She
had thought then that she would never marry, never have a child.
It hadn't been a real marriage until now, but it *was* a real marriage,
their love was real. Cody was her true son. *It can't be taken away
so quickly. It's not fair. Mack and I are just starting.* She wanted to
cry but couldn't. She needed to be strong for Cody. She wanted
to scream but wouldn't.

Even men as wealthy as Mackenzie Bryson didn't have six million
dollars sitting in a bank account, at hand for ready use. Sure, he
had some cash, about five hundred thousand, more than most,
but he needed to liquidate assets for the rest, and he had only
one day to do it. It might be possible to manage that, bend a few
rules, get his institutions behind him when they understood the
urgency, but the easiest and fastest route would be a loan from his
bank. He had been a valued customer for years. He had sufficient
collateral, and the bank could be counted on to be discreet, work
with the FBI, and provide whatever the kidnappers requested.
Monday morning he sat in the office of the bank president, along
with Agent Lanzone, and explained the circumstances.

Manfred Sloane was a family man himself. He listened somberly to Mack, a friend as well as a customer, and to Lanzone. "Of
course, we'll do anything you need," Sloane said. "I assume they

won't want bills over a hundred. That would attract too much attention, and bills lower than twenty will probably be too bulky in that amount. We'll make sure we have enough twenties, fifties and hundreds on hand tomorrow to cover six million."

Mack had discussed with Lanzone the question of marking the bills. Lanzone urged him to do so, saying there were methods that would be undetectable to the kidnappers. But Mack was adamant. He wouldn't take any chance with his son's life. The money didn't mean anything to him. If it were lost, he'd accept that. As long as his son was returned to him unharmed. And Tully? He didn't know whether she, too, was suffering at the hands of the kidnappers or downing beers with them at some raucous bar. If she had done the unthinkable, if the woman he'd come to love had harmed his son, he hoped she'd burn in hell.

Henry was alone in the cabin with the woman and the boy. Julio had left an hour ago for the airport, the next step in the plan. Tomorrow it would be over, the call made, the money delivered, the revenge exacted. He felt restless and paced the living room. An uncomfortable edginess made it impossible to be still. He wasn't worried—everything had gone as planned—but he wished it had just been the boy. Why had he agreed to take the woman, too? With Julio gone, it was he who had to bring them all their meals. Nothing fancy, though. Just something heated from a can, a frozen dinner cooked in the microwave. He supposed he didn't need to feed them at all. What would it matter if they were hungry? By tomorrow they'd be dead. But he didn't want to hear their cries. He didn't want their presence to intrude on his thoughts.

Agnes. That's who he kept thinking of. That's who he couldn't get out of his mind. He hadn't known what it meant to truly love someone until he met Agnes. He hadn't understood what it meant to sacrifice everything for someone you loved. Agnes had sacrificed her life for him. It shouldn't have come to that. Mack Bryson had brought it on her. Now Henry was prepared to sacrifice other lives.

The woman was right—she had been able to keep the kid quiet. He supposed it was better that she had been brought along. It made him feel uncomfortable, though, the way she looked at him when he brought in the meals, the way she'd stare at him, her face expressionless. Was she mocking him? Did she think she was so much better than him? She should have been cowering, but she seemed disdainful of him. He'd show her who was boss. He'd show her she had something to be afraid of. Tomorrow, that's when she'd know.

He unlocked the door to their bedroom and placed the tray of food on the chair. They both sat on the bed, the woman's arm tightly wound around the boy huddled next to her, like a mother bear protecting her cub. She didn't speak. Just that silent stare.

"It's happening tomorrow," Henry said. If your husband pays the money, you'll get out of here tomorrow."

Henry didn't know why he told them anything. They never asked any questions. She made him nervous with her silence, with her penetrating eyes. He felt as if he had to say something.

Alone again in the room, the kidnapper gone, it hit Tully like a bolt of lightning. She had been studying his face, trying to remember. It seemed so familiar, someone she'd seen before, but she hadn't been able to place where. When he brought them their dinner and spoke those few words, it came back to her—she had seen him, heard him speak, at the funeral of Mack's former assistant. It was Agnes's husband, with the same malevolent eyes, the same murderous stare he had fixed on Mack throughout the funeral service.

At that moment, Tully understood, felt throughout her body, that this kidnapping was not about money, not only about money. This man hated her husband, and that meant she and Cody were in jeopardy. They had to find a way to get out.

Her mind raced and she fought to keep her hysteria from rising to the surface, overtaking her. *I must remain calm, I must remain calm.* She repeated the mantra to herself over and over.

She looked around the room and searched for avenues of escape. Two boarded-up windows were on one wall, the locked door on the opposite side. She looked through the closet and found a handful of clothes but nothing else.

"Mommy, are we going to go home tomorrow? I want to go home to Daddy."

Each day he had asked the same question, the expression on his sad face one of incomprehension. Each day Tully had answered, "Soon, we'll go home soon."

Now she looked at her son, looked at his worried eyes, and answered, "Yes, tomorrow we'll see Daddy, I promise."

When Henry came back into the bedroom to remove the dinner tray, she told him she needed to use the bathroom. As he had each previous time, Henry accompanied her to the room and stood outside while she went in. Like the bedroom window, the small bathroom window was boarded up. Tully looked around the room, looked for anything that could help. She opened the medicine cabinet, saw nothing, looked inside the shower stall, found nothing, and then checked the cabinet under the sink. Hidden in the corner was a small hammer. Would that be enough? She tucked it inside the waist of her pants and left her blouse hanging loosely over it. She opened the bathroom door, walked to the bedroom, and waited for Henry to unlock the door and let her back inside.

The second call came at ten-fifteen Tuesday morning.

"Hello," Mack said.

Henry felt good, comfortable with the knowledge that it would be over today. His new life would begin, his old debts settled.

"This is what I want you do to," he said to Mack. Telephone your bank and instruct them to wire six million dollars to MGB Privatbank AG, in Switzerland, account number 00372589-61. The bank's routing number is 302 799 621. If the money is not there in one hour, your wife and son are dead."

Henry had known that the riskiest part of a kidnapping was collecting the money. No matter how many precautions were taken, it was hard to ensure he wouldn't be followed when he collected the payoff. Wiring the money to a bank with strict secrecy laws eliminated that risk. But while it was difficult for a foreign government to get information from a Swiss bank, it also wasn't an easy matter to set up an account. To protect against participation in a crime or assistance in money laundering, banks wanted to meet with the account holder and receive assurances as to the legitimacy of the funds. Rarely, they would permit a third party to open an account, but usually it had to be a local attorney.

Again, Julio had been instrumental. His gambling contacts, the guys who ran the organization, had a local man in Zurich for such purposes. For a substantial fee, he would open an account at a private bank in his own name but earmarked for his client. They trusted him because he understood he would be killed if he stole their money.

Henry arranged with him to open a Swiss account in his name, on Henry's behalf, with instructions to immediately transfer the funds to a bank in the Grand Cayman Islands, where it had been easier to open an account in the name of a dummy company. The attorney was to call Henry on another cell phone as soon as it was confirmed that the money had been received in Switzerland and rewired to the Caribbean. For this service, the Swiss man would receive $250,000. If the FBI managed to get the Swiss bank to open its records, it would take weeks, if not months, and the money would be long gone.

Julio had flown down to Grand Cayman Island and would withdraw the money as soon as it arrived, ending the trail in the event the government managed to get that far. Henry would meet him in the Dominican Republic, where they would split the money.

"How do I know they're not already dead?" Mack asked.

"They're both OK, for now."

"I need to be sure. I want to speak to my son."

"Your son is alive. If you want him to stay alive, wire the

money. Once I get confirmation it's been received, I'll call and let you know where they are. You're not going to speak to him. If you want to gamble with their lives, go ahead."

"The money will be there. Where will my son be?"

"You'll know when I have my money."

"But—"

Henry ended the call. The first part of his plan was complete.

"This is a problem," Lanzone said. "With a wire transfer, we lose the chance to catch them at the drop. I don't think you should do it without knowing your son is alive."

"I don't care about the money."

"I understand, but the kidnappers do. Make them prove they have what you want."

"I can't." Mack choked back sobs. "I can't chance it." He telephoned Manfred Sloane and gave him the kidnappers' instructions. "Please, make sure it's there on time."

Mack wanted to believe that Tully hadn't deceived him, that she hadn't planned this kidnapping. Yet a piece of him hoped Agent Lanzone was right, hoped Tully had orchestrated the kidnapping. Despite his uncertainty of everything else, the one thing Mack knew was that Tully would never harm Cody. Tully's involvement in the kidnapping increased his chance of getting Cody home alive.

Chapter 31

Henry had left Tully and Cody alone in the cabin before driving into Denver to make the call. He had no choice, since Julio was away. He didn't think they'd be able to escape the locked bedroom, but why take a chance? He didn't think their shouts could attract anyone, but again, why take a chance? He entered the bedroom, rope in one hand, gun in the other, and walked over to Tully. He handed her the rope. "Tie him up. Hands behind his back."

Tully didn't move. "Why are you doing this? You don't need to tie us up."

"Shut up and do what I told you," snarled Henry.

"Let me tie his hands in front of him, at least. Please, it's painful pulled behind him."

"I told you to shut up. Just do what I said."

"Please, don't do this."

Her pleas were lost on him. He raised his gun and pointed it at Cody. He didn't need to say anything. Tully went over to Cody, reassured him that he would be OK, and tenderly brought his hands behind him and tied the rope.

"Tighter."

She pulled the rope tighter, careful not to burn his soft toddler skin, careful not to draw cries from his perfect child's mouth.

"Now his feet," Henry said after examining the knot.

When she finished, he picked Cody up, threw him onto the bed, and turned to Tully.

"Now your turn." Roughly, he pulled her hands behind her and tied them, then her feet. He shoved her onto the bed as well, next to her son. Henry examined his handiwork and then took masking tape from his back pocket, tore off two strips, and taped Cody's mouth and then Tully's. "I'll be back in two hours. It'll all be over then," he said as he left the room.

There was no doubt in Tully's mind what *over* meant. She knew Mack would pay whatever he was asked, but she didn't believe their captor would set them free after he received his ransom. She had seen the rancor in his eyes. They had two hours to free themselves, two hours before certain doom.

Expecting to be tied herself, her mind had raced while tying up Cody. She remembered how swollen her fingers and hands became while jogging, and before being tied, she repeatedly clenched her fists. She hoped that would induce swelling, hoped the rope would loosen when the swelling subsided. As she lay in bed, she felt no loosening and despaired at the continued tightness of her bindings.

Think. There must be a way.

She flipped her body around so that she faced Cody. An edge of the tape had lifted from his mouth. She sidled close to him, lifted herself, and turned around, her tied hands close to his mouth. The ropes bound her wrists together, but she could move her fingers. With difficulty, she managed to grab the loose end and strip the tape from his mouth.

"Mommy," he cried. "I'm scared, I'm scared of that man, my hands hurt, help me, Mommy."

Tully flipped over again to face Cody. She could only grunt, the tape still over her own mouth. Cody's hands and feet were still tied. He didn't have Tully's dexterity with his fingers, but his mouth was free now. He studied his mother and inched his face close to hers. With his teeth, he grabbed the tape and slowly pulled it from her mouth. Tully wanted to cry with joy at Cody's industriousness.

"We're going to get out of here, Cody. I'm going to try to untie your hands, but first I want you to push as hard as you can against the rope and see if you can loosen it at all."

After ten minutes spent twisting his hands against the rope, pushing and pulling with all his might, Cody lay on his stomach. Tully brought her mouth down to the rope and tried to loosen it further with her teeth, grabbing on to the knot to pull it open. The process was slow and painstaking. Success was measured by small fractions of movement.

A half-hour later, her jaw aching from the effort, she told Cody to lie on his side. With her back to his back, she groped with her fingers for the knot, found it, and manipulated it with her fingers. The knot became looser. Her fingers worked quickly to tug and pull, tug and pull, and then, at last, the rope slipped from Cody's wrist and tangled around his hands, and he slid his hands free.

"Untie your feet and then come untie Mommy's hands."

Cody's hands were small, not as dexterous as Tully's, but he was patient, sometimes using his mouth to loosen the rope as Tully had, and soon Tully was free as well. She pulled Cody close to her and hugged him, kissed him all over his face and head and stifled tears. They were still a long way from being safe, though. Their bedroom door was locked, the window boarded up.

From underneath the mattress, Tully pulled out the small hammer she'd taken from the bathroom. With its head, she struck the doorknob, hoping it would loosen. Nothing. She struck again, then again, over and over, unleashing her pent-up fury on the door. Nothing.

Her whole body trembled. She dropped to the floor, overwhelmed by a sense of helplessness.

"I want to go home, Mommy."

Cody's plaintive voice went through Tully like a knife. She couldn't fail him again. There had to be a way out. Looking around the room, her eyes focused on the small boarded-up window. She pulled the chair over to it and stepped up and examined the boards. She'd never been handy; having grown up in a home without a father, she was unfamiliar with tools. Common sense was all that guided her now. She looked at the hammer, at the claws at the end of the head, and thought she might be able to pull out the nails with it.

It wasn't easy—she needed all her strength—but it worked. The nails loosened. She stuck the prongs of the hammer underneath the boards and pulled them free until the window was bare and she could see the thick forest outside. She looked at her watch. Almost eighty minutes had passed since their captor had left.

She slid the latch locking the window and pushed it open. The drop to the ground beside the house was over four feet.

"Cody, I'm going to go out the window first, then you climb on the chair, put your leg over the windowsill, and I'll reach up and take you out."

Cody followed her directions and they were free, free from their prison of the past four days, free from the monster who'd abducted them. Tully knew it was too soon to relax. They had to find their way out of the forest before he returned, but she felt the tension seep away nevertheless. She would get them home safely.

The kidnapper had said he'd be back in two hours, but Tully knew they couldn't count on that. They had to be prepared for an earlier arrival. She glanced at the dirt road leading to the house. That would be the quickest route to the paved road, the road that would lead to other homes, other cars, but it was also exposed, impossible to disappear on if he should appear suddenly.

She looked beyond where the dirt road ended, into the forest. She wondered whether there were other homes deep inside, accessible from elsewhere along the paved road. She wondered whether they'd find someone inside if they were lucky enough to stumble upon another cabin in the woods. They couldn't take a chance. They needed to follow the dirt path, but not on it, parallel to it, among the trees and brush. It would be slower, but they could seek cover if they heard his car.

Tully grasped Cody's hand. "Stay close to me, sweetheart. We've got to go fast." They ran through the woods, following the direction of the dirt road. Fallen logs and rocks slowed their travel.

"I'm tired, Mommy."

"We can't stop, Cody. Daddy's waiting for us. We have to hurry for him."

They made slow progress. When they heard it, the unmistakable hum of a motor, the crunching of tires going over small pebbles, they couldn't have been far from the main road. Tully stared hard at Cody.

"Shh," she said, putting her finger to her lips. "We have to be very quiet now. Lie down, Cody. Make believe we're playing hide-and-seek and we're hiding from that man." They fell to their stomachs and flattened their bodies against the ground. Tully hoped they were hidden by the dense foliage.

Henry's vehicle slowed as it neared their position and then came to a stop. Henry got out of the car and looked in their direction, his hand over his eyes to shield them from the glare of the sun. He'd started to walk toward them when suddenly, from deeper in the woods, past where their bodies were pressed to the ground, the crackling of branches could be heard, and then, out of the corner of her eye, Tully saw the thin brown legs of a fawn crashing through the woods. Henry smiled, turned around, and strolled back to his car. He continued his drive past them, moving slowly on the gravel roadway, not yet aware they had escaped.

When he was out of view, Tully and Cody stood up. "Good job, Cody. We have to be superfast now. Can you run faster if we go over to the road?"

Cody nodded.

They headed to the dirt road, and within minutes they reached the two-lane paved roadway.

Now Tully was faced with a choice—one that could mean safety or death. If Henry caught up with them before they found refuge—another car, another house, another person—all would be lost. Turn right or turn left? Up the road or down the road? Tully was disoriented. She didn't know where they were, didn't know which way led to Denver, which way led to the mountains. They were surrounded by trees and couldn't see beyond them to tell in which direction the high peaks lay.

Look to the sun to see what direction you're heading in, Adam had taught her. She looked up at the sky, the sun still in the east, the long days of June delaying its ascent to mid-sky, and determined that left was to Denver, right to the mountains. In each direction, the road curved ahead. They would be hidden from sight once they reached the bend if Henry came after them and chose the other direction.

Which way would Henry expect them to go? Which way were they more likely to meet help? She thought Henry would have come from the direction of Denver and would realize he hadn't seen them on the road and try the other direction.

She chose left, back to the city, toward what she didn't know.

Chapter 32

As he drove back to the cabin, the sky shone brightly on the concrete pavement and the embedded pigments sparkled like multifaceted diamonds. A rich man's roadway, Henry thought. He felt exultant. He'd done it! He'd beaten Mack Bryson, whipped him helpless like a whimpering dog, taken his money and soon his wife and son. The vitriol that had burned a hole in his gut ever since Agnes's death no longer consumed him. A sense of satisfaction had pushed it aside ever so slightly.

He had wanted to kill Mack's son, take something precious away from him, hurt him as he had been hurt. It was no longer anger fueling that compulsion, though. He even felt some sympathy for the little kid. Instead, Henry knew he had to finish what he'd started, had to fulfill his posthumous promise to Agnes to avenge her death. He needed to kill them to erase that nagging apprehension that kept swirling through his head that she had died because he, her husband, was a coward.

When he walked inside the house, everything seemed the same as he'd left it. He wasn't in a particular rush. The feds didn't know who they were looking for. They were unaware of the cabin. Still, he had a plane to catch at three o'clock. He needed time to kill the boy and his mother and drag their bodies deeper into the woods and leave them for the animals. He quickly gathered his few belongings, tidied up the cabin, and packed his car, all in preparation for the next step, the last step.

The open window was the first thing Henry saw after unlocking the bedroom door.

"What the hell?!" He stood frozen, unable to comprehend their disappearance, at first almost relieved, the final act taken out of his hands. And then he snapped out of it and stirred himself into action. They might still be around, in the forest or on the road.

He ran outside. "You can't hide from me," he shouted. "I've got people posted all around. They've got orders to shoot on sight. Come on out and you'll get to go home. You've got my word." Henry stood quietly and listened for any sound but heard nothing. He ran into the woods looking for signs of them. Nothing. He hopped back into his car and slowly drove down the dirt path. He looked into the dense forest on either side of the road and checked for movement or a glimpse of clothing. He got to the paved road, looked right, looked left, saw no sign of them. He had come from the left, from Denver, and so turned his car to the right and drove down the road, determined to find and kill his prey.

Tully was exhausted, weak from the days of captivity and terrified that their captor would overtake them. No one passed them on the road, no one to flag down and bring them to safety. Just an empty straightaway of road for about a mile, she estimated. At least fifteen minutes to get around the curve, she thought. Cody wouldn't be able to go any faster. Would that be enough time?

She bent down and looked directly at Cody. "See where the road turns up ahead?" she said, pointing in that direction. "We need to run there as fast as we can."

"I'm tired," Cody whined.

"I'm tired, too, but when we get past that spot, we can try to find someone who'll call Daddy for us. And then Daddy can drive here and take us home. Can you go fast now?"

"I'll try."

They proceeded in spurts, running a few minutes, then walking, then running again. Tully kept looking back to see if Henry was closing in on them. As they rounded the bend, Tully couldn't believe her eyes. Just ahead of them was a gas station, with an attendant inside the small building. She and Cody ran toward it, breathless, sobbing to the startled worker.

"Help us, please, we've been kidnapped, please call the police. Hurry, he may be close. He may be looking for us."

The attendant, a slight young man with the remnants of acne on his chin and forehead, no more than twenty-two, immediately took charge.

"Here's the key to the bathroom. It's on the side of the building. Go inside, lock the door, and I'll notify the police. What are your names?"

Tully told him, asked him to call her husband as well, and then left for the restroom. She collapsed on the floor inside the dingy bathroom and tugged Cody close to her chest. She could feel both their hearts pounding.

"We'll be back with Daddy soon," she whispered in Cody's ear, unable to stop the flow of tears streaming down her cheeks.

If Mack's living-room floor had been carpeted, he'd already have worn a hole in it from his pacing. He stopped in front of his Steinway grand piano tucked in the corner and stared at the pictures sitting on top. They were mostly of Cody, from babyhood to his fourth-birthday party, a look of glee on his face in one snapshot as he watched a clown make animal balloons. And then the photo that had been his favorite, of him, Tully, and Cody. It had been taken at the same birthday party, the three of them cuddled together, the parents' arms around their son. They were a family in that picture, a happy family.

"It's been two hours," Mack said. "Why haven't we heard from them? They must have gotten the money in the Swiss account by now."

The phone had been silent since the kidnapper's instructions had been given. Lanzone and his crew were still present. Nick remained by Mack's side, and all they could do was wait. Wait for a message from Tully and Cody that they were safe, wait for a call from the kidnappers telling him where his wife and son had been released. Wait for the end of his nightmare.

Lanzone looked up from papers he'd been reviewing. "There are two possibilities if your wife is behind this. She may be hiding out somewhere outside of Denver and waiting long enough for her accomplice to get back before she calls and says he released them. In that case, she and Cody will both come home. My guess is, her plan is to wait a month or so, then tell you she's leaving, join her boyfriend in New York, but with her share of six million dollars at her disposal. Or she might want more than the money. She might want to keep Cody and disappear with him and the cash."

"Oh, God, no," Mack said, his voice hoarse.

"We have a tail on the boyfriend and a tap on his phone. I don't think he knew anything about the kidnapping plan, but she may still try to contact him. We also have a trace on your wife's credit cards. If she uses any of them, we'll know where she's been and can start tracking her. We're not walking away from this. And we're already working on getting information from the Swiss bank. We're going to find them. It may take a while, but we will."

Mack didn't feel reassured. The thought of his son being taken from him, dragged off to an unfamiliar place by Tully, not understanding his father's absence, was sickening. But another scenario was even more horrifying.

"What if Tully isn't behind the kidnapping? Why are they waiting to call?"

Lanzone crossed the room and stood next to Mack. "We have to face that possibility," he said, looking him directly in the eye. "If your wife isn't involved, she and your son may be stashed far away, and the kidnappers still haven't gotten back there, or—"

Mack sank into the armchair and buried his face in his hands. He knew what Lanzone was going to say.

"Or," Lanzone said, his voice soft, "they may already be dead."

Mack couldn't speak. Tears welled up in his eyes, and a sharp pain ran through his chest.

Nick came over to Mack and put his arm around his shoulders. "Don't give up hope yet. It's too early."

Mack looked up at Nick gratefully. He wanted to have hope. He needed to have hope. But he knew that he was being punished, that he deserved to be punished. He thought about the superstitious belief that his mother voiced often as he was growing up: Bad things happen in threes. His wife had died. His assistant had died. Was Cody number three?

It hit him suddenly. Agnes. He remembered her husband at the funeral. In the condolence line, he'd told Henry how sorry he was. Henry stared at him. "You did this to her," he said under his breath. Mack had been shaken. They hadn't spoken to each other after that, but Mack felt Henry's hatred toward him.

"Agent Lanzone, you asked me once if anyone had a vendetta against me. I just thought of someone."

Mack filled him in on the events leading up to Agnes's death. Lanzone immediately had the agents begin tracking down Henry Woodman, the house alive again with a flurry of activity. Amid the turmoil, Mack's sense of doom intensified. He knew Henry Woodman was capable of murdering his son and wife.

Henry drove his car down the roadway, looking for his prey. When he didn't see them alongside the roadway, he turned the car around and headed in the opposite direction. Passing the gas station, he saw the young attendant inside the building. There was no one else around, no one at the pumps, and he wondered if they had sought refuge there.

He had gone too far to turn back now. He had only wanted to kill Mack Bryson's son, his son for Henry's wife, an even exchange. But he was resigned to having to kill the wife, too. If the attendant was protecting her, caught in the crosshairs, it was unfortunate, but he had a job to finish. After pulling his car in, he got out and sauntered over to the office, opened the door and walked in. No one but the attendant was inside. Henry asked for the bathroom key. They could be hiding in there.

"I'm sorry, sir, it's being used," the kid answered.

Henry walked outside looked toward the door to the restroom as he thought about what he would do. Who was using the bathroom if no cars were at the service station? If the wife and boy were inside the bathroom, he couldn't leave them. They'd seen his face. His mug shot was on record. He'd served time. His prints were all over the cabin, and there wasn't time to go back and wipe it clean. He walked back into the building, dawdled over the snacks, and picked out a bag of potato chips. He brought it to the register. "I really need to use the restroom. Have any idea how long it'll be?"

"They should be out soon."

They? Damn, it is them.

"I need the key to the restroom now."

"Sorry, sir, you'll have to wait."

Henry put his hand inside the light jacket he wore and pulled out Julio's handgun. "I'm not in the mood to wait. I said now."

The kid's face blanched, but he didn't move.

"Don't be a fool," Henry said. "Are they worth you dying over?"

The kid reached under the counter, pulled out the spare key, and handed it to Henry.

"You're gonna walk over there with me. Just walk real natural, and if you open your mouth or try to run, this bullet is going in your back."

The kid nodded and they walked outside together. Henry knew what he had to do.

Chapter 33

The wait inside the bathroom seemed interminable. It felt like hours rather than the fifteen minutes since they'd taken refuge inside. And then, finally, a loud knock.

"Mrs. Bryson," a deep voice said. "It's OK to open the door now. It's the police. You're safe, your boy is safe."

Were they safe? Would she open the door and find the welcome sight of the police, or was it a trick, their abductor waiting on the other side, waiting to kill them? The knock came again. The voice urged her to open the door. She sat paralyzed, Cody wrapped in her arms.

A minute passed and then she heard a key being inserted into the lock. She watched the handle turn. The door burst open and a young policeman, his starched uniform neatly pressed, entered and held out his hand for her.

"I'm Officer Kramer. You're safe now. It's OK, no one's going to hurt you."

Overwhelmed by relief, unable to speak, Tully remained seated on the floor, exhausted. As she was helped up, she said, "My son and I were kidnapped by two men. One man is Henry Woodman and his cabin is nearby. It's not far. I can tell you how to get there."

The young officer smiled down at her. "We'll send a car there right away, ma'am. In the meantime, we've been instructed to take you to our police headquarters and the FBI will meet us there."

Tully described the dirt road and its location and then asked, "Has my husband been called? He must be desperate."

"Yes, ma'am, he's on his way."

As the policeman walked Tully and Cody to the police car, she saw the young attendant sitting on the step of the building, his hands cradling his head.

"Is he OK? Did something happen to him?" Tully asked the officer.

"He'll be fine. An ambulance is coming to take him over to the hospital, but it's just a precaution. He's pretty clearheaded now. He was a real hero. The guy you're talking about drove in just after you locked yourselves in the bathroom. Johnny—that's his name," Officer Kramer said as he pointed to the attendant, "he tried to bluff this Henry guy, told him he'd never seen you two. But your kidnapper didn't buy it. He pulled a gun on Johnny and would have gotten you both if he hadn't heard our sirens. He knocked Johnny out with his gun and drove off just as we pulled in. After we revived him, he told us where you two were."

Tully walked over to the young man. "I can't thank you enough. That man was going to kill us, I know he was. We'll be eternally grateful to you."

Johnny blushed. "Anybody would have helped you. I didn't do anything special."

"You're wrong. You did something very special. I know my husband will want to reward you for your bravery."

Johnny shook his head and mumbled, "It's not necessary, really it's not."

Tully shook Johnny's hand and thanked him once more before she and Cody climbed into the backseat of the police car. They drove into the town and stopped at a one-story building on the main road with a flagpole in front. In large block letters over the door of the building were the words MARBLEHEAD SPRINGS POLICE. Tully and Cody were ushered inside and given seats.

Although they were offered refreshments and made as comfortable as possible, the wait for the FBI agents seemed endless. All Tully wanted was for the ordeal to be over, to be home, back in her familiar surroundings, back with her husband.

Twenty minutes later, Agent Lanzone walked into the building. Tully looked up from where she was sitting with Cody on her lap, leaning back into her body, a lollipop in his hand.

"Mrs. Bryson, we're relieved you're both safe. My name is Rick Lanzone, with the FBI. I've been handling this case, and I have a few questions for you, if you don't mind."

Tully looked up at him, standing over her, his face somber. "Where is Mack? I just want to go home."

"He'll be here soon. I know you must be exhausted, but we need to talk to you first. Please come with me."

Reluctantly, Tully got up from the chair, standing Cody on the floor next to her, and took his hand.

"Cody can wait here. This is agent Tom Jennings and he'll watch over Cody until your husband arrives."

Tully held tightly to his hand. "I don't want to leave him. This has been very traumatic for us both."

"I'm sure it has, Mrs. Bryson, but we need to speak to you alone." Agent Jennings took Cody's other hand and gently pulled him away from Tully.

Cody began screaming, "Don't go, Mommy, don't go away."

"It's OK, Cody. I'm not going away. I'll be real close if you need me," Tully said. "Daddy is going to be here very soon. This is a nice man, not a mean one. He'll take good care of you."

Agent Jennings bent down to Cody's level. "There's a candy machine in the next room. Why don't you come with me and I'll let you pick out any candy you'd like."

Cody looked up at Tully and she nodded. He smiled at the agent. "I like M&M's."

"You know what, I think there's some of those in the machine."

After Cody walked away with Jennings, Tully followed

Lanzone down the hallway to a small room. Inside was a table, two chairs on each side, and a mirror on one wall.

"Please sit down," Lanzone said.

Before he had a chance to speak, Tully broke the silence. "Have the kidnappers been caught?"

"No. The guys who found you radioed for another car to try to catch up with the car that left the service station, but they couldn't find it. They searched the cabin, but it was bare. No sign of any inhabitants. A crew is being brought in to dust for fingerprints. Don't worry, we'll find the men responsible, Mrs. Bryson. Now, can you tell me what happened, from the beginning? And try to remember as much detail as you can."

She began with the early return from Paris, surprising the kidnappers, and offering herself as a hostage to protect Cody. She described the men, the van, the cabin, the bedroom they were placed in, the boards on the windows. As she began to describe her growing awareness that her captor was not a stranger, the kidnapping more than a greedy grab for riches, her body shook uncontrollably and her tears flowed once more.

Lanzone reached over and patted Tully's hand soothingly. He passed her a box of tissues and waited for her to regain her composure. As she continued, she described her shock when she realized the identity of her attacker.

"I don't know the second man, but the bigger one—I saw him at the funeral of my husband's assistant, Agnes Woodman. He was her husband. I think his first name is Henry. I know he held Mack responsible for his wife's imprisonment. Maybe he thought Mack was responsible for her death as well."

Lanzone pressed on. "Mrs. Bryson, the gate house attendant at Belle Vista Estates said four days before the kidnapping you called and told him Ames Carpet Cleaning would be coming on Friday and that he should let them through."

Tully shook her head vehemently. "I don't know why John would say that. I didn't call in authorization. I didn't need the rugs cleaned."

Lanzone stood up from his seat and paced. "Here's our problem, Mrs. Bryson. We know all about Adam Landau."

"Adam? How do you know Adam? Has he been told I was kidnapped? Oh, please, somebody has to let him know I'm OK. He'll be so worried."

"What was your relationship with him?"

Tully stopped for a moment, wondering if she should just describe him as her illustrator or be completely forthcoming. *If they know his name, they probably know all about him.*

"Adam is my illustrator, my friend, and my lover. My marriage was unusual, our arrangement was unusual, and having lovers was acceptable to both my husband and me. At least it was then. It's different now."

"Yes, I've seen your prenuptial agreement. I'm aware of the provisions. Were you thinking of leaving your husband for Mr. Landau?"

"Adam wanted me to. He wanted to marry me. But I said no. I know our agreement seems strange to you, but I love my husband and I love Cody."

Lanzone stared at Tully for a moment and silence filled the room. Then, quietly, he said, "If you had changed your mind about Adam, about leaving your husband, you wouldn't get any money under your agreement. You'd be giving up the wealth you'd grown accustomed to."

Tully was stunned. "What are you saying?"

"I'm asking, did you hire some men, maybe even this Henry guy, to grab your son and extort a large sum of money from your husband? And then did you fake your escape when the ransom was paid?"

Tully didn't know whether to cry or laugh. The question was so ludicrous, so incredible, she felt like she must have fallen through some flimsy tear in the universe to a parallel world, one in which everything was topsy-turvy, left was right, right was wrong. With every fiber of her being, she tried to remain calm, but as she spoke her mouth quivered, her eyes misted up.

"Are you insane? Hasn't my husband told you about our

relationship, that it's the closest it's ever been? That we love each other? Did you speak to Adam? Didn't he tell you I wouldn't leave my husband? That I wouldn't do anything to hurt Cody? Henry Woodman would have killed us if we didn't escape."

"I don't mean to upset you, Mrs. Bryson, but I needed to ask. I needed to see your reaction. Given the evidence against you, we had to be sure you weren't involved. Your husband told us your marriage was unusual, but he also told us he was suspicious of your involvement with another man. He didn't dismiss the possibility that you had taken Cody."

Nothing could have crushed Tully more. She felt as if a herd of elephants had stomped on her chest.

"No, that can't be true. He couldn't have believed I would do that," she said, her voice weak.

How could he not know how much she loved him, how devoted she was to Cody? She felt forsaken. After Mack's stunt in Chamonix, she'd been determined to prove to him she was trustworthy, and now it hit her, a revelation that made her heart sink to a depth she hadn't thought possible: Mack was incapable of trusting her, incapable of believing in her. She put her face in her hands and sobbed.

The interrogation lasted almost an hour. Tully was drained, could barely keep her head up, and when told the questioning was over, wearily asked, "Where's Cody? Where's Mack?"

"They've gone home. I'll take you there."

Tully wasn't sure she wanted to be taken home. She wasn't sure any longer where home was. She had liked Mack from the first time she saw him, but it was the man she lived with whom she had grown to love. Paris had been the culmination of that love, the realization of her dream. But now, all that seemed a mirage. Before Paris, before he'd said he loved her, Tully had been prepared to spend the rest of her life with Mack, knowing he didn't return her love, secure in the knowledge that Cody was thriving, that she was thriving as his mother. Now everything had changed.

"Did you tell Adam you thought I had planned the kidnapping?"

Lanzone nodded.

"What did he say?"

"He said it wasn't possible."

It was after seven o'clock when she walked through the front door. Mack was waiting for her, waiting to hold her.

"Thank God you're back, thank God you're safe," he said as he took her in his arms.

Tully pulled away. "I'm exhausted, Mack. I just want to go to bed, to my bed. We need to talk, but not now. In the morning."

Tully thought she would fall fast asleep, but she didn't. Instead she tossed and turned for hours. Thoughts about the trauma of the past few days, the shock of Mack's distrust, swirled through her head despite her efforts to shut them off.

I thought he loved me. How could I have been so wrong? After Chamonix, after the pictures, I forgave him for not trusting me, for not knowing I'd never harm Cody. Now, after living together for so long, how can I forgive him? He should know me now, know I'd be incapable of such treachery. How can I live with someone who doesn't trust me? But if I leave, how can I live with abandoning Cody? He needs me. I'm his mother, his only mother. I gave up Adam to stay with Cody. Gave up the possibility of true happiness. But everything seems different now.

Exhaustion finally turned off her brain and allowed her body to drift off to nothingness. She slept deeply, awakening after Cody had already eaten breakfast. Children were so resilient. He was already playing with his toys while the television showed an episode of *Clifford the Big Red Dog* in the background. Mack was in the kitchen when she padded in, still sleepy-eyed. He beamed when he saw her.

"God, you look so beautiful. Sit down, let me get you some breakfast."

Tully wasn't ready to sit down, wasn't ready to return to normal. "Is it true you thought it was possible I planned Cody's kidnapping?"

Mack froze. "I was distraught. Both you and Cody were gone; Rosetta had been attacked. I wasn't thinking clearly, and Agent Lanzone was convinced you had a hand in it."

"But you know me. You've lived with me for a year and a half. You said you loved me. How could you think I would hurt you or Cody? How could you think I would care about money more than both of you, no matter what anyone else would say? Lanzone doesn't know me—you do. Why would you let him think I could be so heartless? Why would *you* ever think that?"

Mack tried to approach Tully and put his arms around her, but she shook him off. "I wasn't thinking," he said. "I wasn't being rational. I was desperate."

As she'd tossed and turned in her bed the previous night, Tully had wrestled with a decision. When she'd entered the marriage with Mack, she didn't want or expect him to fall in love with her. Neither had she anticipated that she'd be able to open her heart to him. And she certainly hadn't realized how strong her feelings for Cody would become, how she would feel like his true mother and want to protect him like a true mother.

Marriage had changed her, motherhood had changed her. She thought she couldn't love another after Scott and had resigned herself to a life alone. She thought she could share a loveless marriage and not feel lonely. The love for a child would be all she'd need.

Facing the venom in that man's eyes, fearing that death was imminent, had changed what she was willing to accept. Yes, Mack claimed to love her now, but if he did, nothing Lanzone said could have allowed him to believe her capable of kidnapping and extortion and unspeakable cruelty toward a child she loved so much. Was it the specter of Joanna that held him back from truly loving her? She didn't know. The reason didn't matter.

Leaving Cody was the obstacle she'd struggled with. He had always been the reason to stay, but she knew now it wasn't enough.

She wouldn't be able to hide her unhappiness from Cody. It would inevitably infect him as well. He would always be part of her life, and she hoped Mack would allow her to be part of his.

The tears started falling from Tully's eyes as they had so often in the past few days.

"I risked my life for Cody. I'd have done the same for you. Yet you doubted me when I needed you the most, when I was in danger myself. I want to be with someone who would sacrifice everything for me. I deserve to be with that person. I'm leaving, Mack. I can't stay here any longer. I can't stay with you. I hope you'll let me see Cody again. I hope you realize it's best for him. But it feels wrong staying here with you now. I don't belong, I don't belong here."

"Please don't leave. Stay, not because Cody needs you but because I need you. I'm begging you to forgive me. I can do better. I can be better, I promise."

Tully shook her head and walked out of the room. It was too late for promises.

Chapter 34

Tully booked a flight to New York on American Airlines for the following Monday. She and Cody both needed time to decompress from the ordeal, and so Cody stayed home from school the remainder of the week. It was impossible for her to explain to him that his mother was leaving their home. Instead, they played games together, went to the playground and stopped for ice cream on the way home, and cuddled next to each other on the couch while watching *Barney* on television.

Mack wanted to stay home from work as well, but Tully asked him not to. "Please, I want to spend my last week with Cody alone. You'll have your time with him after I leave."

When she tucked Cody into bed that night, he hugged her tightly and asked, "Will those bad men come back?"

"Never. They're far away now and can't hurt us," Tully said. *It's not bad men who'll hurt you now. It's me who's going to hurt you.*

On the morning of her flight, she woke Cody up and said, "I have something important to tell you. Mommy is going away, to New York, like I went before. Only this time I don't know when I'm coming back." She couldn't bear to tell him the whole truth. She couldn't allow herself to imagine his despair. The true story would have to wait, wait until the nightmare of the kidnapping had receded, wait until she was strong enough to withstand his cries.

"Mommy loves you, sweetie, and I'll call you every day."

"I don't want you to go, Mommy. I'll be a good boy, don't go," he cried.

Tully stroked his hair. "I have to."

When her time came to leave, they hugged each other tightly, both sobbing over their loss. Tully pulled herself away and walked out the door. She got into the waiting limousine and pressed her face against the window, unwilling to tear her gaze away from her son. Rosetta stood in the doorway and held Cody in her arms to stop him from running after Tully. As the car pulled away from the house, Tully's anguish was more intense than anything she'd ever experienced—worse than what she'd felt upon her mother's death, Scott's death, the days spent in their captors' cabin, not knowing whether they'd survive.

As her plane taxied down the runway, Lauren's warning played over and over in her mind. She had tried to stop Tully from accepting Mack's proposal, had tried to make her understand the ramifications of her decision.

"I can leave if it doesn't work out," Tully had told her sister.

"But there's a little boy involved here, with little-boy emotions," Lauren had retorted.

As the airplane took off, carrying Tully two thousand miles from the child she loved dearly, her sister's words cut through her like a knife stabbing at her heart.

"And that's the whole story. No more lies, no more pretending." Tully was back in New York City, sitting in Haley's living room and having a glass of wine, and she'd just revealed the truth about her marriage.

"I don't know where to start. Everything you've told me just seems so incredible." Haley took a deep breath. "OK. First of all, are you all right now? My God, a week ago you were running away from a madman."

Tully nodded. "I know. It doesn't seem real to me. While I was locked up in that room, all I could think about was protecting Cody. When I recognized the kidnapper, I was afraid for Cody, not for me. After it was over, when Cody was back home and asleep in his bed, I realized that it's time to think about what I need. And for the first time in my life, I felt—"

"Strong?"

"No—empowered. I wasn't afraid anymore. I didn't fall apart, I didn't freeze up. Cody is alive because of me."

"I'm not surprised," Haley said. "I always thought you were courageous. You picked up and moved to New York City without knowing anyone, without any family nearby. I don't think I could have done that."

"It *was* hard at first. Then you and I became friends and I didn't feel so lonely. And, of course, after a while I had Scott."

There was a moment of silence, and then Haley said, "I knew you were depressed after Scott died, but I never dreamed you'd felt so hopeless. I wish you had opened up to me then."

Tully took a sip of her wine. "It wouldn't have made a difference. When Mack offered me a make-believe marriage and instant motherhood, it seemed like enough. I wasn't ready then to believe I could have more."

"And now what? Are you going to marry Adam?"

Tully sighed. "I don't know. I love Adam—that is, I think I do—but I'm not ready for another commitment. For now, I just want to take care of myself.

After two weeks on Haley's couch, Tully began her search for a furnished apartment. "Two questions only," said Amy Lewis, the real estate agent. "How much money can you spend and what area of Manhattan?"

Tully still had a lease on her fifth-floor walk-up on the Upper East Side, but her tenants' sublease didn't expire for another six months. And then they had an option to renew it for one more year. Tully had paid nine hundred dollars a month for the rent-stabilized apartment but knew it was next to impossible to find another like it. There was another factor: Two years ago a fifth-floor walk-up in a dusty apartment building was part of her adventure in Manhattan, but since then she'd enjoyed a life-style that had provided her with every comfort. Her kitchen in Colorado was bigger than her old apartment.

"Two thousand a month and first choice is the East Village." Adam lived in the East Village. He'd wanted her to move in with him, but she wasn't ready for that. It was better to find an apartment close by.

"For two thousand a month in that neighborhood, I can get you a toilet, not necessarily running," scoffed Amy.

Tully thought about it. She had seventy thousand dollars in her bank account, almost all the money Mack had given her as part of their agreement. Every time she'd tried to use her own funds for anything, Mack insisted he'd pay. The only expense she'd covered was her birthday present to him. And, of course, the money he gave her wasn't taxable. It was a gift from husband to wife. She'd never had so much money, but she knew it had to last her. She had decided to take a year to work on finishing her novel before finding a job.

"Twenty-five hundred and I don't mind not having a doorman," Tully countered.

"Well, you're certainly making it challenging, but let's see what we have," Amy said as she scrolled down a computer screen. "Aha," she said after a few minutes. "I hoped this was still available. A darling little apartment. It just came back on the market, not too far from the East Village. The owner's been transferred to Europe and just extended his stay for another year."

They hailed a taxi at the corner of Amy's midtown office. "Take us to Thirteenth Street and Broadway," Amy told the driver.

The apartment was as Amy promised. It certainly was little, with only one room, a walk-through kitchen and a cramped bathroom. But it was darling as well. The creamy yellow walls were wainscotted, and the large window overlooked a garden in the rear of the building. Best of all, there was a built-in Murphy bed, leaving plenty of floor space for the gingham sofa, the large desk and the dinette table.

"How much?" asked Tully.

"Only twenty-three hundred a month. It's a steal, believe me."

Tully didn't hesitate. "I'll take it."

As she looked around the apartment, she realized that she had returned to the city where she started a new life almost five years ago, when she made the decision to leave the town she'd grown up in. Now she was starting a new life all over again.

"What do you think?" Tully asked Adam after she gave him the tour of her apartment. A pan of lasagna was cooking in the oven, and the smell of garlic wafted through the one room.

"It's cozy, I guess."

Tully laughed. "Yes, but I think it suits me perfectly."

Adam took both of Tully's hands and pulled her close to him. "You know you could have stayed with me."

"I know. I need time by myself, to sort things out."

"When you're ready, I'm here for you."

"You may not want to be after you taste my cooking."

"I'm serious."

Tully pulled away. "I'm not sure what I want, Adam, except I know I want you in my life. I'm just not sure how. Can you accept that for the time being?"

"I love you, Tully, you know that. And that means I want you to be happy. With or without me."

Tully had just finished her nightly call to Cody when she asked him to put his daddy on the phone. Before he got off, Cody asked, "When are you coming home, Mommy?" She had been in New York for three weeks now, and he asked that less frequently. At first, he had started every conversation with that same question. "Not for a while," she answered, the same answer she always gave. "But I'm thinking about you every day, and I love you so-o-o much. Now go get Daddy."

"Tully? Are you OK?" Mack asked when he picked up the phone. She rarely spoke to Mack when she called Cody. It was too painful. Instead, each evening at half past nine, two hours later than Denver time, she dialed his number and Rosetta answered the phone. Sometimes Cody picked it up directly.

"I'm fine, but I've moved into a new apartment. Now that I'm getting settled here, we can't put off talking to Cody any longer about what's happening."

"Your new apartment—are you living there alone?"

"If you're asking me whether Adam is living with me, the answer is no."

Tully thought she heard a release of breath on the other end of the phone.

"You left so quickly after your ordeal," Mack said. "I sort of hoped it was because you were still in shock from the kidnapping. You know, like war veterans who come home with post-traumatic stress syndrome and nothing seems right. Isn't that possible?"

"I know it seems that way, but it's not. So much has happened between us. I'm not the person you married, I'm different now."

"I know you're not, Tully. But I'm different, too. Maybe if you spend some time away, maybe later we can talk about what happened, talk about us. Before we talk to Cody."

Tully hesitated. "I don't want to give you false hope, Mack."

"At this point, I'll take any kind of hope at all."

Chapter 35

Even in the concrete metropolis of New York City, a person can find the dramatic red, orange and yellow foliage that signaled the beginning of a new season. The brilliant hues of autumn surrounded Tully as she jogged in Central Park. Saturdays were set aside for her long run—ten miles—and she often headed uptown to the park for it. Runners, bicyclists, roller-bladers all surrounded her. A mile into the run, she settled into a rhythm and let her mind meander. She thought back to her first outdoor training runs along the roads of Belle Vista Estates. She missed the Saturday jogs with Mack, and yes, she missed Mack as well. At the same time she felt at peace. Her novel was progressing nicely and she was confident it would be completed before her savings ran out.

She was meeting Adam for lunch after her run. Over the past three months, he had cared for her as he'd done when her ankle was sprained, only this time it was her psyche that needed to heal. He was attentive and loving, giving her the space she needed to recover yet always ready to give more, always hoping to give more. There was nothing holding her back now from accepting his marriage proposal. Nothing except the memory of what it had felt like in Paris when she and Mack made love and every nerve of her body seemed to explode with joy. It was comfortable with Adam and he would always be her friend, a dear friend, but she had learned in Paris what it felt like to love deeply and passionately, and she was no longer willing to settle for less.

She still spent many nights talking on the phone with Adam. They still met for dinner, for a movie. She loved his kindness, his warmth, his gentleness. But she wasn't *in love* with him. She knew it was wrong to mistake affection for love, attraction for passion. She cherished his friendship and at the same time recognized that it was not meant to be more.

Tully finished her jog, walked for a bit, and then sat on a park bench while recovering. Two toddlers chased each other as their mothers watched nearby. It was impossible to look at them without thinking of Cody. Twice she'd flown back to Denver and spent the weekend with him while Mack was at his ranch. Twice her heart had broken as she hugged him goodbye.

After a while, she got up from the bench and walked to the subway. She took the number four train to Fourteenth Street and walked to her apartment. She had just enough time for a quick shower before leaving again to meet Adam. As she entered her apartment, she noticed that the red light on her telephone was blinking. After pressing the button for her message, she heard a familiar voice. "Mrs. Bryson, this is Agent Lanzone, from the FBI. I have some good news for you. Please give me a call."

Lanzone had called Tully occasionally to give her updates on his search for the kidnappers. The first break in the case had come with the identification of Henry Woodman's accomplice, Julio Martinez. He was a small-time bookie who'd had just one arrest, as a minor, a drunk-driving charge that was thrown out when the defense attorney uncovered a malfunction in the breathalyzer equipment. However, it was enough to have his fingerprints on file, and they matched those found in the cabin, along with Henry's. Both Julio and Henry had disappeared, their apartments emptied of personal belongings, their bank accounts cleaned out.

The second break had come after questioning Henry and Julio's neighbors. From one, they learned Julio had a girlfriend, Anna Lopez, who worked as a nanny for Angie Johansen, one of Tully's friends at Belle Vista Estates. It hadn't taken a genius to figure out that Anna had been the one to call in the clearance for Ames Carpet, pretending to be Tully. Angie had been one of the women at Tully's luncheon the day of the call. Anna was easy to crack when they brought her in for questioning. She quickly admitted her role when threatened with a kidnapping charge if she didn't cooperate and a substantially lesser charge if she did. "I only called the gatehouse. That's the only thing Julio asked me to do," she told the FBI. "It was easy to pretend I was Mrs. Bryson, since that's who John expected to hear. He said I'd get $10,000 just for making a call. I know the money means nothing to these people, but for me it makes a real difference. Julio said they were going to burglarize the house, that's all. He promised me no one would be hurt." When asked why she hadn't come forward when she learned that it was a kidnapping, that two lives were at stake, she'd said she was afraid she'd be held responsible.

Julio had asked her to run away with him, maybe to one of the Caribbean islands, maybe New York. He didn't know where he'd end up, but Anna had family in Denver and didn't want to leave everyone behind. And Julio had been true to his word—a week after the kidnapping, she received a check for $10,000, drawn on a bank in the Dominican Republic.

Armed with a warrant, the FBI obtained a copy of the check from her bank and was able to track down Julio's Caribbean bank account. Secrecy in Dominican banks was strict, but not quite as strict as in Switzerland, and eventually the FBI was able to seize his account. They obtained the bank records, including Julio's address. He was picked up, still in the Dominican Republic, a month after the kidnapping.

Finding Henry had proved to be more difficult. They had checked the records of the bank where Julio's money was found, but no account for Henry surfaced. They tried other banks in the Dominican Republic, but without a basis to believe the money was secreted away there, they couldn't get warrants and couldn't extract any information from the banks.

Tully dialed Lanzone's phone number. "Agent Lanzone speaking."

"Hi, Mr. Lanzone. It's Tully Bryson."

"Mrs. Bryson, I have good news for you. We've got Henry Woodman."

Still cradling the phone, Tully sank to the floor. A sense of relief flooded through her. "How? When?"

"We got lucky. We put the word out to the people in his neighborhood, you know, if they saw or heard anything from him to contact us. And then we did the same with Agnes's friends and family. One of her sisters went to the cemetery to pay her respects and saw fresh flowers. Turns out Henry was having flowers delivered weekly to his wife's grave. We found the florist and he identified the purchaser as 'Hank Wallis,' then gave us the credit card used for the payments."

"How did that help?"

"Well, the credit-card company gave us the address where bills were sent. Turns out he settled in Paradise Island, in the Bahamas. Bought himself a little house and apparently was busy gambling away his payoff in the hotel casinos. He was arrested two weeks ago. I didn't want to say anything until extradition was finished. We got him back here in Denver yesterday."

Tully felt as if a weight had been lifted. Most of the time she successfully blocked memories of the kidnapping, but occasionally she awoke from nightmares drenched in sweat, the image of Henry lingering in her mind. She'd held on to the hope that arresting him would still those nightmares. Now, finally, that hope might be realized.

Moments after she'd hung up with Lanzone, the phone rang again.

"Tully, it's me. Have you heard the news?"

Mack's voice on the other end of the phone startled her. They'd spoken only infrequently since she left Denver three months earlier, and when they did, it was always about Cody. In those calls, Mack assured her that Cody hadn't regressed to his formerly clingy behavior since she moved back to New York. It seemed Tully's calls to Cody each evening provided the reassurance he needed that he still had a mother, a mother who loved him.

"I have, Mack. I just got off the phone with Agent Lanzone."

"It's an ending, don't you think? Now that he's behind bars."

"Yes, I suppose it is."

Mack cleared his throat. "I was wondering—hoping, I mean—that it could be a beginning as well."

Tully remained silent.

"I love you, Tully. I know I've disappointed you and I understand your anger at me. I can't imagine what it must have been like for you and Cody, locked up in the room, terrified you'd both be killed. But I was afraid, too, afraid that I was going to lose the two people I loved most. I barely slept the entire time you were away. When Lanzone suggested you were behind the kidnapping, all I could think of was ..."

"Was what, Mack? How you didn't know me? How you could have invited a monster to live in your house?"

"No," he said quietly. "I kept telling Lanzone you wouldn't have done this. But as the days went on, I couldn't stop thinking of how Joanna had deceived me, how blind I'd been because I loved her. I kept wondering if I was doing the same thing all over again, whether I was deceiving myself about your feelings for me and Cody because I loved you so much. And then anything seemed possible."

Mack had never spoken of Joanna to Tully before. He had refused to discuss her. But Tully had imagined her as the perfect wife, the perfect hostess, the perfect mother. The woman whom Mack couldn't forget. "I don't understand. How did she deceive you?"

Mack told her about his last night with his wife. "Before you," he said when he was done, "before I realized how much I love you, I was afraid of getting close to another woman and failing her, as I'd failed Joanna. I thought my armor was impenetrable, but you shattered it to pieces. Still, I fought my feelings. Until I thought I was going to lose you. And then I knew—in order to keep you, to let you fully into my life, I had to first forgive myself for not understanding Joanna's sickness. I had to accept that in the heat of the moment, I can make a mistake."

"I always thought of Joanna as my competition."

"No. She was the source of my shame."

"Anyone would have reacted the way you did."

"But I didn't think I was like everyone else. I thought I was better, smarter, more in control than others. I never considered failure an option for me. And then I failed the woman I cared most about. I've lived every day with my guilt over sending Joanna away, sending her to her death. And when I was tested again, I failed you, Tully. I know I did. When you walked out, I knew I deserved to lose you. I knew that once again I'd failed the woman I loved. But when that happened before, I crawled inside my shell, hid from everyone, hid from myself. I'm not doing that now. You're too important to me. I love you too much to run away. Or to let you run away."

Tully was stunned by Mack's revelation. She wanted to forgive him but was reluctant, afraid to let herself hope, afraid another disappointment would be unbearable. "I don't know what to think, Mack. I need more time."

"Yes, darling. Of course. Just promise me, as you think it over you'll remember what we had in Paris."

"I will," she said before hanging up the phone. Mack didn't need to remind Tully of Paris. The memory of their last trip was always with her. It defined what she wanted in a relationship. But whether it was with Mack or someone else, she just wasn't sure.

Chapter 36

Lost in thought at her computer, trying to figure out a tricky scene in her novel, Tully didn't hear the knocking at her door at first. When she did, she looked at her watch and smiled. One o'clock on Saturday meant that Billy was at her door, making his weekly delivery of flowers. Mack had sent her two dozen red roses every week for two months. The first delivery came the day after they'd spoken about the capture of Henry Woodman, when Mack had asked Tully to forgive him. She called him to thank him and they talked for almost an hour.

It became their routine, flowers followed by a lengthy phone call. During these calls, she began to realize that although he had disappointed her, grievously disappointed her, she wasn't blameless. She hadn't been willing to understand how the overwhelming fear of losing his son could obliterate all thought of anything else. How it could displace everything Mack knew about Tully. She had rushed to judgment, wouldn't allow herself to forgive him, wouldn't let him explain. She hadn't let time heal them both. When she walked out of their home, leaving Cody motherless again, not listening to Mack's explanation, still loving him but unwilling to fight for that love, she failed him as well.

Her months back in New York taught her that she was strong enough to withstand loss. She had realized, at last, that she could create her own happiness. Yet she never stopped loving Mack and over the months appreciated that his love for her was genuine, that they shared a bond that had begun with an impulse but had grown to be durable.

Christmas was two weeks away and they were both spending the holiday at their sisters' homes. It would be their first time seeing each other since Tully had walked out.

"Hi, Billy, come on in," she said as she opened the door. The florist's only grandson delivered Mack's flowers each week, and Tully had become fond of the young man. However, instead of seeing the usual two dozen roses, she was greeted with a burst of color. A huge bouquet of orchids, calla lilies, gerbera daisies and pink roses hid Billy's face. "My goodness, Billy, this is a surprise."

"It's not Billy," Mack said as he lowered the basket of flowers. "I hope it's a good surprise."

Tully burst into tears.

Mack put down the basket and drew Tully to him. "Darling, what's wrong? I'll leave right now if I'm upsetting you."

"No," she said between sobs. "It just—I haven't seen you in such a long time and now you're here. I've missed you so much. I don't think I wanted to admit it to myself." She wiped the tears from her cheeks and took Mack's hand. "Come inside, come sit down. Tell me why you're here." She led him to her couch and they both sat down.

"I flew in yesterday for a programming-industry dinner. I know we agreed to wait until Christmas, but it killed me to be this close to you and not see you."

Tully looked him over. He was as handsome as always but looked changed. The sadness in his eyes she'd noted when they first met was gone. They were both different from the two people who'd met almost two years ago.

"I'm glad you didn't wait." Tully leaned over and kissed him, first tentatively and then, as he responded, hungrily. They remained locked in each other's arms for a few minutes, and then Mack pulled away and looked around the room.

"Wait, where's the bedroom? Have you rented this just for your writing?"

Tully laughed and pointed to the built-in cabinet along one wall. "That's where I sleep. It's a Murphy bed."

"Show me."

Tully pulled the bed down and they both fell onto it, tearing their clothes off as quickly as they could. It was unlike Paris, where they had explored each other's bodies slowly, deliciously. Now Tully clutched Mack tightly, her need for him urgent. Afterward, they lay entwined in each other's arms.

Hours later, they got out of bed and took a shower together. "Are you sure two of us can fit in this bathroom?" Mack asked when he peeked into the room.

"The apartment *is* tiny, smaller than my last apartment in Manhattan. But I've been happy here. And that's all it takes for it to feel like my home."

Mack spent the rest of the weekend with her. They walked all over the city. They talked—about Cody, about themselves. They laughed and they sat quietly side by side, no words needed. When it was nearly time to leave for the airport, Mack led Tully to her couch and they sat down.

"I wanted to wait until New Year's Eve, when we were with our families. I wanted to wait until we were back at the country club, where it all began, and take you outside like I did that night. I wanted to ask you then, propose to you the right way, the way a man proposes to a woman he loves. But I can't go back to Colorado without knowing."

He got down on one knee, reached into his pocket and pulled out a ring box. "Tully Gordon, would you do me the greatest honor of becoming my wife? I can't promise you I'll never disappoint you again. I can promise I'll try my hardest not to. And I promise that I'll always love you."

He gazed into Tully's eyes. So many thoughts swirled through her head—thoughts of Cody, of how she'd started to feel happy living on her own, of her friendship with Adam. But one thought kept pushing itself to the forefront: She was in love with Mack. She pulled him up to his feet, put her arms around his neck and said just one word.

"Yes."

THE END

Acknowledgements

As always, my thanks begin with my husband, Lenny, who has always supported and encouraged me.

Writing a book is a long, slow process, and for the most part, a solitary one. But once the initial manuscript is completed, the revision process starts. During this phase, the input of many people have helped shape the final product. For her expert counsel on the overall manuscript, I thank Danelle McCafferty. In addition, my son, Jason, and daughter-in-law, Amanda, gave invaluable advice about early drafts.

This book couldn't have been put together without the expertise of the people at The Editorial Department: Doug Wagner for his copy-editing, Christopher Fisher for his book design, Morgana Gallaway for the e-book design, and Beth Jusino for her uncanny ability to perfectly capture the essence of a story for the back cover description.

Finally, thanks go to Derek Murphy for his beautiful book cover design.